PAYBACK
WITH YA LIFE

WAHIDA CLARK

GRAND CENTRAL
PUBLISHING

NEW YORK   BOSTON

Grand Central Publishing
Hachette Book Group USA
237 Park Avenue
New York, NY 10017

Visit our Web site at www.HachetteBookGroupUSA.com.

Printed in the United States of America

First Edition: May 2008

10 9 8 7 6 5 4 3 2 1

Grand Central Publishing is a division of Hachette Book Group USA, Inc.
The Grand Central Publishing name and logo is a trademark of Hachette Book Group USA, Inc.

Library of Congress Cataloging-in-Publication Data

Clark, Wahida.
    Payback with ya life / Wahida Clark — 1st ed.
        p. cm.
    ISBN-13: 978-0-446-17808-2
    ISBN-10: 0-446-17808-X
    1. African Americans—Fiction. 2. Drug dealers—Fiction.
    I. Title.
    PS3603.L3695P4 2008
    813'.6—dc22
                                                    2007033395

To all my brothers and sisters on lockdown. Stay up, stay focused and know that this too shall pass.

ACKNOWLEDGMENTS

All Praise is Forever due to the Creator. I thank Him for everything and pray that He always finds me among His most grateful servants.

Wow! This is my first time writing the acknowledgments section while I am free. Well almost. I'm on home confinement this very moment and being out of prison is a wonderful feeling. My husband, Yah Yah, you are such a blessing. What would I do without you? To our two beautiful daughters, Hasana and Wahida, Mommy is home and we are on our way. Hajj, aka Gina, thank you so much for everything. You've been holding it down for a long, long time, as well as Kisha, Samataha, Aisha and the rest of the sisters. Hadid, Hakim, Willie, Hussein and the rest of the brothers. Birdie and Princess, thank you so much for being there for Hasana. I love you sisters for that.

Keisha Caldwell from the D, you know what's up and you are one sister who always remained the same. Antoinette Boxley, thank you so much for your help with the outline on this one and the original title, *Final Payback*. You worked me hard on this one. Shawn James,

ACKNOWLEDGMENTS

I thought *Payback* was a done deal. I had no plans for doing a sequel. Ladies in Alderson, Danbury, Tallahassee and prisons throughout the country...thank you so much for the continuous love and support. Sis. Aminah Gargani, what's really good?

I get so much mail asking me to shout them out in my next book, sorry. Those letters are in boxes. I'll try again next time. But those I can remember: Writa'z BLOC, much love; Latif Lamar, Yalonda Burgess, Kaywan, Ron Red Handed Thompson, Fish, Slymm Brown, Steve Dixon, Doggy Mac, Zach Tate, Fajr Bint, Mike Sanders, Shadee (sorry for doggin' you out in *Payback*). Those names are for starters. My helpers, Intelligent Tareef Allah, thank you so much for your editing skills, Lashawn James, Dee Favors, Pamela Frye, Sylvia Webster, Teresa Hodge, Tamara and Marcus from the D. I can't leave out the author of *Prison Stories*, Seth "Soul Man" Ferranti. My Web guy Roka, you are the bomb. Lil' Wahida, thank you again for holding my MySpace page down and keepin' it hot for a long time. Tru and Teesa of Tru Books in CT.

Y'all be on the lookout for my anthology, *What's Really Hood? Vol. I*, guest starring Bonta, Victor Martin, Shawn "Jihad" Trump, L. L. Dasher and myself. Y'all are going to love it.

To all of my fellow authors who showed me love as soon as I hit the bricks: Jason Poole, Joe Black, Endy, Crystal Perkins Stell, Treasure E. Blue, Noire, Cash, Kiki,

ACKNOWLEDGMENTS

Swinson, Nikki Turner, TuShonda Whittaker, T. Styles, Tracy Brown, Danielle Santiago and Valencia Williams, but a very special shout-out to Kwan, Erik Gray and J. M. Benjamin. Those brothers were the very first to stop by and showed this sister lots of love. It was real.

To my editorial director, Karen Thomas. My Shero. Thank you for believing in me. That sister is tha bomb, y'all. I can't leave out her busy assistant, Latoya Smith. Thank you, ladies. For everything.

Marc Gerald, my agent. Thank you for everything and looking forward to taking it to the next level.

To my production editor, Mari Okuda, you run a tight ship but I love your work.

Oh, my mama, Berta, Aunt Ann, Aunt Ginger, Aunt Marva, Aunt Sis, cousins Carla, Rob and Brother Melvin. Thanks for years of support while I was in the belly of the beast.

To my special friend and publicist, Jerry, aka Courtney Moran, aka Al-Jermiqua. I got a lotta love for you. Jon "Barney" Jones, let's make it happen. Paula Edwards, Cyrus Webb. Thank you, vendors and bookstores, for selling my books. *Essence* magazine, *Black Issues Book Review* and *Don Diva*...I'm back!

Last but definitely not least, to my fans: I love y'all and I love writing the books that make you want to laugh, cry, beg me for the characters' phone numbers, the whole nine. Thank you so much for the continued love and support.

ACKNOWLEDGMENTS

Peace and Love
Wahida Clark
The Queen of Thug Love Fiction

PO Box 8520
Newark NJ 07108
wahidaclark@hotmail.com
wahidaclark.org
myspace.com/wahidaclark

Holla at ya girl!!!

CHAPTER ONE

The image of yellow tape and bystanders began to fade as Shan's eyes were glued to the rearview mirror as the thought of Brianna being gone forever twisted up her insides. The only thing she had now was the memories of her road dawg, her sister, her best friend...Brianna was gone. "Why, B? This can't be happening." She slowly turned the corner and was lost in thought. Then minutes later she pulled up into a busy Memphis service station on Chelsea. This joint was always jumpin'. They called it "In and Out" as well as "The Corner Grocery." She needed to gas up, get some more snacks and call her brother, Peanut.

She flipped open her cell phone and dialed her brother. Apparently he checked the caller ID because he started screaming on her as soon as he answered it.

"Yo, I was hoping you changed your mind. Why you gotta be so damned hardheaded? Way the fuck out in California, and driving on top of that! How the fuck am I supposed to be able to look out for you?" He spazzed out on her.

"She's dead, Peanut," she whispered.

"What? I can't hear you."

"She's dead...Brianna. She's gone."

"Yo, back up. And speak up, maine." His Memphis accent was no longer subtle.

Shan let out a huge sigh. "I said she's dead, Peanut. Brianna is dead."

"What? W-what happened? What are you talking about?" Peanut didn't want to believe what he was hearing.

Shan swallowed and exhaled before speaking. "She took her own life, Peanut. My girl blew her own brains out." Shan started talking to herself, now oblivious to Peanut being on the line. "I can't believe those words are coming out of my mouth. I wasn't there for her. Why didn't she say something when she came to see me?" She swiped at the tears that were streaming down her cheeks. "Why would she go out like that?"

"Shan," Peanut yelled into the phone. "Where are you? How did you find this out?" Peanut was pacing back and forth. "Aww damn. No, not Brianna. Are you sure?" His voice cracked. Even though he was mad at her for doing him dirty, by setting him up to be robbed, he couldn't deny he still had love for her.

"I wasn't there for her, Peanut," Shan mumbled, ignoring her only brother.

"Where are you, Shan? I'm coming to get you. Where is Brianna?"

"You wasn't there for her neither and now she's gone," Shan sobbed.

"Shan. Where the fuck are you?" he pleaded. "Come on, baby girl. Tell your big brother where you are."

"It doesn't matter. I'm out."

"What you mean it doesn't matter? This shit doesn't make any sense. You mean to tell me that our sister Brianna is dead, and she killed herself? Come at me better than that."

"It is what it is, Peanut. I'm out of here. Don't worry about me, I'll be fine. I'm grown, remember? Plus, I'm already on the road."

"Well get off the fuckin' road and come back home. How the fuck you gonna up and leave after this shit? You don't need to be leaving like this."

"I'll call you every couple of hours." She ended the call and turned off her phone.

"Shan! Shan!" Peanut yelled before he threw the phone at the wall.

Shan got out of the car and filled up her tank. Placing the nozzle back into its slot, she headed inside. The scent of grilled hot dogs smacked her in the face and made her nauseous. She grabbed a handbasket and a few napkins and covered her nose.

She began walking the aisles, filling up the basket with graham crackers, smoked turkey, bagels, cream cheese, orange juice, ginger ale and a few pieces of fresh fruit. She backtracked and threw in paper cups, napkins, plates and plasticware. She paid for the items along with the gas and headed for her car.

After she got everything situated, she slumped into the driver's seat and squeezed her eyes shut. She began to tremble. She saw Brianna. Her face was crystal clear. She had this huge smile on her face.

"B, why the fuck are you smiling?" Shan screamed. "Bitch, you left me here and think the shit is funny? Why the fuck did you blow your brains out? Was life that bad, B? You took the sucka's way out! Why, B? You could have waited a few more hours. I was coming for you!" She reached in the bag that she had packed for Brianna. "See?" she yelled out. "I was coming to get you. You could have waited. We was going to Hollywood, bitch!" She began pulling the clothes out of the bag. "Look at this, B. I was coming for you. Me and you. I forgave you.

"Peanut is home now, B. I had so much to tell you, about the setup, Forever and Briggen being fuckin' blood brothers and I'm getting ready to be a mommy," she sobbed as she smoothed out Brianna's clothes as if she were getting ready to put them on. "You were getting ready to be an auntie, bitch. See what you are going to miss out on!" she screamed. "That nigga Forever, he wanted me to get an abortion. But I said, 'Fuck him.' I'm a rida. I don't need him to help me with my baby. If he wants to be a fuckin' sperm donor, so what! It's his loss. Between me, his uncle and auntie, this baby will be spoiled rotten and won't want for nothing. B, I was feelin' Forever. But he was only playin' me to get his dick wet and to get paid. I still can't believe I was that dumb. Shit's really been crazy." She wiped her tears away and continued to talk. "And that bitch Nyla, I know she was behind the setup. I bet you could have brought that bitch for a penny when I didn't show up. Good lookin', B.

"Oh wait." Shan grabbed her bag and pulled out an envelope. "This is the letter that you sent me. I was so mad at you that I never bothered to open it. I brought it with me so that you could read it to me while I drove." Her hands were shaking as she opened up the envelope, pulled out the letter and saw the check for seven thousand dollars. "Damn you, Brianna." She gritted her teeth as she looked at the check again. She proceeded to read the letter. After she finished she balled it up and threw it forcefully at the window. Then she began banging on the steering wheel and screaming.

She was unaware of the figure standing in front of her window tapping on the glass. "Shan! Shan!" Briggen looked at the bags sprawled across the front seat. *Where the fuck is she off to?* He felt his heart rate speed up. "Shan!" He banged harder on the glass. "Open the door!" he ordered.

She looked up at him and like a robot she unlocked the door. He snatched it open. "Are you hurt? What the fuck is going on?" He was looking her over for signs of foul play. He breathed a sigh of relief when she appeared to be fine…physically. But emotionally, he sensed that she wasn't right. "Where are you on your way to?" he gently asked her.

"Why?" she snapped. "And where did you come from?"

"What do you mean why? I did you a favor, remember? I'm on your team. If you're gettin' ready to bounce at least you can tell me."

5

She glared up at him, embarrassed to be caught like this. "Where did you come from, Calvin?" She called him by his government name.

"You in my hood, Shan. I have businesses in this area, remember? I own this gas station." He smirked. "So, can you tell me where are you on your way to?"

"It's none of your concern, Briggen, so what difference does it make?"

He took a handkerchief out of his back pocket, squatted down and began to dry her face. "You're in no shape to be on the road. Look at you. You got your shit all packed. I'm worried about you. What the fuck has you so upset?"

She took the handkerchief from him and blew her nose. "I'm okay," she blurted unconvincingly.

"Woman, please. Like hell you are. You're gonna tell me something. Who and what are you running from?"

"I told you, it's none of your business. Now can you please move so that I can be on my way?"

"I ain't going nowhere until you tell me where you're going and why you look like you're having a nervous breakdown."

She sucked her teeth and blushed once again from embarrassment as she went to start the engine. He snatched the keys out of her hand.

"What do you think you're doing, Briggen?" She was almost screaming.

"If you want to be on your merry way, then I suggest you start talking."

"Unngghh," she growled. "You are such a pain in the ass, Briggen," she pouted as she banged her head back against the headrest. "Since you must know, I'm moving to the West Coast and my best friend just blew her fuckin' brains out. There! Now can I have my keys?"

"Who you talking about? Which girl? The one I met at the club?"

She nodded her head yes and the tears began flowing once again.

"Damn. That's fucked up. I'm sorry to hear that." He used his thumbs to dry more tears off her cheeks. "Why the West Coast? That's kind of far, isn't it? You got peoples out there?" She shook her head no. "Nobody?"

"No, Briggen. I just need to get as far away from here as possible. I need a fresh start."

"Baby, that's too far. Plus you don't know anybody. I'm not feelin' that at all, Shan. And you're driving? Nah, I ain't feelin' that."

"I didn't ask you how you felt about it."

"I still ain't with that. It's too far, and you're traveling by yourself? That's not a smart move, baby girl. Don't you think you should rethink this? At least for a week or two. Give yourself a chance to get your head right. Fo'real. You really need to rethink this. You are not in your right mind." He began thinking out loud. "Nah. You can't have these keys back." He stood up and yelled, "Hey, Woo! Come here, maine."

Shan jumped out of the car and began following him. "Briggen, give me my damn keys. You ain't my damn daddy." She was trying to grab them out of his hands. He threw them to Woo, who snatched them out of the air. "Briggen, now...is...not the time," she stammered. "Why are you doing this?"

"Somebody has to do it. You're not being rational."

"Rational!" she screeched as she screwed her face up. "Spell rational! Nigga, I am a grown-ass woman."

"So? You're still not being rational." He grabbed her hand. "Get into my car. Woo is gonna drive yours and follow us."

"Follow? Nigga, you have lost your fuckin' mind. Give me my damn keys, Briggen." She stomped in place as he held open the passenger door to his Denali. "I'm not going nowhere with you. Remember what happened the last time I was with you!" She was referring to the ass-whooping his girls had put on her at his club.

"Seriously, baby girl. We need to map out a plan. You can't just up and go somewhere without having a plan. What's the rush? The West Coast ain't goin' nowhere. We need to map shit out."

"We? We? We need to map shit out? When did you learn French? *We* don't need to do shit. You can get the fuck on so I can go on about mine." She was still standing in her same spot looking like a spoiled brat who was just told that she couldn't go outside to play.

"After I'm sure that you got a plan you can get your keys back. Now come on, get in my ride, it's starting to rain," he commanded.

"I *have* a plan, Briggen." She turned to Woo, who was getting into her car. "Can I have my keys please?" Briggen smiled at her, not wanting to believe he was going to get a second chance with her. He slammed the door and locked it. "Come on, Shan. Get in now. It's raining." Briggen watched her as she stomped over to the Denali and climbed in.

After they had been driving for ten minutes in silence, she asked, "Where are we going?"

"To my place. Why?"

"Well, how far is it? I need to use the bathroom."

A few minutes later Briggen pulled into a Waffle House on Raleigh Street in Lagrange.

"I need my cell phone."

"Where is it?"

"In my car."

"I'll get that while you use the restroom."

She sucked her teeth and rolled her eyes at him. "I'm sure you will." She got out and slammed the door.

When she came out of the bathroom, Briggen was standing at her car talking to Woo. He passed her the cell phone.

"Glad you rejoined us. I was wondering if you were going to jump out the back window and try to escape. What happened? They got bars on the window? And you look like you saw a ghost." Woo was trying not to laugh at Briggen's wisecracks.

Shan ignored him and headed to the Denali. As soon as she got in she called Peanut.

"Yo, Shan. Where the fuck are you?" Peanut barked into the phone. "You need to stop bullshittin' around. I'm worried about you, maine."

"Peanut, I'm bleeding. It's coming out in clots," she whispered as she looked out the side view mirror for Briggen. "Meet me at the emergency room. I think I lost the baby."

"What baby?"

"I'm pregnant, Peanut."

"Pregnant? By who? How? When the fuck was you gonna tell your brother? And don't say it's by that nigga at the prison!" he screamed on her.

"Okay...I won't say it then."

"I'ma kill that nigga and all of his family!"

"Peanut, stop it. Just meet me at the hospital." Briggen jumped in the ride just as she ended the call. "I need you to take me to the hospital. I still have to make my doctor's appointment."

"Hospital? What's wrong?"

"I'm scheduled for a physical. My job requires it before I transfer."

"Why at the hospital?" Briggen was skeptical.

"My doctor's office is on Med Place, Briggen. That's why. Now do you need any more info? If not then drop me off and I'll call you when I'm finished. It'll give me some time to clear my head."

"You don't want me to stay? Why do I feel like this is a trick?"

"Don't worry, it's not." Her stomach was cramping. "You got my car, and here, take my cell. I'll call you when I'm ready." She leaned her head back and closed her eyes, trying to hide the fact that she was in pain.

CHAPTER TWO

Janay was livid as she headed to see her dad, Big Choppa, the number one dope runner in Memphis and the one who had groomed her for the game. His bodyguard, Boomer, was sitting on the porch when she pulled up. Boomer stood six feet three inches, at three hundred forty pounds with no neck, and was black as tar. The whitest thing on him was his eyeballs and the prettiest was his teeth. He had been Choppa's bodyguard and right-hand man ever since she could remember.

"Boomer," Janay spoke as she climbed the front porch. He grunted, but the way he looked at her always made her feel exposed. Those eyes...his eyes seemed as if they were piercing her mind, reading her innermost thoughts. Other than that she loved him to death. When everyone else feared him, he was like her second father. Yes, his bite was most definitely meaner than his bark but he had nothing but love and loyalty for Big Choppa and his family. She quickly turned her head and eased the front door open. She took a deep breath before stepping inside.

She found Big Choppa relaxing in his La-Z-Boy, chin on his chest, appearing to be sound asleep. She knew he wasn't because he always slept very lightly. His bald head was shining in the dimly lit room. Old age and liver cancer were definitely taking their toll on her father. He had gone from a robust and healthy two hundred sixty pounds to a sickly one hundred seventy in less than six months.

He ignored old age and the liver cancer, continuing to hustle as if the hands of time were standing still or even pushed back to twenty years ago. Big Choppa wasn't hearing of getting out of the game. As a matter of fact, every time Janay would bring up the subject of chilling he would fuss her out.

The aroma of a down-South breakfast of catfish, eggs and grits filled the air. Big Choppa's favorite meal. Sure enough, as her gaze traveled to the tray next to the La-Z-Boy there was a plate with the remains of catfish bones, dried egg yolk and traces of grits. The hot sauce bottle was missing its top. The tall orange juice glass was almost empty.

Janay drew back the heavy olive drapes, giving some light to the dim living room. She stuck her fingers into the soil of several of the houseplants before getting the vase to give them some water.

"What I tell you 'bout messin' with my plants, Nay?" Big Choppa's voice boomed.

"They're very dry, Daddy. If I didn't mess with your plants they would have been dead a very long time ago."

They had this exact same conversation every time she came over.

"And why you gotta be openin' my drapes?"

Janay ignored him as she busied herself cleaning up his dishes and straightening up the living room. His oldest daughter was the spittin' image of her mother: her doe eyes, long slender frame, dark flawless complexion. Today she even had her long hair pulled into a bun, just the way her mother had worn hers. Janay's biological mother passed away when Janay was five. She suffered from the same disease as Choppa. From then on Big Choppa's girlfriend Ida stepped up and had been playing the mother role ever since. The whole family referred to her as Mom. After watching Janay go back and forth for twenty minutes he wanted to know what was up.

"What's botherin' you, Nay? You ain't over here to just clean up."

"You feel up to riding with me to check on the traps?"

He shook his head no and motioned to the front door. "Take Boomer with you. And what I tell you about callin' 'em traps? You're going to business establishments, not no corners."

"Daddy, please. Since when did dope houses become business establishments? They're traps. Niggas buying dope, niggas sellin' dope and niggas like us coming to collect the money. That's a trap. Now come on, Daddy," she whined. "I want you to ride with me."

"If there's somethin' you want to talk about, spit it out. Shit, girl, what I tell you about that?"

"It's personal, Daddy." Her voice trembled. "And it's not that easy to spit out."

"It's easy if you just go on and say it." Janay flopped onto the couch, and the tears came streaming down. "Aww, girl, what's the matter? You pregnant?"

"No," she sobbed.

"You and Shadee fighting again?" When she didn't respond, he shook his head. "Did that lil' negro put his hands on you?"

"No, Daddy." She was now crying harder. Shadee was no doubt the love of her life. They shared a son, Marquis, and had been together for the past six years. She was wifey. Every bitch knew it and respected that...except for Brianna. He wouldn't leave that gold-digging bitch alone for nothing in the world. She remembered the first time she had followed Shadee over to her house; his excuse was that she was holding his dope. What could she say? Brianna had been a thorn in her side ever since. But when she brought her ass over to Janay's house looking as if she had been smoking crack all night, that was it. Then when Brianna went on and put Shadee on blast saying that he had asked to marry her, that was the last straw. She went on and told Brianna, "Kill that nigga!" Janay had then stormed out the house and sped over to Big Choppa's.

"Nay! Don't lie to me. Now, tell me, did that nigga put his hands on you?" Choppa belted out once again.

"No, Daddy, he didn't. I wish he would have. An ass-whooping would be easier to deal with. Listen, Daddy, you can't tell nobody...not even Miss Ida, what I'm about to tell you. Okay?"

"Girl, if you don't say what it is you got to say, I'ma—"

"Daddy, this is serious. You gotta promise me you won't say anything," she cut him off. "Swear on Mommy's grave, Daddy."

Choppa rolled his eyes in disgust. "Girl, I'm the parent. Spit it out girl, damn."

"Dad, Shadee got that monkey."

"He what?"

"He is HIV-infected."

"My God! Nay...what about you? Don't tell me—"

"I don't know. I already made an appointment to get tested. We really hadn't been doing anything and I don't even know how long he's had it. He wouldn't tell me," she cried.

"I'ma break that nigga in two. So you're tellin' me y'all ain't been doin' it? Who has he been fuckin' since y'all ain't been doin' shit? Who did he get that shit from? He had to have got it from somebody!" Choppa was trying his best to get to the bottom of the story.

Janay squeezed her eyes shut. "I...I caught him..." she sobbed.

"You caught him with some bitch? Good then. I'm sorry, baby, but dammit to hell they deserve each other."

"Daddy, I caught him going up in his boy Doc."

"What!" Big Choppa yelled. "Going up in his boy?" He needed a few moments for that to register. "Awww damn! Hell naw, you tellin' me this nigga is a fruitcake?

A homo thug-ass nigga? Awww, Nay Nay, tell me it ain't so," he pleaded. "And...he passed that shit on to my baby?" Choppa was looking at Janay, hoping and praying that she was getting ready to say no.

"I have to get tested first, Daddy."

"This is some fucked-up shit." Choppa jumped out of his La-Z-Boy. "Oh that nigga gone tell me how long he's been fuckin' faggots in the ass. He got an old head like me fucked up," he mumbled as he headed for the stairs, leaving Janay wanting a hug from her father.

"Daddy, you can't be getting your blood pressure all up," she called after him. "Ain't shit we can do about it now...but deal with it. So chill out. Have you taken your medicine today?"

"Don't try to sidetrack me." He was fussing all the way up the stairs and was still fussing as he was coming back down. "The nigga should of thought about whose daughter he was fuckin'. After I finish with him he ain't gonna fuck nothin' else."

"Daddy, stop it."

"I'ma stop it all right. I'ma break his ass in two then cut off his dick and stop it up in his ass. They don't call me Choppa for nothing. And let me find out he done gave my baby that shit. I'ma bury that nigga and then pull his ass up, kill him and bury him again. Get him on the phone, Janay. Find out where he is. Boomer!" he yelled out.

The front door flew open. "I'm right here, Chop." He had an ugly scowl on his face. He knew from the tone of Choppa's voice that something wasn't right.

"We gotta make a run. I told you to call that boy, Nay. Get his faggot ass on the phone."

"Daddy! You promised you would keep this between us. Excuse us, Boomer." Boomer peered at Janay, then at Choppa, and slowly backed out the front door. Janay turned to her father. "You promised, Daddy."

"You promised for me. And I didn't tell Boomer shit."

"Whatever Daddy. You might as well tell him. You called Shadee a faggot. All he has to do is put two and two together. Plus, you always include him in my business."

"Then what the hell you complainin' for? Just get the nigga on the phone," he barked at Janay as he flipped out a nine-inch switchblade.

"I know where he is. He's at my house."

"What house? Why in the fuck do you got the nigga in your house?"

"He came over this morning."

"What, Janay?"

"Daddy, we still have a son together and I do still love him."

"Naw...fuck that bullshit! Your son spent the night at his grandmother's. And love him? His sorry ass ain't ask for your hand in marriage!" He shook his head in disgust. "Janay, don't tell me you still layin' up with this nigga!" He was in her face, and he grabbed her by her shoulders, shaking her. "Answer me, dammit. You still layin' up with this nigga? Why is he still at your house?" he yelled out.

Janay couldn't stop crying. "Daddy, stop screaming. He still lives there, have you forgot?"

"You should have put his ass out when you caught him stickin' his dick in another nigga's ass! Girl, have you lost yo' damn mind? He done told you he got HIV, you caught him fuckin' a nigga and he still in yo' damn house?"

"Daddy, we've been together for six years. I don't know. I-I don't know what I was thinking. I wanted to try and work it out...shit just happened so fast. Then to add insult to injury," she heaved and cried out, "his girl-friend Brianna came over to the house earlier, screaming. She was mad because she is infected and he promised to marry her and I got mad. I had had enough. She even had a burner. I told her to blast that nigga. I freaked out and just left them there. I *wanted* her to split his wig. I am through with him, Daddy, so stop trippin'."

"Hold up. Hold up. Janay, you left his other woman in your house holding a gun on your man? Aww, Janay. Sometimes you're so smart, you're stupid. What if she kills the nigga in your house? Boomer! Come on, girl." He snatched her arm. "We need to get over there."

Boomer drove the Lincoln Continental, Big Choppa sat in the backseat and Janay was in the front. She was dialing her house phone and Shadee's celly but no one picked up.

"If he is fucking in my house again, this time I am going to kill him and whoever it is he's fuckin'." She dialed the numbers again.

"Boomer, make some calls. Put it out there that I'm lookin' for this clown," Choppa ordered, and Boomer immediately began dialing his phone while still handling the wheel.

Ten minutes later they turned onto Janay's block in Cordova. "There go the nigga's truck right there," Choppa growled.

"Yeah that's it." Janay's heart was pounding uncontrollably. She pushed the car door open before the car could come to a complete stop.

"Girl, hold up," Choppa hollered after her. By the time Boomer parked and the both of them, Boomer especially, struggled out of the car Janay was already inside her house. When they opened the front door, Janay was running toward them screaming and crying. She jumped into her father's arms. Boomer pulled out his heat as he rushed past both of them. Choppa was trying to calm down Janay, who was releasing gut-wrenching screams.

"Chop, come look at this main man," Boomer called out.

Choppa pulled out his heat. "Get some fresh air, baby. Go on the porch for a few minutes."

"No...Daddy, I gotta see him again," she cried.

"What the hell for? Go get some fresh air." He pushed her toward the door and waited until she went outside before going to see what it was that had his daughter freaking out.

"It smells like dog shit up in here," Boomer commented as they both covered up their noses.

When Choppa got close up on Shadee's body, he stifled a gag. "Gotdamn! Ain't no bitch did this to a nigga. If she did, I need her on my team."

"He is fucked up," Boomer added. They took a few steps forward and were leaning directly over him. Shadee was naked from the waist down and lying on his side. His ass was covered in blood. They leaned in closer to peek at his face and both jumped back when his eyes fluttered open.

"Shit!" Choppa said in surprise.

"H-help...me," Shadee faintly whispered.

"Well I'll be damned! Ain't this a bitch!" Choppa yelled out. "Nigga, you is fucked up. I thought you was dead. This fool must got nine lives."

"H-help," he groaned.

Brianna had aimed three shots to his head. One of the bullets was in his jaw, one had grazed his head and the final one had skinned his ear and gone into the carpet. She was definitely a lousy shooter.

Boomer was looking around the living room. The lamps and end tables were knocked over, sofa cushions were tossed all around the room and the smell was undescribable...sex, dogs and dog shit permeated the air.

"Nigga, I'ma call an ambulance, but what you want me to tell them what happened up in here? Shit, boy, you gotta give me sumthin' to work with." Choppa was holding a conversation with Shadee as if he were up and about and not on the verge of meeting on the crossroads.

Shadee just stared blankly at Choppa, who had pulled out a handkerchief and was covering his nose. When he saw Shadee close his eyes he yelled, "Man, don't die on me now. You are my grandson's father. What happened? Who did this here shit?"

"T-the dogs," he gasped.

"Dogs? How many?"

"I d-don't...a lot."

"Gotdamn. Boomer, call this boy an ambulance. I was gonna fuck you up my gotdamned self but shit, they ain't leave me nothing to do."

"Daddy." Janay was coming through the front door. Boomer rushed over to stop her.

"No, baby. You don't need to see this." Boomer pushed her back out toward the door.

She was trying her best to break away. "Is he dead? Let me see him, Boomer."

"No, baby, he ain't dead. He's gonna be okay. The ambulance is on the way."

"Please, let me see him." Her knees buckled as she held on to Boomer and started crying.

"Are you clean? You know the po-po is coming."

She nodded her head yes.

Big Choppa and Boomer stood by the squad car as Janay was getting out. Three different officers had questioned her for almost an hour apiece and she was exhausted. She had to report to the station first thing in the morning to be interrogated some more.

Detectives were still inside the house and Janay was ready to go crash at her dad's. As they walked over to

Big Choppa's car, the white officer of the crew called Janay as she jogged over to where she was.

"Ma'am, the young lady who was here with your boy-friend, Ms. Brianna Russell, she committed suicide."

"Suicide?" Janay questioned.

"She blew her own brains out."

Janay gasped and her knees got weak. Big Choppa held one arm while Boomer held the other as they led her to the car.

"I'm sorry about that." The officer then pointed at Choppa. "Hey, Big Choppa Mr. Devlin, we got our eyes on you," she taunted.

"We got our eyes on you too," he shot back.

CHAPTER THREE

When Briggen pulled up in front of the emergency room, Shan picked up on his hesitancy. "I'll be okay, Briggen. I'll call you when I'm done."

"Girl, you think I'm just gone leave you here, not knowing what's the matter with you or if you're okay? Man, I'm comin' with you."

"Boy, I told you, I'm tight. It's only a physical, Briggen. It's not like I'm going for surgery or something." At least that's what she hoped.

His cell rang and he quickly flipped it open while motioning for Shan not to move. Her stomach was cramping and it was taking everything within her power not to double over and scream out. *If he doesn't hurry up and end that call, I'ma—*

"Nigga, what?" he yelled into the phone. "Maine..." He jumped out of the truck and slammed the door. "Fuck the bullshit!" she heard him yell. "I'll do the shit myself. I'm headin' over that way right now." He turned the phone off. "Woo, you ain't gonna believe this shit."

Shan exhaled a sigh of relief as another cramp subsided. Then she slowly got out of the truck. Briggen ran over to her. "Baby, hold up."

Shan looked at her watch. "Briggen, I'll be fine. It's only a physical exam. My appointment is at two and it's almost a quarter after." He shook his head no as if to say he wasn't buying her story. "Briggen, trust me. I'll be all right. Plus you sound like you got some business to handle. I'll be all right. I'll call you when I'm done. Just be ready and don't keep me waiting." She slung her Louis Vuitton bag over her shoulder and headed for the emergency room entrance. She looked back and Briggen was standing there with a frown on his face. She mouthed, "I'll be fine," waved and stepped through the sliding double doors.

It being a Friday night, the ER was in full swing. It smelled like funk, blood, sickness and death, all rolled into one. An orderly rushed past her with an old white guy with his head wrapped in bloody bandages, almost knocking her over.

"Damn, I wish I didn't have to be in this bitch," Shan mumbled under her breath. The waiting room reminded her somewhat of a battle zone. Homeless people were sleeping on three chairs put together. If it was somewhere to sit, who would want to sit down? There were prostitutes lumped up from one of their pimps or tricks, trifling-ass mommas with four of their five kids sick as hell and most likely been sick all week, feens sitting in the corner throwing up everywhere. "Ughhh." Shan pulled the ticket and it read 02 while the digital sign

25

read 76. *Oh hell naw.* Just as Shan was about to try to slip through the doors that separated the waiting room from the treatment areas, a herd of medical staff came rushing through, pushing a young boy who couldn't be no older than thirteen. He was shot up and covered in blood.

"Excuse me, Doctor." She boldly stepped in front of the one who was lagging behind.

He turned, stopped and raised an eyebrow. "How can I help you?"

"I'm about seven weeks pregnant. I've been under a lot of stress. Earlier, I started bleeding and now I'm cramping."

"That isn't a good sign...Mrs.?"

"Ms. McKee. Shan McKee."

"Ms. McKee, follow me."

"Nurse Smith," he called out. "Can you get Ms. McKee here prepared for an examination? Call OB. We need someone stat."

"Okay, Ms. McKee. Have you been triaged yet?" he asked as he led her to a wheelchair.

"No."

"When did you say the bleeding began?"

"About two hours ago."

"And the cramping?"

"About forty-five minutes ago?"

"Is this your first pregnancy?"

"Yes." Her voice cracked.

Nurse Smith returned and he smiled. "This is my wife, she'll take real good care of you. Good luck." He patted her shoulder as Nurse Smith wheeled her up to one of the triage nurses and ordered that she immediately get Shan prepped for an examination.

Shan then was put in a treatment room, handed a gown and told to undress from the waist down.

Two and a half hours later, Peanut was pacing the waiting area and Shan was getting a D&C. She had suffered a miscarriage.

Losing all patience, Peanut marched up to the receptionist station for the third time. "Excuse me, ma'am. My sister, Shan McKee, can I see—"

"Yes." She cut him off. "Here's your visitor's pass. Follow the yellow dots to the elevators."

"About time," Peanut mumbled, snatching the pass. He stopped at the gift shop, bought some get-well balloons and flowers, then headed toward the elevators. Arriving on the third floor he stepped off the elevators and followed the signs to room 313. The door was cracked and Shan was getting dressed.

"What are you doing?" Peanut asked, poking his head in and startling the hell out of her.

"I'm getting dressed. You scared the hell out of me, Peanut."

"What happened?" he asked, setting the flowers on the desk next to the bed and tying the balloons to the bedpost. The patient in the next bed turned up the volume on the TV. "What the fuck is going on? You scaring the hell out of me. First, you tell me that you're moving

27

way across the fuckin' country, then you tell me Brianna blew her own fuckin' brains out! And now you're pregnant!"

"I'm not pregnant anymore. I had a miscarriage, they gave me a D&C and now I'm ready to go," Shan stated matter-of-factly.

"A miscarriage? You keeping secrets from me now? How far along were you?" Peanut was beside himself.

"I wasn't that far along. Seven, eight weeks."

"Who is the nigga?"

"You already know who it is."

"Don't tell me no jailbird-ass nigga. Please tell me it was a guard or something."

"An inmate, Peanut. I told you about him already. Yeah. I fucked an inmate. So the fuck what? I was feelin' the nigga, until I told him I was pregnant and he said he already had a family. Then he calmly told me to get an abortion."

Peanut stood there staring at his sister with a blank look on his face. He definitely had a lot on his mind. He had never thought that his baby sister could hide so much shit from him. His thoughts went back to the day when he finally made bail and she was there to pick him up. He knew something was bothering her but he chopped it up to her being stressed out.

Shan on the other hand had had all kinds of crazy thoughts going through her head. She was trying to figure out how to tell her big brother that she was pregnant by an inmate, how she did what she had to do, illegally, to pay for his attorney and post his bail and how that led from one thing to another.

When they both stopped trying to read each other's minds, Shan finally said something. She mainly spoke about how mad she was about Brianna flipping the script on the family by setting Peanut up. He was shocked but happy when she told him that she got some niggas to go over to Brianna's house and fuck her up. He told her that Brianna should've been glad that was all she did, because when he caught up with her ass, he was going to slowly torture her to death.

Shan reluctantly broke down and told Peanut that she was talking to some inmate named Forever. She decided out of fear to leave out the being-pregnant part. She reminded him that while he was locked up, none of his people was coming through with any bread, for lawyers or bail. She told him that Forever made her an offer that she couldn't refuse. All she had to do was pick up the dope and drop it into a trash can. Even though he was short on the bread, most of the money she had hustled up came from him.

She then went on to tell Peanut that Brianna was the one who told her that Forever's wife was going to set her up because she found out that they were fucking. She made sure to leave out the part about her approaching his wife, Nyla, as she was going on a visit, right there in the parking lot.

Peanut could not believe what he was hearing. He wanted to choke the shit out of her. He couldn't believe that she would jeopardize her freedom and safety like that. Before he knew it, he had smacked the shit out of her. Shan was stunned. She knew of her brother losing his cool at times, but she never thought that it would happen with her. Shit, she was grown and his own flesh and blood.

Shan burst into tears and started screaming, "Let me paint a picture for you, Peanut. While you was stressing and making sure niggas didn't take that ass, yeah, I fucked a prisoner. But he was the only one that was helping with lawyer fees, transfer fees and bond tickets. Nigga, and let me remind you about those bitches you fuck with. Them hoes ain't come off of nothing but a few dollars. If it was up to them, where would you still be sitting? So miss me with all that drama. If I had to do it all over again, I would. So fuck you. And I *am* moving to Cali."

Peanut felt bad for smacking her. Because she was right, everything she did was for him, when no one else on his team stepped up to the plate. She also told him that it was useless to look for his so-called main man Nick or anyone else because they were ghost. To Peanut's surprise Shan handed him almost a half brick and four stacks that she had gotten from Forever. She told him to take it, that it was just a little something for him to get on with. Fuck the losses. Charge it to the game. After that he really felt like shit. On top of that he was responsible for getting her caught up in all the madness. Now he needed to figure out how he was going to keep her from moving to Cali.

"Damn, I'm all right. You straight?"

"I'm straight. Now will you say something and stop looking at me sideways. Hello! What are you daydreaming about?" She interrupted his train of thought, and brought him back to the here and now. "I made a mistake. Everything's cool. Say something."

"Mistake?" He frowned. "That's an understatement." He looked at her as if he didn't know her. "I'm just in shock. You fucked my head up with this. This ain't like you. Selling drugs, fuckin' with a nigga that's locked up and at your fuckin' prison job? This shit is...just crazy."

"You're right. This ain't me. But guess what? I ain't have time to sit and ponder over if this was the right decision or not. I had to do what I had to do. And I'm over it and now you need to get over it. Now let the shit go, Peanut. I'm kicking myself in the ass enough."

"All right. I'ma let that go for now. So let's talk about what's the real deal with you moving out West? Did they transfer you because they found out you was fuckin' an inmate?"

"Ms. McKee," the nurse interrupted, "since you're leaving against the doctor's orders, as soon as you're ready at least stop at the nurse's station to sign your discharge papers and pick up your prescription. And be sure to follow up with your own personal doctor." She popped back out.

"Peanut, I explained to you why I'm moving to Cali, I just want to get away. I don't like it here anymore. Cali is where they have an opening for me, so I went for it. And no, they didn't find out about me and…him." She stood up and wobbled.

Peanut grabbed her arm and helped her back down to the bed. "Are you all right? Maybe you should stay for a couple more days. Why the fuck are you leaving against the doctor's orders?"

"I don't want to stay overnight. This place is depressing. Please get me out of here."

"Stay put. Let me go get a wheelchair."

"Boy, just hold my arm. I'm ready to go."

"No. I'm getting a wheelchair." He rushed out of the room.

After she was formally discharged and made it downstairs to the lobby, Shan said, "Let me use your phone."

He passed it to her. "Hold up while I go and pull my ride around. What about your ride?"

"I have a ride. My friend Lisa is coming to pick me up. She has my car."

"Lisa? Who is Lisa?" His phone vibrated and he checked the caller ID.

"A friend from the job. I'll be fine. Answer your phone." He stood there looking at her. "Answer it, Peanut."

"I think you need to come home with your brother."

"Peanut, I already told the girl that as soon as I was done, I'd call her."

"We need to have a serious sit-down before you head out West."

"Yeah, we need to kick it about a lot of things. I'ma chill for a minute. Shit is crazy. Brianna…dead. I just lost the baby I was carrying. Give me a few days. I'm gonna call you."

"Shan, don't try no slick shit. You better make it your business to holla at me. I'm not fuckin' around with you, girl."

She cut him off. "Boy, answer your damn phone."

"As long as you got my point."

She stood up, rolled her eyes and walked over to the pay phones. Slipping two quarters into the pay-phone slot, she kept an eye on Peanut.

"Yeah," Briggen answered.

"I'm ready. How far are you?"

"Shan, you on some bullshit. Don't no damn physical take five hours."

"Briggen, my brother came up here and I hung out with him. Are you coming or what?"

"I'm on my way."

She hung up and went over to Peanut, who was in an intense conversation. She wanted him to hurry up and leave before Briggen pulled up.

"Damn," Peanut gritted as he ended his call. "C'mon and let me drop you off. I got a run I need to make."

"Peanut, do you pay attention? I told you my girl is on her way and I'll call you when I get to her house. I'm fine."

"Where she stay?"

"In Germantown."

"Germantown? How the fuck a guard can afford to stay in Germantown?"

"Who said she was a guard? And for your info she lives with her parents."

"I still ain't feelin' you going with some strangers. Fuck that shit, you need to come with me."

"Come with you where? All your shit is in storage. And you need to get yourself together. Where are *you* going? Because the last time I checked your bitch Keke had a nigga all up in your spot and them other bitches you was fuckin' caught amnesia. I suggest you focus on getting yourself together and don't worry about me."

"Oh, so you got advice for big brother now?" He smirked as he leaned over and kissed her on the cheek. "Aiight then. I'ma go ahead and dip."

Thank God. Second time today I was saved by a phone call. "I'll call you later."

"Oh, and by the way, Cali ain't a good look. Don't run 'cause you slipped and fucked an inmate then got pregnant with his seed. We all fuck up, sis."

"Please tell me that you are not going to keep throwing that shit up in my face?"

"Sheeit, I'm not even sure if I should be calling you Shan anymore. Your name should be Vicky with all the secrets you got."

"Ha ha ha. Very funny. Bye, nigga. We'll discuss this when I'm feeling better." She let out a sigh of relief as she watched him rush out the double doors and walk right past Briggen's truck. She had been beginning to believe that he wasn't going to leave. She waited until he pulled

34

out of the parking lot and decided to leave the miscarriage behind her.

As soon as Briggen saw her he jumped out of his truck. "You straight, shawty? You look a little weak for somebody only having a physical." He opened the passenger door and helped her inside, while eyeing her skeptically.

"I'm fine. Tired but fine." She leaned back into the soft buttery leather, reclined the seat all the way back and closed her eyes. The inside of his ride smelled like Lacoste.

When he jumped into the driver's seat and pulled off, he started to grill her. But when he saw how tired she looked he decided to wait. They drove to his house in complete silence. No conversation, music...nothing. She gave him a cool point for that. She had a bunch of shit to mull over. Right now she was supposed to be enjoying a nice long ride out West, starting brand-new, her and Brianna leaving the city of Memphis behind. She had been looking forward to it. Without B to keep her company, she was actually having second thoughts.

Brianna...she was really gone.

Peanut. She shouldn't have given him Forever's package. Now he was going to hit the streets with a vengeance. But then why was she fooling herself? If it hadn't been Forever's package, it would have been someone else's because he was going to get his hustle on...regardless. But if Nyla, Forever's wife, would of had her way, that package would have been the Feds' package.

Forever. She was feeling that it was a blessing in disguise that she lost the baby. A new job, a new state, by herself and with a baby? A baby by a nigga who told her to get an abortion? What in the hell was she thinking?

Then there was Briggen. How did she fall into his web...once again? She recalled the day that they met. She had taken her car to get some work done on it. It was his shop. He introduced himself as Calvin. He was a businessman. A legit businessman. They started kickin' it over the phone for about two months straight. He took her to Las Vegas for her birthday and that was the first time that they fucked. After that she didn't hear from him again. He didn't even return her messages. Then there was that night at the club...his club. She and Brianna went out to celebrate her new job at the prison. When she saw him she didn't know if she wanted to embrace him or spit on him. When Brianna explained to her that he wasn't Calvin the businessman but Briggen the dope dealer, she had heard enough and decided to leave. However, he managed to talk her into sticking around so that he could explain his disappearing act. She reluctantly agreed, which resulted in her getting her ass beat by not one but two of his bitches. What were the odds of her running into him on this very day?

Entering the gated community, Briggen coasted to a stop in front of his condo and jumped out to take the mail out of his box, then pulled up into the driveway. Shan's car was already parked.

"Welcome to my humble abode."

She cracked a smile as she followed him inside. The first thing she noticed was the large chess coffee table with pieces the size of hot-sauce bottles. "Where did you get this from? This is amazing." The pieces were obviously handcrafted. The queen looked like a real queen and the knights were covered with authentic horsehair. "Impressive," she mumbled.

Then she took in the rest of her surroundings. The color gold overwhelmed her senses. Next was a pair of carved wooden seahorses that caught her eye. Even the living room furniture was gold with splashes of olive.

"Oh my God! Are those real?" She went over to an open glass frame that held about ten seahorses suspended on fine wires.

"Yeah."

She snickered. "Why do I get the feeling that I'm at the beach?" She twirled around and her gaze fell on the huge chandelier hanging from the ceiling. "That chandelier looks like a giant octopus. You got real seahorses in a frame, carved wooden seahorses over there, huge wooden seahorses on the desk, the seashell lamp and the colors? What the fuck?"

Briggen laughed. "Why are you insulting my taste? I love the beach. This is my own little private beach house. I know you gonna let me have that."

"I'm not insulting you. But—"

"But what?"

"Why don't you move somewhere where there is an actual beach or an ocean?" She couldn't stop giggling.

"I will one day. But for now, this is it."

"Let me guess. You brought this house from a clucker for a couple of rocks?"

"Oh, you really got jokes, Shan. You really got jokes."

"So you said private. Does that mean that none of your hoes will be running up in here?"

"You have nothing to worry about. Trust me. No hoes will be running up in here. So you can get comfortable and chill here as long as you like."

"Can I see the kitchen?"

"Not if you're gonna be insulting me and laughing in my face."

"Where is the kitchen?"

"Just turn to your left."

She headed for the kitchen. It looked like an old ship. It had ship-replicated windows, an anchor and fishnets. It was very spacious and even with the stainless steel appliances it was still beachy and ocean-like. Even down to the wallpaper. "Aye, aye, Captain," she joked. It was definitely beyond Shan's imagination. "This is...so not you, Briggen," she mumbled.

Leaving the kitchen, she went to inspect the bedrooms. The master bedroom was olive green and had an impressive Gregorius-Pineo Moragas four-poster bed. The linen drapes went around the entire room. He had a La-Z-Boy, ottoman and huge flat-screen TV. The carpet was linen and olive. It was obvious that he hardly stayed here. She didn't want to believe that this was his house. It had to belong to a couple of white yuppies.

She ventured off to what appeared to be the guest bedroom. The walls were cream-colored, and the geometric espresso drapes made her dizzy. The bedspread was Horizon in espresso. A few pictures on the wall. Simple. Very different. The bathroom was old-fashioned with freestanding bowl sinks, something she had never seen outside a magazine. She backtracked to the master bath, which was huge. The shower was all glass. He could lie in the bed and watch whatever ho he had over for the night take a shower.

"I brung most of your things in," he said, startling her.

"Thanks. I would love to take a nice hot shower, eat something and go to bed. You think you can accommodate a sister?"

"I'm at your beck and call. I just want you to enjoy your stay at the beach house."

"Since you got jokes, you can take my bags to the guest room."

He smiled. "Just make yourself at home."

She called Peanut and left him a message on his voice mail, then she was finally able to indulge in a hot, steamy, relaxing shower. By the time she finished and threw on something comfortable the house smelled good. Her toes gripped the thick carpet as she followed her nose.

"A brother that can cook. At least it smells like you can cook," she teased.

"Maine, you looking at a master chef." He pulled off his apron and went to pull out a chair for her. She had slipped into a pair of shorts and a T-shirt. And so had he.

He fixed a plate and set it in front of her.

"What do we have here?" Shan licked her lips.

"Briggen's famous crab cakes, glazed carrots, roasted parsley potato wedges, and"—he went to the refrigerator and pulled out a huge bowl of spinach salad and placed it in the middle of the table—"to drink, your choice of vintage white or red wine."

"Impressive. Very impressive." She poured a glass of the red wine. "Are you going to allow me to dine alone?"

"Nah. I'm just making sure you're straight before I sit down."

"I'm straight. Come on. I'm hungry."

He laughed, fixed himself a plate and sat down to join her. Her mouth hung open as he said grace.

"Oh my God," she mumbled. "How many faces of Calvin aka Briggen are there?"

"Stick around if you really want to find out."

"I'ma stick my fork in this crab cake first." And she did. "Oh...oh...Briggen. I love you." She closed her eyes and savored the spicy seasoning. "Ohmygosh, these are so good. Look at me with a straight face and tell me you cooked these."

"I cooked them, girl."

"You are scaring me."

"I don't know why you trippin', brothers can cook."

"But—"

"But what?"

"Nothing."

"Enjoy the dinner, Shan, and stop insinuating that a baller can't cook."

She started laughing. "I didn't say that."

"Because I didn't give you a chance to. Am I right?"

"Okay. Okay. You got me."

"Umm-hmmm. Just enjoy your meal."

Shan had been chillin' up at Briggen's crib for the past week. At first he was in and out, basically stopping by to see if she was okay and to cook her dinner. She spent her time relaxing and getting her mind right as well as healing from the D&C. He eventually went to Detroit for four days.

She was lying across his bed watching TV One on his flat screen, which was the only TV in the house, when she heard his Denali pull up. She glanced over at the clock and it read 1:48 a.m. She hadn't seen him for a couple of days.

He stood in the bedroom doorway staring at her. She pressed the mute button and tried to read his facial expression. They gazed at each other for several minutes before Briggen broke the silence.

"You done fuckin' with Forever?"

That caught her off guard. "Where did that come from?"

"I need to know. I mean I'm feelin' you. Plus, we really haven't taken time out to talk."

"Well, yes I am finished with your brother. I would have never—"

Briggen cut her off. "I don't need an explanation. All I needed to hear was yes."

He walked slowly over to the bed as he tossed his Detroit fitted cap over to the dresser and dropped the Al Wissam leather jacket onto the ottoman. He lowered himself on top of her and began playing with her nipples and gently planting kisses all over her face, shoulders and neck.

"I missed you," he whispered into her ear. "I'm glad you decided to stay."

She moaned as she wrapped her legs around his waist and began stroking the back of his neck. "You're...so... tense," she whispered in between moans.

He paused with the kisses and playing with her nipples to look into her eyes. He eased up, kissed her chin and then went for her lips. She opened her mouth to play with his tongue. "Mmumm," she moaned as she pressed up against his hard dick and continued to massage his neck. He gently slid her silk tee over her breast and began sucking on her nipple.

"Briggen," she whimpered. His mouth was now taking in as much of her tatas as he wanted to taste. "Briggen, hold up, baby."

He slowly allowed her breast to ease out of his mouth. Planting kisses along her shoulder and neck, nibbling on her earlobe and finally landing his lips on hers. "You've... got...the sweet...est lips," he groaned in between kisses as she slowly ground her pussy onto his strong thighs. Her breathing was getting faster and their grinds more intense as Shan dry-fucked herself to a quick orgasm. Briggen's dick was about to break as she trembled beneath him with her eyes closed. His huge hand massaged her ass, and then tugged at her shorts.

"No, Briggen," she purred.

"No what?" He was still tugging on her tight shorts.

"Briggen, what do you want from me?"

"Oh, you done got yours, so now you want to talk? I want to fuck, that's what I want."

"We can't."

"Why not?"

"I'm on my period." She was still bleeding from the miscarriage.

He looked down to her face to see if she was playing. "Awww damn." He rolled off her onto his back.

She smirked as she seductively straddled his thighs, undid his belt buckle, unsnapped his jeans and slid his zipper down. He was breathing heavily as he looked on, anticipating what she was getting ready to do. His massive hard-on pushed through the slit in his boxers.

"You're too little to handle this nigga." He pointed down at his dick.

"Nigga, please, you obviously don't know who I am. I have a master's in brain surgery. They call me the head doctor."

"Well, I need some help, Doc." He watched her as she stroked him. "Show big daddy what...ungh...you got."

"Uhmm-hmmm. Listen to yourself. Big daddy can't even form a sentence and I ain't even got started yet."

She leaned down, blew on the head and then began sucking him. One hand massaged his balls while the other hand was gripping the base of his dick, sending Briggen on a frenzy and whining like a bitch. Grabbing on to her head, he grunted and then released a warm load of semen all down her throat.

She slowly released his limp dick and was on her knees with a smirk on her face, both hands on her hips, looking down at Briggen, who had his eyes closed.

"Nigga, if I didn't know what your dick game was all about I would call you the one-minute man. I hadn't even got started yet."

His eyes remained closed but he smiled. "Don't let that shit go to your head. I bet you can't do that shit again."

"Nigga, what! Look at this." She lifted his dick with a couple of fingers and it flopped back down.

"Oh, so now you got jokes." He pulled her on top of him and greedily kissed her. "I gave you a cool point. I thought you was gonna leave a brother hangin'. But you showed me that you got skills. I'ma have to hold you hostage," he teased.

"I don't think so. I'm leaving in a couple of days."

"A couple of days?"

"Yeah. I gotta call Brianna's mother to see how the funeral went and I gotta talk to my brother and convince him that I'll be all right."

"I don't want you to go. You can stay here. You got the joint all to yourself. I need you, Shan."

"Need me? Briggen, don't start. This is something I have to do for me. I can't stay in this town much longer. I can't."

"I need you, girl."

"Briggen, you don't *need* me. Now I'm trying to be nice and not bring up all those bitches you got. But you're really pushing me."

He grabbed her by her locks and kissed her again. "I need you, Shan. There's no way I can compare you with them other broads." He traced her jawline with his thumb while gazing into her eyes, forcing her to look away. He turned her face toward his and kissed her again. "I need you. And you know it's not for selfish reasons. I need you. I can't let you get away this time."

"Well, if it's not selfish and you really do need me, leave this shit and come with me."

"Cali is too far, but we can go someplace else, not too far, not too close. And I bet your brother would like that much better. You don't have to answer me now. Think about it."

"So, you would leave all of this shit behind? For me?"

"Not in a day. But I could do it in a couple of months."

"There is no way in hell I could stick around for a couple of months."

"I'm not asking you to. What I'm saying is that I could go back and forth but it will take me a few months to get shit wrapped up. Don't answer me now. I want you to think about it. All right?" he asked her again.

"Why me, Briggen?"

"You know why. Them bitches are a one-hit wonder, in it to win it for themselves. You know they don't give a fuck about me. They just want the money. I may get grimey sometimes but I'm still human. I do have a heart, Shan. At the end of the day when the dust settles, I gotta have somebody to be in my corner, not just in it for the paper. Somebody with that bulletproof love. And you know you the one."

"I can't believe this shit!" Shan stormed out of Brianna's mother's house. "Two damn weeks and they haven't even buried the girl." Shan yanked at her locks as she talked to herself.

Shan was in for a shock when she stopped by Brianna's mother's and was told that they were too distraught to bury Brianna but would cremate her when they got over their grief. Of course they hadn't been too distraught to go over to her house and clean out her closet and take the furniture. Her sister and her mother both had on her clothes and jewelry. Shan couldn't stomach being in the same room with them. She was in absolute disbelief. They gave her the key to Brianna's condo and wanted Shan to clean it out for their trifling asses.

As soon as she got in the car she picked up her celly and called Peanut. When she was getting ready to turn off her phone he decided to pick up.

"Yeah."

"It's me. I need you to meet me at Brianna's. I got the key."

"Give me a half hour."

"Hurry up."

"Twenty minutes, Shan. Damn."

"I'ma sit outside until you show."

"I'll be there."

When Shan pulled up in front of Brianna's it felt eerie. "Damn you, Brianna," Shan spat as she hugged herself. She dialed Peanut again, crying.

"Ten minutes, Shan, damn. Hold tight."

"Why you gotta holler? I can't stop shaking. I can still feel her. Her mom and her sister had on her clothes and her jewelry. I think them bitches are crazy."

"Everybody deals with death differently, Shan."

"It's just fucked up, that's all I'm saying. They haven't even buried her yet. Who lets a body sit up for two weeks? We just as bad; we didn't even have plans to go to the funeral."

"You muthafuckin' right! Fuck burying her. I sure didn't have any plans to go nowhere near her bitch-ass funeral. I would have done some ignorant shit."

"You still feel like that?"

"I hate that bitch!"

"It doesn't matter. We gotta bury her. I don't even know how much shit like that cost." Shan was rambling.

"Don't sweat it. I got it," Peanut assured her.

"Where are you?"

"Almost there. Sit tight."

"Hurry up, I'm waiting." Shan hung up and called Briggen.

"What's up, shawty?" Briggen asked.

"Hey."

When he noticed that she wasn't going to say anything, he asked, "You all right?"

"Not really."

"What's up?"

"I'm getting ready to go into Brianna's house. It just feels...weird."

"It's supposed to. That was yo' girl. Y'all were tight."

She sighed. "You know I gotta bury her. Her own mother told me that she is not up to the task."

Briggen chose his words carefully. "Look at it this way, your girl wouldn't want it any other way."

Shan thought about it for a couple of minutes. "You know what? I didn't look at it like that. Thanks. I needed to hear that." She dried her eyes and they kicked it for several minutes before Peanut pulled up next to her. "I gotta go. My brother is here. See you when I see you." She hung up.

"Damn." Briggen looked down at the phone. He and Woo were kicking it at their meeting spot. "She didn't even ask where I was or was I coming by the crib. She just told me, 'See you when I see you.'"

"Nigga, you ain't all that. Not every shawty is gonna sweat you. It ain't like you the best thing since sliced bread," Woo teased as he laughed at him.

"You don't understand. I am the best thing since sliced bread. I'm Briggen, nigga. I'm that nigga," Briggen said with a straight face. "And she chillin' up in my spot talkin' 'bout see you when I see you." He even had to laugh at that one.

Just then his dope broad Tami came in. She walked over to him, gave him a duffel bag and kissed him on the lips.

Peanut and Shan were cleaning up Brianna's condo in silence. It was weird for both of them. She had been a big part of their lives. And the condo was just as much theirs as it was hers. Peanut took the kitchen and living room and Shan took the rest of the house. Brianna's mom and sister had taken only the clothes and the big stuff. Peanut had called a locksmith to come open Shadee's safe. They didn't understand how the greedy broads had overlooked it. The way they left everything in shambles, it was obvious that they were in a big hurry.

Shan was seated on the floor, going through a briefcase of papers. The last two documents caused her to break down.

"Peanut," she cried out. "Peanut!" she then screamed.

He ran into the bedroom and she was sitting on the floor crying. "Shit, you screaming as if someone was jackin' you, girl, damn."

"This ain't good. This shit ain't good." She handed him the documents, pulled her knees up to her chest and was rocking back and forth.

Peanut took his time going over the top document. He finally said, "Yo, this is a life-insurance policy for a hundred g's. You are the sole beneficiary. Damn. What if we hadn't come over here? What if you would have left for Cali? You would have never found this out. See! This is a sign. You don't need to go, baby sis."

"It's not that document," Shan screamed. "Look at the other one. Plus, she committed suicide. I can't collect the money."

Peanut continued thumbing through the life-insurance policy. When he finished, he opened up a closed document. When he saw the test results stating that Brianna Russell was HIV-positive, he turned pale white as the papers fell to the floor.

"Peanut, I can't lose you too. Go get tested."

"What?"

"Go get tested. I know you was fucking her, Peanut," Shan screamed. "I'm not dumb." She jumped up off the floor. "If you got that shit, I will kill you myself." She stormed past him and headed for the door. "I'll holla at you later."

CHAPTER FOUR

W hat the fuck happened to him, yo? Won't nobody tell me shit. They wouldn't even let me see him." Born was crying out of frustration. "He's not just my uncle; he's like my pops, yo."

The entire crew was in Shadee's apartment, upset, confused and trying to get some answers. Here their leader, brother, fellow soldier and mentor was laid up in a hospital bed in critical condition under police protection. Janay couldn't be reached and no one was giving them any answers. They could feel it. Shit was about to be fucked up.

Born was sitting on the floor, his back against the front door. Jo Jo, Teraney and Slim were seated on the sofa. Kay-Gee was sprawled out on the love seat and Doc had the floor. He was pacing back and forth chugging on a forty ounce of Budweiser. Tears were flowing nonstop down his cheeks.

"Maine, you making me dizzy, sit yo' ass down," Kay-Gee snapped, causing Doc to hurl the now empty bottle at him. It slammed onto the back of the love seat and bounced onto the floor. The room already smelled like a wet bar.

"Will y'all cut that shit out," Slim ordered. "All of us are stressed out and we'll continue to be until we get to the bottom of this shit."

"Shit's gonna be fucked up," Born yelled. It was obvious that he was taking it the hardest. Most likely because he was the youngest and the closest to Shadee.

Teraney sparked up the purple haze. "No it ain't, lil' nigga. Sha wasn't the only soldier. We all hustlas but we're soldiers first. That's how Sha did it. You know that and that's how he taught us."

Born was gently banging the back of his head against the door. His eyes were bloodshot and his nose was beet-red and running.

"Yeah, and we still got to eat," Jo Jo reminded everyone.

"I can't believe that bitch did that to my uncle. I should go and do her whole family," Born gritted.

"Maine, her family ain't have nothing to do with that gold-diggin' sac-chaser's bullshit. They didn't even fuck with Brianna like that," Teraney told him. "So don't go and do something stupid." Born was now banging his head harder against the door. "Born!" Teraney yelled. "Her family ain't have nothing to do with her bullshit. Don't go and make us hotter than we already are over some shit we ain't have no control over. We still gotta get this money." He shot Born a look that sent a serious warning.

"How you know Janay ain't have nothing to do with

this? The shit went down at her house! Now all of a sudden we can't get in touch with her, her pops, her sister...everybody's ghost," Doc spat as he used this opportunity to show his hate for Janay.

"Maine, what you been smokin'?" Jo Jo asked him.

"Yeah, don't you think she would have been arrested by now?" Kay-Gee wanted to know. "Her nosy-ass neighbors would have told us that as well as the police. But everybody is talkin' about Brianna going off and then blowing her own fuckin' brains out."

"Doc, nigga, you know Janay didn't do that shit. I don't know why you always got beef with her," Born snapped.

"Aiight, yo. Y'all muhfuckas sleep on Janay if y'all want to but I ain't. And speaking of beef, Sha's connect wants three extra g's for a key. I got at him last night." Doc figured this was the opportune time to slip that in.

"What?" Jo Jo snapped.

"Maine, fuck that! He on some bullshit," Teraney added.

"Hell yeah," Slim agreed.

"Fuck him. We can get weight from Janay and Big Chop. That's Sha's wifey." Born said it as if the shit was a no-brainer.

"Hold up everybody. Y'all didn't even give me a chance to finish. I got this. I've been working on something that's almost three and a half cheaper than Sha's connect," Doc assured them.

"Nigga, when did this come about? And who is this connect?" Kay-Gee wanted to know.

"Ray-Ray, my cousin down in Dyersburg."

"Nigga, how you gonna take food out of Sha's son's mouth?" Born was ready to spaz out on Doc.

"Boy, three g's less than what we already payin' plus half on consignment? That's not takin' shit outta nobody's mouth. Young nigga, that's how you do business. Plus in Sha's absence I'm in charge. I ain't gonna let Sha's son starve. Let's make this paper." Doc was letting them know that he was now the HNIC.

Then all of a sudden everyone in the room started yelling at once.

"Y'all niggas shut the fuck up!" Slim jumped up screaming and stood in the middle of the room. "Damn, yo, what the fuck?" He shot daggers at everybody until the room was so quiet you could hear a dollar bill hit the floor. Then he turned to Doc. "Nigga, we know who's in charge."

"I can't tell. Everybody got somethin' slick coming out of their mouths," Doc countered. "Y'all act like I don't know what the fuck I'm doin'. Shit, I ain't new to dis, I'm true to dis."

"Nigga, everybody can voice their opinions. I know you can understand where Born is coming from. Sha copped from Choppa most of the time and Janay, that's wifey, so we should keep doin' that. You was actin' like coppin' from her was out of the question," Slim barked.

"Naw, it ain't like that. I'm just tryna get as much paper as possible as long as my peeps is givin' it to us on these terms. I already gave him my word that I was gonna get at him."

Slim yanked at his beard, as he always did when he

was weighing his options. "Aiight, nigga, go ahead and get that because time is of the essence. We don't know how long he'll keep those terms. Plus we can't get in contact with Chop and 'em."

Born couldn't believe what he was hearing. He looked at Slim as if he had sprouted three heads.

Born and the rest of Sha's crew had been blowing Janay's cell phone up. Of course she understood they wanted to know what happened to their boy, but damn, right now everything was just too much to handle. So she got her father to take her to his hideaway crib that no one knew about but her, Boomer and her sister Crystal. The four of them packed a bag for a couple of days and headed out as soon as they dropped Marquis over at his grandmother Ida's.

Janay was really fucked up seeing her baby's daddy laid up in the hospital helpless, fucked up, bandages covering his head and face, tubes sticking out of his mouth, nose and arms. She was feeling some kind of way at first. She was ready to cry and was wishing that she could carry his pain for him. That is until she remembered the night she walked in on him getting his dick sucked by another nigga then turning the nigga over on his ass and diggin' his back out as if the nigga were a bitch. *His faggot muthafuckin' ass needs to die. Here this nigga is trying to hold on for dear life. And for what? To get well and fuck up somebody else's life?*

That painful night she stood at his bedside, if the

po-po hadn't been at the door she was contemplating pulling out all the plugs. But instead she stormed out of the hospital room and swore that she would never go back.

"Aiight, man," said Ray-Ray, Doc's cousin, then gave him dap and watched him pull off.

Doc had just copped seven keys from his cousin and now he was headed back to the crib. He picked up his celly and dialed Teraney. "Yo, it's me. I'm on my way in. I'll call you when I get to the crib."

"Aiight, we waitin'." Teraney sounded as if he was gettin' lifted.

Doc hung up and focused on his four-hour drive back, compounded with the turn of events with his boy Shadee. He didn't know why the hospital wasn't allowing everyone to come and see him. Shit, he wasn't the muthafuckin' president. And that bitch Janay...it's as if she had disappeared off the face of the earth. That was an admission of guilt as far as he was concerned. Shadee was at her house, was shot at her house, and now she was gone. C'mon now, he figured it don't take a rocket scientist to figure that shit out. Plus, since Janay caught him and Sha fuckin' he knew it was only a matter of time that she was going to flip out and want some get-back. So the fuck what! That's how he and Sha got down. Damn, his dick was getting hard at the thought. The more he thought about Sha the harder his dick got. His mind was clouded so much that he found himself driving to the hospital while jackin' his dick off. He was imagining Sha bustin' off in his mouth. He picked up his celly and dialed Teraney.

"Yo, you in?" Teraney yelled over some loud music.

"Almost; I'm at the hospital to see if I can see Sha. I'll call you."

Teraney was trying to be rational. "Maine, what the fuck you smokin'? You got all that shit on you and you stoppin'?" He could hear Doc sniffin'. "Nigga, pull yo'self together and get yo' mind right. Swing by here first, then I'll go to the hospital with you, aiight?" Teraney could still hear sniffin'. "Aiight, maine? Come see me first and we'll go together."

"Aiight." Doc hung up.

"Ay, Slim!" Teraney called out. "Let's roll, maine. I just got off the phone with Doc. That nigga trippin' off of somethin'. First, he say he on his way to the crib. Then he calls back cryin' and shit, talkin' about he on the way to the hospital to see Sha."

"What!" Slim exclaimed. "The fool on his way to the hospital with seven birds? That stupid muthafucka! We need to get to the hospital and take his car. Fuck it! He can find a way to get home. Nigga talkin' about we need to get this paper and here he is throwin' bricks at the penitentiary...and with our muthafuckin' shit." They both were heated.

"You got his key ring?" Slim asked as he put on his jacket.

"Yeah, I got 'em." Teraney tossed them to him.

"Let's be out den."

Doc was already sweet-talking the receptionist as she popped on her chewing gum and blushed. He slipped her a twenty and his phone number as she gave him a visitor's pass and watched him head for the elevators.

When Doc stepped off the elevator and headed toward ICU, the first thing he looked for was the po-po. There was none. His eyes scanned for room 510; he bypassed the busy nurse's station and came up on Sha's room. He stepped into the dark room and took a deep breath. The only lighting was from the moonlight and the monitors. He stepped up cautiously to the bed. Seeing all the equipment and tubes had him stuck on stupid. This was not the nigga that he had grown to love.

After overcoming the initial shock, he was finally able to speak. "Sha, Sha, can you hear me? What happened, yo? Everybody is worried about you." He picked up Sha's hand and began stroking it. "I miss you, dawg, I don't know what all happened to you and why, yo." He kissed Sha's palm. "Get well, man, you gotta pull through. Don't leave all of us like this."

"Excuse me." The heavyset nurse on duty interrupted by turning the lights on. "Are you on the patient's special visitors list, and where is Officer Polk?" she rattled off.

"Yeah, I'm his brother and Officer Polk is on break. He knows I'm here. However, I'm leaving. I just had to check on him. You know, make sure he's all right. You takin' good care of him, right?" Doc flirted as he eased toward the door.

She still was looking at him with suspicion. "He's in good hands. Good night Mr.—"

"When he becomes conscious tell him his nigga Doc was here and I got much love for him." He turned and rushed for the elevators.

By the time Doc reached his car the tears were streaming down his cheeks. As he pulled off, Teraney and Slim were pulling up, missing him by a minute.

"Let me out here; I'll take this side and watch the front door while you drive around. Stupid nigga," Slim snapped, referring to Doc, as he jumped out. Teraney pulled off to continue cruising the lot looking for Doc's ride.

When Doc pulled up in front of his house, he started to call Teraney but changed his mind. He decided that he would call him when he got inside. He hit a few switches before getting out and popping the trunk. His secret compartment was in the amplifier in the trunk and was activated from the inside. He slid the lid off the amplifier, grabbed the heavy navy blue duffel bag and slid the lid back. He wiped more tears from his face, slung the bag over his shoulder and slammed the trunk. He went around to the back entrance and took out his keys and opened the door. That's when he felt the cold steel kiss the back of his skull. When he went to turn around he heard...*click*.

"Don't move, muthafucka, 'cause if you do I'ma send you to meet your maker." Doc felt a gloved hand frisk him and snatch Duke, his Smith & Wesson.

"Man, what the fuck you want?" Doc based up.

"Shut yo' bitch ass up! Who the hell you think you talking to?" Skye barked as he pushed Doc inside the house. He was glad that the living room light was already on. "This here is my show, partna, and you gonna do what the hell I tell you to. Now drop the muthafuckin' bag and strip, then you can get on your knees and suck my dick." He laughed. "Nah, fool, I'm fuckin' with you. I don't get down like that. Hurry the fuck up, nigga, you takin' too long to strip." Skye grew impatient from the usual adrenaline rush he always got when jackin' and smacked Doc several times in the back of his skull for not moving fast enough.

While Doc was standing in all his glory butt-ass naked, Skye told him to lock his hands behind his head and commanded him to walk to the bathroom. Skye struck Doc two more times, just because.

"Nigga, that's on GP just in case you think about pullin' some funny-ass shit. Now stand the fuck up before I shoot ya dick off and make you suck ya own shit."

"Man, just take the—"

"Just take what, nigga?" Skye cut him off. "And what the hell you looking at? You thought you was gonna see who's jackin' yo' ass? Nah, playboy, shut the hell up and speak when spoken to, bitch. This is my game. Get ya ass in the bathtub," Skye barked as he kicked Doc square in the ass, sending him flying headfirst inside the tub.

Doc grunted.

"Get yo' clumsy ass up! Hurry up, fool!" As soon as Doc stood up Skye tossed him the roll of duct tape.

"Tape one arm to the shower rod." Skye impatiently looked on as Doc, who was bloodied up, fumbled with the tape. As soon as Doc had one arm wrapped up Skye snatched the tape and began taping up the other hand. "You a slow-ass nigga." Then he bound his ankles together and turned the shower on, making sure the water was cold.

"Where's the money at?" When Doc wouldn't answer, Skye busted him in the mouth with the butt of his burner. Doc again grunted in pain. "I bet you'll speak now. Where the money at? And don't make me ask again."

"In the bedroom. Top drawer." Skye left and found the bedroom. He went to the top drawer and found five stacks.

Oh I know this nigga sittin' on more than five stacks, Skye was thinking to himself. He began to tear the room up, flipping the mattress over first, emptying the drawers out and then going through the closet. As he cased the closet he hit a spot on the floor that felt as if it was gonna give. He rocked back and forth on it with his foot.

"Ahhhh, yeah...this some slick shit here," he was saying as he started to rip up the carpet. "Oh yeah, this here is some real slick shit. Gotdamn, money in the bank." Skye was looking down at twenty-five stacks. He put it in the bag along with the ounces of weed he ran across. Skye ran back into the bathroom where Doc was in and out of consciousness, and shot Doc in his shoulder. "Nigga, that's for lying to me about yo' otha stash. Bitch-ass nigga. I'll catch yo' ass slippin' again."

CHAPTER FIVE

Behind dark shades, Sonya and Miss P, two of the leading Memphis gossip queens, sat in the back during Brianna's funeral doing what they do best: gossiping.

"Umph, this cheap-ass funeral. As many niggas as she was fuckin' she should have been buried like Princess Di. I just knew she would have more people than this show up," Sonya whispered to Miss P as they looked around at the sixty-something guests.

"I thought she would have more people than this show up myself. And she should have more flowers than that," chimed Miss P. "Ooh look. Ain't that Artie and his wife? Ain't no way in hell I'll be comin' to a bitch's funeral who was fuckin' my husband. That's some crazy shit. It couldn't be me," Miss P continued to pop off.

"Girl, me neither." They watched as Artie and his wife walked up to the closed casket with a bouquet of flowers. As soon as Artie laid the one red rose on Brianna's casket, Artie's wife stepped back and kicked her casket so hard it slid over. The entire room gasped. She then began screaming all kinds of obscenities. Artie hauled off and backhanded his wife across the face. That was the only way to shut her up and stop her from disrespecting Brianna's funeral any further.

"Lawd have mercy!" Brianna's neighbor Miss Hattie yelled out.

Sonya was giggling and Miss P was mad that she didn't have a camera phone to have caught the whole thing. Artie was dragging his wife out of the funeral by the back of her neck.

Several men rushed to the casket and began replacing it on the stand.

Brianna's sister was now up there motioning for more of the funeral workers to clean up the mess. Her mother looked as if she was going to faint. Shan was stunned beyond belief as she leaned over and said in Peanut's ear, "I can't believe she did that."

"B pissed off a lot of people. I thought the shit was rather funny myself," Peanut told her with a smirk.

"You are so ignorant," Shan gritted between clenched teeth.

"Look what the cat drug in," Sonya said, referring to the brother who favored the reggae artist Sean Paul.

Miss P unashamedly craned her neck to get a good look at the brother with the black fedora and dark shades. "It looks like that nigga Nick but I ain't sure."

Sonya smacked her lips and whispered, "Gurrrl, it's him. That nigga got a lot of nerve. Ain't nobody seen or heard from him since Peanut went to jail. Him and that bitch used to fuck around, but just like every other nigga, the bitch kicked him to the curb too. But Nick is a keeper. I don't know what that bitch was thinkin', not holdin' on to that one."

Nick nodded at the two ladies as he looked around to see who was in attendance. He fell back, trying to keep a low profile. He didn't want anybody to recognize him, especially not Peanut, and was glad to see him and Shan sitting way up front. He knew he shouldn't have come but he just wanted to know for himself: was she really gone? He spotted Brianna's mother and sister. Even though the crowd was small, Nick noticed a few faces that had decided to show up. The hoes who were there didn't like or probably didn't even know Brianna. They knew she fucked with get-money-type niggas, so they were most likely there to pick up her slack. And the niggas in attendance were those who you rarely caught at the club. But you could bet your last dollar they would be at the *Who's Who* funeral. The fellas were looking sharp, and the ladies were looking even sharper. Instead of a funeral service it was more like a meet-and-greet.

Oh shit, Nick said to himself as he held his head down to avoid being noticed by Peanut or Shan. He was so into checking out the so-called mourners he wasn't keeping an eye on the man who, without a doubt, if they were to come within a few feet of each other, somebody was gonna get their wig split. He didn't know what they were looking at but everyone's attention was now turned to the young lady who was standing in the middle of the room. Nick used this opportunity to slip out of the funeral without a confrontation. Especially since he had already been recognized by the two broads who had been talking throughout the entire service.

"Fuck this nigga at?" Teraney spat, tossing the cell at Slim. After circling the Med, the only Memphis hospital that served all of the hood folks, for almost thirty minutes and Doc not picking up, they were now expecting the worst as Teraney floored the pedal.

"Born, we lookin' for Doc. Round all them niggas up," Slim barked before hanging up and dialing Doc's number once again. "This nigga Doc better quit playin'. If something happened to the work I'ma do this nigga. Ain't no room for fuckups." They rode lost in thought until they came up on Doc's block.

"Yo, this nigga's car is parked." Teraney skidded on the brakes because he had almost passed right by it. They both inspected it and then looked up at the house.

"Shit ain't right, maine," Slim said. "Find a spot to park."

Teraney double-parked and they got out, hands on their pieces, looking around. They checked out the front entrance first and it was locked. They went around the back, stormed up the steps and stopped at the door, which was wide open. Slim, leading the way, flicked on the living room light, and then made it to the kitchen. Nothing looked out of the ordinary.

"Bathroom." Teraney pointed. Slim nodded and led the way. Slim held his hand up when they got to the bathroom and put his ear against the door. They could hear the shower running but no movement. He slowly turned the knob and pushed the door open and saw Doc's silhouette hanging from the shower. Slim flicked the light on.

"Fuck," he spat as he put his burner away and pulled out a switchblade. "Check the rest of the crib, Raney." He turned off the ice-cold shower and cut the tape from around Doc's wrists.

Teraney came back. "The bedroom is fucked up and of course, I don't see any signs of the work. Is he gonna be aiight?"

"Fuck if I know. The nigga is shot. Help me lift his heavy ass." They carried him to the bedroom and wrapped him in several blankets.

"Do you feel a pulse?" Teraney asked.

"He *is* breathing. Get a street doctor over here. The nigga is unconscious and is probably freezing to death. This big-ass lump on his head doesn't look good and we need to stop this bleeding."

Briggen was sittin' in the back of the prison visiting room waiting on his cousin Zeke to come out. He looked at his watch and it was almost one-thirty. *This nigga needs to hurry up. I got shit to do.* Briggen had no clue as to what was so important that Zeke needed him to come up here. The last time he visited was to see his little hardheaded-ass brother, Forever. That's when he'd found out that Forever was fucking Shan and using her to bring in his dope. Briggen told Forever to leave Shan alone, and that she was his first and he needed to use her. But Forever ignored him and kept on doing him. Forever hadn't called or reached out to him since. Briggen glanced up, and four inmates were coming through the door. Zeke was leading the way. Briggen stood up and frowned at his smiling cousin.

"Nigga, don't be smiling at me. What the fuck you got me up here for?"

"Good to see you too, punk!" Zeke grabbed Briggen, pulled him to him and gave him a hug. "Go get a nigga some vittles out them there machines," Zeke barked and playfully punched Briggen in the chest.

"Maine, I don't know who the fuck you think you are. Go get the shit yourself." Briggen pulled out some bills and tossed them at him.

He watched as Zeke came back with an armful of snacks. "Nigga, you still greedy as shit." He snatched the bottle of Cherry Coke out of Zeke's hand. "So what's up? And how's my hardheaded-ass brother? I have a feeling this is what this visit is about."

Zeke got comfortable, opened up a bag of potato chips and stuffed them in his mouth. He turned serious. "Man," he began, "blood is supposed to be thicker than water. And I'm a very loyal muthafucka but I ain't no damn fool and a nigga still gots to eat. I need to take over this whole operation. We need to make some changes . . . and fast."

"What the fuck is up? You and Ever been gettin' money together since y'all was shawties."

Zeke gobbled up the last of the chips and swallowed the last of Briggen's Cherry Coke. "Your brother on some shit and it ain't a good look."

"What about him? I had an idea he been on some bull-shit, since I haven't heard from him. What's the bizness?"

"Maine, shit is deep. You know he had shawty bringin' in that work."

"Yeah, I know all about that. I put a stop to it."

"No, you didn't. Shawty was trying to get her brother's bond money together and Forever was breaking her off with a little bit of change at a time. She was bringing the shit in long after you said stop."

"Say what!? Where the fuck he was gettin' the work from?"

Zeke put his palm up to silence Briggen. "Then Nyla found out and she stepped in and talked Forever into set-tin' shawty up. That's why shawty quit the day she was supposed to make the drop. She didn't even show. She bounced with the dope and some dough. Now, Forever and Nyla is beefin' big-time. It's a whole lot of drama. Ever been trippin' hard. I need to do my own thang and let him do his. I gotta distance myself. Do me. Bottom line." Zeke was looking at Briggen, who had on his game face. Zeke couldn't tell what was going through his mind. Finally Zeke said, "Your brother turned straight snitch, Brig."

Again, Zeke watched Briggen as his words set in. Zeke wished that things hadn't gone down the way they did. He hated to be the one to break the bad news...but snitchin'? That shit was jeopardizing everything and everybody.

"You ready to hear the rest?" Zeke wanted to get everything off his chest.

Briggen was speechless. Would his own flesh and blood snitch him out? Naw, not Forever. "Give it to me raw, nigga."

"The reason why he ain't re-up with you is because he's using another connect and owes dude mad bucks. From what I'm hearin' that's why it has dried up around here, 'cause dude ain't fuckin' with Ever no more. Now Forever tryna get in touch with Skinny and dem."

"Who is the connect that he owe?"

"Some cat named Polow. I don't know why Ever think he can just straight-up jack niggas for they work. That ain't like him. But, yo, Brig, you know I don't trust the nigga no more. He's too hot."

Finally Briggen said, "Aiight, fam, thanks for puttin' me up on what's happening." He stood up to leave and gave Zeke some dap. "I gotta dip."

As he stepped away he turned back around when he heard Zeke call his name. "I'm lettin' you know now. If I think that nigga is gonna jeopardize you or me, we gonna have some problems. Just let me know the bizness if you want me to handle it."

He and Briggen locked eyes and then Briggen turned and left.

Everyone was in Doc's living room. The street doctor had got Doc to the point where he was all right. The bullet came out without a problem and he meticulously dressed both wounds, the one on Doc's head and the one on his shoulder. He then gave Doc a sedative that he chased down with a pint of vodka and now Doc was pissy drunk and in his bed sleeping like a baby.

"So we all agree that we coppin' from Janay, right?" Slim asked.

Everyone said yeah.

"So Doc ain't in charge no more?" Born wanted—needed—to know.

"We'll vote on it when he's able to be present. He's pissy drunk and talkin' out of his head. Y'all ain't gonna get no valuable info from him in that condition," Slim announced and left it at that.

"Fuck that!" Teraney barked. "Wake that nigga up. We lost seven birds."

"Hell yeah," Jo Jo agreed. "Born, you and Raney go drag that nigga outta that bed."

The whole room was in an uproar and they all started moving toward the bedroom. Slim said, "Fuck it." He got up and went out the front door.

CHAPTER SIX

"Hey, luv, you aiight?"

"Who is this?" Nyla snapped.

Peanut laughed. "Oh, it's like that now? A nigga can't even check on a beautiful lady nowadays without getting snapped on. What is the world coming to?" he joked.

"Peanut?" She finally recognized his voice. "I'm sorry about that. Wait. What am I apologizing for? You called me collect the last time I spoke to you, so what's up? Wait a minute. You're out?" She sounded excited. "Oh my God, you're out!" she squealed.

"Yeah, I'm out. I've been home for a couple of weeks."

"A couple of weeks? And you're just calling me? I should hang up on yo' ass."

"Nah. You don't want to do that. Go easy on a nigga. I'm out here trying to get back on track. So how you holdin' up and when can I see you?"

Shit. Peanut had caught her off guard fo'real. It's like he always knew to call when she was straddling the fence. Here she had just gone out on a limb to set Shan up so that Forever could come home and the bitch didn't even come to work. Instead she did one better and quit, making Nyla look and feel stupid. So now she was still pissed at Forever for fucking the bitch raw and getting her pregnant. She was at the point of love him or leave him. Unfortunately, she just couldn't see leaving him since she had put in so much work. They were married and had their beautiful daughter, Tameerah. But that hadn't stopped her from thinking of a get-back and Peanut just may be the answer.

"You still there?" Peanut interrupted her flashback and train of thought.

"I'm here."

"A nigga tryna see you, so what's up?"

Damn. He's coming on strong. But shit, I wouldn't mind seeing his ass. Beep. "Can you hold on a sec, that's my other line." She pumped her fist. *Yes! Saved by the bell . . . or should I say the beep? And right before I got into something I ain't have no business getting into.*

"Hold on? Do I look like a secretary, maine? Just tell me when can I see you."

"You gonna let me take this call or what? If you ain't got time to wait, then call me back," she went back at him and then clicked over. Whoever was on the other line hung up, so she clicked back over to Peanut. "Now was that so hard? It didn't even take long," she teased.

"Naw, but tell me how long I'm going to have to wait to see you." Yeah, he was pressin' her. But he couldn't help it. He couldn't stop thinking about her. She was the ultimate picture of a lady in his eyes. He wanted her to be his lady. There was an attraction between them that he couldn't control…no matter how hard he tried…and he knew that she could feel it as well. It didn't matter to him that she was holdin' a nigga down on lock. He wanted her to be his lady.

"Actually—" *Beep.* "Shit, that's my line again; do you mind holdin' on?"

"Damn, your line is bumpin'. I'm glad I called when I did or I probably would be the one struggling to get through. But go ahead. Do you need me to take some messages for you?" He was bein' real smart with it.

"You got jokes. Nigga, don't be like that. I promise it won't take long. Hold on." She clicked over.

It was Forever.

Oh shit, oh shit. She hopped around as if she were stepping on hot coals. *Just my luck. Does this nigga have ESP?* When the recording said *Press five to accept,* she hesitated. "Oh God, calm down, Nyla, breathe." She finally did…as she pressed five.

"Damn. I thought you wasn't going to press five. Did I interrupt something?" Forever was nonchalant about it but she knew he was dead serious.

"Hold on. Let me get rid of this call." She clicked over before Forever responded. "Peanut, I gotta take this call."

"Is everything aiight?"

"Yeah. Well, no. I'll get back with you."

"You don't even have my number. I'll get back at you. Handle your business, shawty." Peanut hung up.

73

Nyla sighed as she clicked back over to Forever. "Yeah," Nyla spoke drily.

"Yeah? That's all you got to say? Straight up, what dick got your mind gone?"

"Forever, did you just call here to argue?"

"I'm just sayin' you—"

"You're just saying what, Forever? Huh? Why it got to be some dick? I can't be tired of your shit? Of course not. You think your shit don't stink."

"Damn. And your mouth fly. You can't tell me another nigga ain't in this equation. What's the nigga's name?"

"Why?"

Forever chuckled. "I knew there was a nigga in the equation. I don't believe this shit. You fucked him already? Can you at least tell me that?"

"What difference would it make?"

"You bitch."

"Fuck you, Forever. Unlike you, I haven't crossed that line or broken my marriage vows."

"The way you poppin' off you expect me to believe that bullshit?"

Nyla was fighting back her tears. "I'm starting to hate you, Forever."

"Ain't this a bitch. So it's over?"

"I answered your call. I'm still here, ain't I?"

"Fo'real, I can't tell. You got niggas callin' the crib and shit. Are we through?"

"Do you really care, Forever?"

"Nyla go 'head with the bullshit, this is me, Forever, baby. Fuck you mean do I care?"

"Yeah, the same Forever that fucked a bitch and got her pregnant. That Forever, right? How many more bitches you up there fucking, and getting pregnant?" Nyla now had tears streaming nonstop down her cheeks.

"C'mon, Nyla."

"C'mon my ass, Forever. Nigga, I got your last name and your daughter," she screamed.

You have one minute remaining, the recorder chimed.

"Nyla, don't do this."

"You already did it, Forever. And fuck you. You need to sweat for a minute." The phone disconnected.

"Fuck!" Forever slammed the phone down. He had waited exactly fifteen minutes to call her back but now she wasn't answering. He picked up the phone and dialed again. Nyla still wouldn't pick up.

"Yo, man, can I jump on the phone right quick? Shit!" one of the inmates standing in line quipped.

Forever ignored him and walked away. He spotted his cousin and codefendant Zeke going down the hall. He needed someone, preferably Zeke, to listen to him vent.

"Zeke!" Forever yelled out. Zeke turned around, nodded and kept it moving.

"What the fuck?" Forever was really confused. *This nigga has been acting standoffish for the past few days.*

"Zeke," Forever called out again as he picked up his

pace, determined to catch up with him. "Zeke, hold up, nigga, I need to holla at you."

"Nigga, I gotta take care of something. I'll get with you later," Zeke yelled back and strolled off.

Peanut ended up calling Nyla back and talked her into meeting him at the movies. They went to see *The Pursuit of Happyness* with Will Smith, and now they were standing in the parking lot, leaned up against Peanut's Denali. He was holding both of her hands.

"I enjoyed our little date. Even though we took separate cars," he teased.

Peanut was massaging her palms. Her short haircut, beautiful smile and petite body were a complete turn-on. She had on a jeans outfit with some stiletto boots, and she was still a little itty-bitty thing.

"I enjoyed myself too." The gentle massage she was receiving was making her tingle. Add the fact that his Jean P cologne was making her head swim. "I think it's time for me to be going."

"You don't sound so sure. You want to get something to eat? I'm hungry fo'real, how about you?"

"I'm nervous and I feel guilty. He asked me for your name today."

"Is that why you're nervous, lil' mama? I can take care of myself. If I was in his shoes I'd be asking the same thing. Yo, but listen, it was just a movie, right?"

"Yeah. Just a movie."

"When you're ready to do a little something more, just

let me know." He reluctantly let her hands go. "Let me walk you to your car." He grabbed one of her hands and she giggled.

"What?"

"Nothing."

"What? You are laughing because I can't stop touching you?"

She took out her keys and unlocked the door. "Good night, Peanut."

He put his hand on the door handle. "You know I want to kiss you, right? What would you do if I kissed you?" He didn't give her a chance to respond, his tongue was parting her lips as one of his arms snaked around her waist and pulled her in close. He felt her hand glide up and caress his chest, and just as quickly she gently pushed him away.

Nyla leaned back and gazed up into his eyes. "We just kissed. Didn't we?"

"Yeah, we did. If you need to blame somebody, blame me. I initiated it. I've been waiting and wanting to do that for a long time, girl."

"I gotta get going. Thanks for the movie."

Peanut grabbed her wrist. "Do you feel guilty for kissing me?"

"Yes and no."

Peanut chuckled. "What's that supposed to mean? Talk to me."

"Later, okay? I need to go and pick up my daughter."

"So when can I see you again?"

"I'll call you."

He opened the door for her and stood by as she started her ride and drove off.

Nyla made it to her sister Lisha's house in record time. She was in a zombie state of mind. She heard Lisha yell out before peeking through the mini-blinds. Nyla heard the several locks being released and then the door flew open.

"Hi," Nyla said to her sister.

"Nyla, what are you doing here after midnight? Tameerah is sound asleep!"

"So . . . can I come in?"

Lisha sucked her teeth and pushed the screen door open. "Forever has been calling here all night looking for you. Where were you?"

"What did you tell him?"

Lisha looked at her baby sister and could tell that something wasn't right. "I told him I didn't know."

"Oh, my God." Nyla gasped. "My plan of making him sweat is in full effect. That nigga ain't gonna get no sleep tonight."

"Don't tell me you were creepin' out on Forever." Lisha stood there holding her robe closed. When Nyla didn't respond, she yelled, "Oh, no you didn't!"

"I went on a date, Lisha." Nyla started crying as she flopped down on the couch and covered her face.

Lisha jumped up to get her sister some tissues. When she came back, Nyla was pacing back and forth, hugging herself and still crying.

"I don't know what to do."

"Start with drying your face. How you gonna get to the end of the bid and start fucking around on him?"

"I didn't fuck around on him!" Nyla spat defensively. Then she said above a whisper, "But part of me wanted to."

"Oookay." Lisha backed away from her sister as if she was in shock.

"Lisha, you don't know what it's like. You never been with a nigga that's locked up. I've been doing this shit for five years. Five long years, Lisha."

"Lower your voice, you'll wake up the kids. And, bitch, please, I know how long it's been. I been doing the damn time with you; that's why I said it's almost over. You can't hang in there a little while longer?"

"Oh, girl, you just don't know how hard I'm trying. I miss him so much. And I used to love him more than I love myself."

"Used to?"

"Yes, used to." She blew her nose. "Forever got some other bitch pregnant, Lisha."

"He what!" Lisha shrieked.

"You heard me. She was the computer teacher up there. He was fuckin' her and he had her bringing in his dope."

"Aww hell to the naw! That's fucked up! He went up in that bitch raw-dog? Damn, Nyla, I would have…shit…" She thought about it. "I don't know what the fuck I would have done. That is so fucked up. When did you find all of this out? And why are you just telling me?"

Nyla laughed. "Girl, I was just as shocked as you are.

The shit happened so fast. Then I had this brilliant idea, since he claimed that it was just business and she was expendable. I said, 'Let's set this bitch up so that you can come home.' The nigga didn't want to do it but I didn't give him a choice in the matter."

"So what happened? What's up with that? And you? Setting somebody up? Forever snitchin'? This story is getting crazier by the minute."

"The shit fell through. He gave her the dope and everything but she quit. Just like that. My baby would have been home, Lisha," Nyla cried.

"Damn, that's some foul shit, Nyla. I didn't know you had it in you."

"Me neither. I was so angry at him, at her, and now he has a baby on the way ... by her, Lisha. I'm still angry with him. More than angry. I'm so hurt. I can't believe he would do this to me. And niggas be wondering why bitches leave them for dead. This is why. After five long years ... this is the thanks I get."

Nyla's cell phone rang, startling both of them.

"Who is that?" Lisha looked at the phone as if it were a snake, then said, "I bet you it's either one of two people, your husband on them gotdamned contraband cell phones or the nigga you was out with tonight. You need to answer it."

"Hell no." After the fourth ring it went to voice mail. Nyla breathed a sigh of relief.

"Girl, this is too much for me," Lisha told her as she looked at the word *unavailable* on the caller ID.

It started ringing again. "Oh shit!" Lisha yelled out. "You need to handle that. It's probably the nigga you were with."

Nyla thought about it, and then smiled. She said, "Hello," sounding all cute.

"Nyla, it's me."

It was Forever.

CHAPTER SEVEN

Here come that nigga now," said Silk, Briggen's man under Woo. He and his sister Tee Tee were sitting in the back parking lot of the mall smoking a blunt.

"I hate this cocky-ass nigga," Tee Tee snapped. Silk started choking, eyes watering, as he passed her the blunt. "Breathe, nigga. You still don't know how to smoke?" She put the blunt out as she watched Skye get out of his truck and go over to the passenger side. He opened the door, pulled out a large black duffel bag and slung it over his shoulder before closing the door.

Silk turned the engine on and flipped a few switches and Tee Tee slid back a trap door. She pulled out four vacuum-sealed Ziploc bags filled with money and gave them to Silk. When Silk stepped out of their ride, Skye was standing there peeking over at Tee Tee.

"Don't be lookin' at her, man. She said she don't like cocky-ass niggas like you." They made the exchange and Silk passed him the duffel bag filled with the birds that Skye had jacked the night before from Doc. Silk walked

Skye away from the car while Tee Tee checked it out and put the dope away.

"What it lookin' like?" Silk asked him.

"Nigga, this me you dealin' wit. It's lookin' lovely."

"It's not like I don't trust you or no shit like that," Silk joked.

"Whatever, yo, I know your sister checking shit out as we stand here." Skye smirked.

Silk started laughing. "No doubt, baby boy. Of course she gonna check shit out." He gave Skye some dap and headed back to the ride. Skye followed but went around to the passenger's side. He tapped on the window.

Tee Tee slowly turned toward him and looked at him as if he smelled like shit.

"So you hate a cocky-ass nigga like myself, huh?" Skye was definitely full of himself.

"Why ask questions you already know the answer to?" She kept her gaze locked with his.

"What kind of niggas you like?" When he saw that she wasn't going to answer he winked at Silk. "Don't tell me you done got used to these lame-ass bamma niggas down here. When you step your game up, holla at a real G."

She sucked her teeth. "Your dough ain't long enough for me," she snapped. "Let's go, Silk."

"Baby girl, my money real long, just like my dick."

Tee Tee threw her head back and laughed.

"Nigga, we out." Silk put the car in reverse and pulled off.

Skye stood there watching as the car disappeared. "Bitches," he mumbled but as always was turned the fuck on. After he put the Ziploc bags of cash into the stash spot he made his way into the mall. Shit, it was Saturday and he was going to get fly and find some bitch to gut out.

He strolled inside the mall and headed straight for the food court. A cookies 'n' cream milkshake was calling his name. He got in line and began eyeing all the honeys that were out and about. "Umm umm ummph," he mumbled at the eye candy all around him.

"Can I help you, sir?" asked the young kid who was working the counter at Baskin-Robbins. Skye was still eyeing all the ass that he could take in. "Sir, can I help you?" the cashier asked again.

"Yeah, umm, give me a cookies 'n' cream milkshake."

"Are you treating?" the two shawties standing behind him asked, causing him to turn around.

"Depends," Skye stated as he checked them out.

"On what?" the shorter of the two chicks asked.

"On your age."

"I'm eighteen," the tallest one said.

"I'm seventeen." Her partner giggled.

Skye thought about it as he looked them over. *Average.* "Yo, money, give these young ladies what they want." He put a ten on the counter. The clerk passed him his milkshake, he took it and said to the two girls, "Y'all be easy."

"Thanks," they sang in unison and then both burst

into giggles. Their mission of coming up on some free ice cream was accomplished.

Damn, I haven't been in here for a good five minutes and already I'm trickin' off my loot. Then he spotted her. The honey-brown shawty that was struttin' through the mall as if she owned it. He imagined himself climbing up those never-ending legs. And that ass! Her ass was outta this world. Her hair was cut in sexy layers, complementing her angelic face with dimples that would make a nigga want to fall in love.

Oh shit, the gods must be smilin' down on me. On further inspection he recognized her as Big Choppa's daughter. Which one? He wasn't sure. They looked just alike to him and fo'real it didn't even matter. As long as he got in.

He found himself following her. She went into the first three stores and came out empty-handed. *Damn, she is ... my fantasy.* He tossed the last of his milkshake in the trash and followed her into Neiman Marcus. He was mesmerized and after about twenty minutes he was ready to fuck her.

She had a handful of items that she took to the shoe section. Skye got bold and sat down. He watched as she matched up several pairs of shoes with her outfits. The sales associate came over to offer her some assistance and his fantasy handed her four different shoes.

"Can I see all of these in an eight and a half?" she asked. Then holding up a pair of Chloe pumps, she asked, "Do you have these in tan?"

The sales associate nodded her head in approval and disappeared.

She sat down across from Skye and locked her gaze on him. "What? Did I tire you out?" she asked as she took her time checking out this big thugged-out, confident-ass nigga sitting across from her. His long legs were stretched out and on the end of them were some Cole Haan Nike boots. The Evisu jeans and Knowledge Tee looked brand-new. The leather Pelle Pelle jacket looked as if it cost a grand. The ice on his wrist, the bling around his neck and the rocks in his ears got her pussy to tingling. *Yeah, I'd do him.* He was smiling. *What a gorgeous set of teeth. What a little cutie, in a thugged-out way. Light green eyes and all.* She smirked.

The sales associate brought out the shoes and set them in front of her.

"Thank you." She took her gaze off Skye and focused on the shoes. Skye watched his soon-to-be new fantasy pussy and lick as she tried on all the shoes and pranced in front of the mirror. He had to have her.

"You don't want my opinion on which pair to get?"

"No. Because I'm getting all four pairs."

"I see." He nodded in approval.

"Can I get you anything else?" The sales associate reappeared as if on cue.

"I'll take all of these, thank you."

"Great." The associate gathered up the boxes as Skye watched his lick gather up the rest of her items. When they headed for the cash register, he jumped up and followed them.

As the sales associate rang up the items, Skye whispered in Shawty's ear, "I got this."

"I'm good, playboy. Maybe I'll grab you a couple of pairs. You see anything you like?"

He smiled. "Bossy." Skye mimicked Kelis, "But, yo, I gotchu."

"All right then. Go right ahead. Be my guest. You've been following me for an hour. It's the least I can do."

"Straight up. We just happened to be going to the same place."

"Yeah, okay," she responded, sounding unconvinced.

"Look. What's good? I'ma grab me a shirt but I'm pickin' out what I want to see you in tonight. Just tell me what time to pick you up."

"That will be three thousand two hundred and eighty-five dollars. Will that be cash or charge?"

"We got a deal?" he asked her as he pulled out a knot, causing the saleslady to blush.

She was seriously mulling it over. *Shit, just because a nigga dropped four grand don't mean shit.* "What if I already have plans for tonight?"

"Cancel them. So we on or what?" he pressed.

"Okay, let's do it."

❦

Born was cruisin' the flea market in an attempt to clear his head. He had been up drinking all night and snortin' mad lines. It seemed that shit just went haywire...over-night. Shadee getting shot, and now he was laid up in the hospital barely hanging on to his life. Then there was Doc. The nigga got jacked for seven birds in his house. That shit was suspect to Born. Then to add insult to injury, the streets were coming up empty as far as who had touched Doc.

Born stopped and picked up a couple of packs of Bayer aspirin and some orange juice. He paid the cashier, stood there and popped the aspirin while chasing it down with the bottle of orange juice. In the background "Side 2 Side" by Three 6 Mafia was blaring. Born let out a loud belch, gave the empty bottle to the clerk and headed over to where the music was. A dude named Datsun had a booth of mix tapes, DVDs, incense, T-shirts...the whole nine.

Born scanned the huge selection. This dude had everything, all of the latest CDs and tons of independent shit. Born thought it was funny that people were getting mad paid off crazy shit like *Bum Fights*, *Bar Brawls*, *Cat Fights Unleashed*, *Ghetto Fights* and *Crackheadz Gone Wild*. What was even crazier, he was a fan of the bullshit. He had a nice collection in his truck. He went back to the DVDs and scanned over *Rump Shaker*, *Katt Williams: Live*, *Gang Wars*, but one stood out that he didn't have: *Shadee Presents: Where My Dawgs At?* Born went back to that one and picked it up. He inspected it closely.

"Yo, money, where you get this?"

Datsun eyed Born as if he were speaking a foreign language. "What?"

"Fuck it! Let me see your DVD player right quick."

"It's broke, man. You got one in your ride, big balla!"

Born pulled out a twenty and threw it at him. He grabbed the DVD and went to his pimped-out Caddy and popped the disc in, expecting to see Sha and the crew doing some dumb shit, like clownin' in front of dope, money and hoes. But what he saw knocked the air out of his chest and made his head spin. He turned the DVD player off and jumped out of his ride. He was practically knocking over the flea market patrons as he headed for Datsun's booth. He stormed into the booth, grabbing Datsun by his shirt, and they both pummeled into a rack of CDs and went crashing to the floor.

"Where the fuck you get that disc from?" Born screamed while shaking him.

"What disc? What the fuck you talkin' about? I got a shitload of DVDs, nigga." Datsun got wide-eyed as he looked up at a crazed nigga, with bloodshot eyes and spittle flying out of his mouth.

"You wanna fuckin' play dumb-ass games?" Born banged Datsun's head onto the floor, stood up and pulled out his forty-five.

"Oh shit! He got a gun!" some little dude said as he backed out of the booth.

Born aimed the burner at Datsun's head. "I'ma ask you one more time. Who gave you that DVD?" Born gritted.

"Okay, maine. Damn, put the heater away."

"Give me a name, nigga."

"Freddie, man, I got 'em from Big Freddie."

Born tucked the heater inside his waistband and stormed out.

"Man, you gettin' all fly. I thought you was going to work." Melky, Skye's little brother, rolled around in his wheelchair circling Skye as he got dressed. Melky had gotten a bullet in his spine during a jacking that he and Skye did almost three years before.

"This is work, nigga."

"I can't tell, boy. What's her name?"

Skye was smoothing out his goatee and started grinning.

"What's so funny?"

"Dawg, I don't even know her name."

"Man, you stupid. How you gonna go out with a chick and you don't even know her name?"

"Nigga, I don't need to know her name. It's Big Choppa's daughter." When he saw the look on Melky's face he said, "Yeah nigga! I told you it was work."

"Damn bruh, how'd you do that? Which one of them honeys is it?"

"What difference do it make?" Skye snapped.

Melky started laughing. "Fool, you don't even know, do you? Let me find out, you slippin', son." Melky was showing his New York roots. They were born and raised in Brooklyn but when things got hot they found their way down to Memphis. And been there for the past three years. "But check it. How many times we went over this one? Son, if it's a lick you planning, you want Janay. She the one running thangs. If it's Crystal, all she do is parlay."

"Damn," Skye mumbled.

"But it's all to the G. We can still work it. Where you meet her at?"

"The mall."

"Well, I could just about guess which one you came up on." Melky smirked.

"Chill out, nigga, I got dis. You know how I do it."

"Handle yo' business, dawg. And don't fuck this up," Melky advised, before wheeling off.

"Where you at, maine?" Slim was asking Born. "They waitin' on you to come through the spots."

"Get Janay on the line. Y'all need to find that bitch!" Born screamed.

"Whoa, whoa calm down, fool. What the fuck is up?"

"A tape...Sha...man...the dogs...they fucked him up." Born pulled over and parked. "I'ma kill that bitch, man." He hung up and broke down crying.

Two days later, in Crystal's bedroom, Skye was laid-back bustin' a nut in her mouth.

"Sssss...oh shit," Skye screeched like a bitch as his body jerked and twitched. Crystal licked his balls and stuck two fingers in his ass.

"Whoa! Whoa!" Skye was spent, but not that spent. He grabbed her hand. Crystal giggled.

"Just checking." She got up and stumbled into the bathroom. She was still fully dressed. Skye's boxers and jeans were down around his ankles. They were both tore up from the floor up. They had been out drinking, smoking and partying on and off for the past two days.

"C'mere girl," Skye called out.

"You come here." She stuck her head out of the bathroom.

"I can't move."

"Punk-ass nigga," she teased.

"Tell me that shit while I'm guttin' yo' ass out." She snivered and looked at his dick. "Yeah, that's what I thought; now come over here."

She hurriedly undressed and strolled out of the bathroom butt-ass naked and crawled up and sat on his face. Skye sucked, licked and kissed up and down her thighs as her juices trickled from her pussy into his mouth and her entire body caught fire. Breathing hard, he grabbed her ass and took his time as he ate her pussy. Her ass gyrated around and around as his tongue teased every nerve ending of her clit. She held on to his head and gave his tongue a slow, steady and sexy ride.

"Right here, baby, right...there," she whispered. He increased his pace as her pussy melted in his mouth. As he slowly eased his thumb inside her, she threw her head back and her tightness clamped around his thumb as she screamed and creamed all over his face. Now it was her body that was spazzing and jerking. She fell over onto her back.

Skye sat up and pulled off his Timbs. He stood over the bed looking at Crystal as he undressed.

"Yo, I'ma fuck you up if I find out you sucking another nigga's dick."

"Let me find out my head game got you sprung already." She turned over onto her stomach, giving him an up-close shot of her ass. She eased onto all fours, clapped her ass cheeks and looked back at him. "I'm gettin' ready to get you sprung on something else, playboy."

"You gotta suck me back to life first," he told her as he flicked his limp dick.

She turned around and crawled over to the edge of the bed.

"I think I picked the right sister. The prettier one." He began stroking her ego. "The sexier one who can suck a mean dick." He was looking at the picture on her dresser of the two of them together. "I seen her some-where before. Don't she fuck with—"

"Shadee, yeah, yeah, yeah. Are we gonna fuck or talk about my sister?"

"Shadee? I thought he was fuckin' with that ho, Bri-anna?"

"You sure is snitchin' the nigga out. But it don't even matter. The bitch Brianna had that monkey. When she found out that she had it, she blew her brains out."

"Hold up, hold up. Go back to what you just said she had." His face was turning pale.

"She was infected." Skye stood there looking at her as if she were crazy. He had fucked Brianna on several occasions. One time raw. "Helloooo! Did you hear me?"

"Shut the fuck up." Skye pulled his pants up.

"Where you goin'? What's wrong?"

Skye was grabbing his shit. "I'ma call you. I'm out."

CHAPTER EIGHT

Peanut, did you get tested yet?" Shan whispered into the phone.

"Why are you whispering?"

"Well, did you?" she snapped.

"Yeah. They told me the earliest they can squeeze me in is Tuesday."

Shan breathed a sigh of relief. "I got something to tell you. You want the good news or the bad news first?"

Peanut tensed up. "Give me the bad first. Nah, fuck it! Just spill it."

"You take all the fun out of everything."

"Shan, just say what you got to say."

"Okay, boy, damn." She sucked her teeth. "I'm not moving to Cali. They have an opening at the Federal Correctional Institution in Milan, Michigan." There was silence. "You can't stop me from going," she continued. "Peanut, my mind is made up."

"So how did this come about? And who or what is in Michigan?"

"I went online since you were having a California

hissy fit to see if they had a job closer. And I won't be out there alone. I have a friend of a friend who's relocating out there as well."

"A friend of a friend, huh? I see you've been busy. So who is this nigga that I'm sure is a friend of a friend."

"You don't know him. Do you think you'll be able to go out there with me for a few days?" she asked in hopes of changing the subject.

"When are you leaving?"

"Thursday or really whenever you're ready. When can you be ready?"

"Since you're really going through with this . . ."

"Relocation, Peanut," she finished the sentence off for him.

"Whatever the hell you want to call it. If you want to leave Thursday then Thursday it is."

"Thank you. Thanks for your support. Even though I had to twist your arm."

"Let's break bread tomorrow," he snapped.

"Yeah, and I love you too. Bye, Peanut."

Peanut hung up with his baby sister feeling stressed out. If this was an indication of what parenthood was all about, he didn't want any children. *Michigan! I know some nigga is behind this move. I'ma find out who he is before she leaves the state of Tennessee. Believe that!*

After Shan hung up with Peanut, she lay there in thought. She knew Peanut didn't want her to leave but hey, it was time to do her. She was all keyed up to go to Cali, but now she had to redirect her energy toward Michigan. She had taken Briggen up on his offer. For one, because it was closer, and two, because Briggen said he would be out there with her and he had family out there. Not because she was feelin' all like that toward him or was she falling head over heels for him? She had to admit that she liked him, liked his style, liked the way he was genuinely concerned about her and wanted her to be all right. Was he like that with all of them bitches he got jockeying for his attention? She was now beginning to understand why. And it didn't hurt that his dick game was very much on point. Even though they hadn't fucked since she was chillin' at his spot it was fresh in her mind, the lovemaking session they had had in Las Vegas. Then she wondered if she was getting with Briggen to get back at Forever.

Briggen and his main man Woo were seated at the bar in his club. Briggen was on his second double shot of Remy and Woo was still nursing some Goose. Jim Jones's remix of "We Fly High" was low in the background. The club wasn't open for business yet but they were discussing business until Woo got personal.

"So...you think lil' mama is going to move down to Michigan?"

"Nigga, what you think?"

Woo grinned. "You a bad nigga if you pull that off."

"Man, she left this morning. It's already a done deal.

I couldn't keep her here. Shit, I got Forever, Sharia, Mia and Tami. And you know I had to keep her. Shit, one got good credit and good pussy. I slipped up and let her get away that last time."

Just then Sharia walked up and handed Briggen his cell phone. She whispered something in his ear and they both started laughing. He smacked her ass and she leaned in and stole a kiss on his lips.

Briggen turned his attention to the phone. "What's up, Cuz?"

"I'm just confirming a few things. Gotta know what I'm getting into," his cousin Keeta said. "And your girl Sharia? She is so fuckin' nosy. She wants to know the bizness real bad."

Briggen smirked as he admired Sharia's ass and thighs as she walked away. He made a mental note to dip his dick up in that before he left up out of there.

"Yeah, you know how that go. I told my girl Shan to call you as soon as she hit the dirt. She'll be with her brother. You already told the Realtor to be on standby, right?"

"Yeah, I told her. But I'm straight on her. I'm talking about *me* and the beauty salon." Keeta had graduated with her cosmetologist license last year and was dying to open up her own spot. When Briggen paid her a visit last week and told her he wanted to come down and invest in something, she thought that she had died and gone to heaven. The shop where she currently worked was called Steppin Out. And it was one of the top-notch spots in the D. But shit, she was a Thompson and the

Thompsons always take shit to the next level. As long as Briggen didn't come to town looking to set up a dope spot everything would be all gravy. She wasn't trying to catch a case for nobody.

"Keeta, I told you my plan. What? You thought I was bullshittin'?"

"I just wanted to make sure because we already came across two buildings. I want you to see them. When are you coming back?"

"In about a week."

"Okay, cool. As soon as I hook Shan up with the Realtor, I'll call you."

"That'll work, you be easy. And Keeta?"

"What's up?"

"Good lookin'."

"Fo'sho, Cuz."

Briggen ended the call. He turned toward Woo. "Them Detroit niggas gettin' that bread, you ready?"

"When were you planning on filling me in?" Woo inquired.

"As soon as I made up my mind as to what I wanted to do. But playboy, I've made up my mind and now it's a go, nigga."

Woo nodded in acknowledgment. "That's what's good."

After they discussed the plan for Detroit, Woo left and Briggen went looking for Sharia. He found her in her office, a phone glued to one ear, counting money with a joint dangling from the side of her mouth.

Briggen went over to her and removed the joint from her mouth, took a pull and put it out. Feeling cocky, he lifted her out of the chair and set her on the desk, causing her to drop the loot. It rained all over the floor.

"Baby, you want to try that new water, Bling? It's that shit that runs forty dollars a bottle. I think the ballers will want to floss with it," she said. Briggen shook his head no as he unbuttoned her blouse and slid his hand over her tits. He leaned over and buried his face between them.

"Hurry up," he told her as he hungrily sucked on her nipples, causing her to have to work extra hard in order to think, breathe and talk business all at the same time. She was able to cancel the order for the designer water. By the time she completed the business transaction and ended the call, her pussy was throbbing and dripping wet. She forgot that she even had the phone in her hand and it dangled loosely before falling onto the desk. Breathing hard, she moaned, "Fuck me."

He stood up and she slid his jeans and boxers down over his ass. His fingers spread wide, he eased up her thighs to her panties. She possessively stroked his throbbing dick as he raised her up and snatched her panties off. She automatically wrapped her legs around his waist. Thrusting into her sweltering, juicy pussy, he felt her fingers dig into his back as her eyes rolled back into her head.

"Ohhh . . ." she whimpered, sliding her fingers down to his ass, guiding him to rub up and down her clit.

"B-Brig..." she stuttered, "right there...baby, like...oh shit, right...like that."

Briggen thrust harder and grabbed her by her hair. "Like this?" He ground into her hot pussy, pressing up against her G-spot. "Like this?" He felt her pussy clamp onto his dick as he thrust faster and harder.

"I'm c-cum c-cumming," she squealed as the pussy showed no mercy on his pipe, squeezing it. Unable to hold back any longer, the both of them erupted at the same time. They were trying to catch their breath and Sharia didn't want to turn him loose.

Briggen ran kisses along her shoulders and neck. Her hands framed his face as they shared a kiss that was interrupted by the club phone and his cell both ringing at the same time.

"This is my time," Sharia moaned in between kisses. "Please...don't answer."

Briggen pulled up his boxers and jeans, then grabbed the cell. "Whassup?" he answered anyway as Sharia sighed.

"Where are you? I need to see you." It was Tami, his dope broad.

"I'm at the club. Can it wait till later?"

"Hold on," she told him.

"I wanted to be with you tonight," said Sharia. She rolled her eyes at him, placed her hand on his chest and pushed him back as she slid off the desk. When she went to walk away from him, he grabbed her and pulled her back. "I want to spend some time with you tonight," she threatened, and pouted at the same time.

"Baby, I'm back," Tami said. "I need to see you. And when you say later, how much later?" Tami wanted to find out.

"Everything's straight, right?" His left eyebrow raised up.

"Yes and no."

Briggen's mind was reeling at all the possibilities. "I'll call you back in an hour."

"Okay, I'll be waiting. Love you."

"Love you too." Sharia broke away from him. Briggen hung up and watched as Sharia put her panties back on. "Who said I was finished?"

"Nigga, don't try to appease me. The liquor tab is almost nine g's, which account do you want me to use?"

"It doesn't matter as long as the shit is delivered by Thursday." He leaned up against the desk. He knew she was pissed. "Come here." He held out his hand and she sauntered over to him. He wrapped his arms around her, whispered in her ear, "You know Daddy will be over later on. Let me take care of my money first, aiight?"

She didn't respond so he slid both hands up under her skirt and was rubbing her ass. Sharia was his baby. She was fine, smart, sexy and loyal. She was also very jealous but she had been working on that. She had even whipped Shan's ass before and any other ho that she felt threatened by.

Mia ran his day care center. She was the bossiest of the crew and didn't take no shit and refused to bite her tongue. He always had to check her about something. She didn't like Sharia or Tami and never hesitated to let them know. Her pussy was to die for and she ran the hell out of the day care.

Tami was all street and loved her some Briggen. She was the ultimate ride-or-die chick. She loved money and loved the dope game. Many niggas wished they had her on their team and had tried to pull her on several occasions.

Was he really willing to walk away from it all? He had to think about that some more.

And now add Shan to the equation. It was something about Shan's innocence that drew Briggen to her and made him want to take care of her. He hadn't decided yet where she would fit in on his team other than by running the beauty salon.

Briggen always sang, "I love girls, girls, girls, girls, girls I do adore." It was one of his favorite joints from Jay-Z.

"Bring Daddy back to life so that I can hit this gushy gushy one more time," he whispered into Sharia's ear.

Sharia smiled as she slid down to her knees. The buzzer rang. They both looked at the monitor and Mia was at the door. Sharia sucked her teeth. "This is some bullshit, Briggen. Make that bitch wait. Why the fuck everybody calling and coming by at the same time?"

He looked down at her. "Now you wouldn't want me to do that shit to you. Would you?" He pulled her up. "Plus, you got me all night. Go let her in."

She walked away from him. "You go let the bitch in!"

"What did you say?" he snapped.

"I *said*, do you want me to let her in?"

"That's what I thought you said."

Shan and Peanut stayed at the Atheneum Hotel in Detroit. They took their time driving from Memphis, taking advantage of the quality time together talking and airing things out. By that following afternoon they both were feeling a little more comfortable with Shan's move and her getting this job at the prison.

She finally told Peanut the name of the guy she was seeing. She gave him his government name: Calvin. Of course Peanut wanted to know his entire life history. Shan filled in the blanks the best she could, while of course leaving out pertinent details.

They were now standing downstairs in the hotel lobby. Briggen's cousin Keeta got tied up so she had arranged for the Realtor to pick them up from the hotel.

Five minutes later a fire-engine-red Porsche pulled up. The valet opened the door and out stepped this pretty cinnamon-colored, deep-dimpled, tall big-booty honey. She had on a tailor-made Escada suit. The skirt stopped right at her knees, her shape was phat. Peanut's eyes traveled down her long shapely and sexy legs to the stilettos, and it took everything in his power to control his hard dick. Her hair was in a ponytail with a bang. *Bossy*, Peanut said to himself.

She strutted into the lobby, looked at Shan and said, "Ms. McKee?"

Shan smiled. "Call me Shan. Ms. Tanner, right?"

The ladies shook hands. "Call me Karin."

"Karin, this is my brother, Anthony, and he will be hanging out with us today."

"Pleased to meet you, Anthony." She held out her hand for a shake and was caught off guard when he kissed it.

"Pleasure's all mine, Karin."

She looked him up and down, and gently took her hand back. He resembled the NBA star Chris Webber but was not as dark. She glanced at his bling. Not too much. *Nah, this nigga is too rugged for my taste. But then again, I ain't never met a nigga I couldn't clean up.* She pulled out her business card and handed one to Peanut and then one to Shan.

"Let's get a table so that we can discuss exactly what it is you're looking for. A good friend of mine told me to take real good care of you," Karin informed them as she turned all of her attention to Shan. "Fishbone's restaurant is right through here."

They immediately got a table and began going over property listings and different areas. Peanut sat back quietly listening to every word as the two women went over several things. Ole girl was on point as far as her real estate game. But she was a little too stuffy for his taste. However, he had a suspicion that it was all a front. All he needed was time alone with her.

By the time the sun started to go down they had looked at four properties and gotten a little acquainted with the city of Detroit and Karin was dropping them back at the hotel.

"Don't forget to call Keeta to let her know we made progress. She had an emergency this morning. She had intentions on hanging with us," Karin told Shan.

"I'll call her as soon as I get upstairs. What time should I be ready tomorrow?" Shan wanted to know.

"How is eleven?"

"That's fine, and thanks a lot."

"Aww girl, you straight. I'll be over to pick you up. Thank you for allowing me to be a major part of your relocation. What y'all gettin' into tonight?"

"I don't know," Shan said.

Peanut got out of the car first and then he opened the door for Shan.

Rude-ass nigga. Ain't even got the decency to say thank you or goodbye, Karin said to herself.

"I'll catch you in a few, let me holla at Miss Lady here," Peanut said to Shan.

"Aiight, mack daddy, but I doubt it if you get any play," Shan teased as she walked away.

"Stay out of grown folks' business," he teased back.

"Can you close my door, please?" Karin asked.

Peanut jumped in the front seat and then closed the door. "So, Miss Lady, what you got planned for a nigga?"

"Excuse you?" She twisted her neck.

"What kind of host are you?"

"You better call Keeta if you want a host. I don't have nothing planned for you."

"No? I want you to take me out, Mrs.?"

Karin smirked. "It's not Mrs."

"I can't tell with that golf ball you got sittin' on your finger," Peanut prodded.

"Rings don't mean shit. Anyway, call my cell phone. I'll see if I can squeeze you in, Anthony." She made an attempt to be formal.

"Don't sleep on a nigga, baby girl. I ain't no country boy."

"Well, show me then. You can ride with me to the mall," Karin challenged.

"Let me grab a couple of stacks. I'll be right back."

"A couple? Nigga, please." She dug in her purse and pulled out a brick.

"Damn. Shawty it's like that?" He had a feeling that she was street.

"Yeah, I'm just like that. You straight, I got you. Besides, you said I was the host. By the time I get finished you'll be ready to move to the D yo'self."

"Bet that." *Damn. I know how to pick 'em. I'm going to pluck this bitch. Once I give her some good dick, she'll bow down. Her ass need to be taken down a notch or two. Hoes will pull a chameleon on a nigga. Bitch acting all professional and shit. She ain't nothing but a gangsta in a dress. Plus, these Detroit girls talk too fast for me.*

"You know what? Why don't you take this address down and meet me later. I got a lot of shit to handle. Let's hook up around nine." Karin instantly flipped the script on him.

See, now that's the shit I'm talkin' about. But it's cool.
"Aiight, I'ma check you."

She watched his swagger as he disappeared into the
hotel lobby.

"Girl, my grandma had another asthma attack," Keeta
was telling Karin, who had stopped by to see if everything was okay. Karin was parked in Keeta's driveway.
"You need to come in, it's getting chilly out here. Plus
you got something on your mind? You keep staring off
into space and shit."

"What do you know about the brother?"

"What brother?"

"Shan's."

"I don't know shit. My cousin Brig told me to make
sure Shan was taken care of. He's putting up the dough
for her. He ain't say shit about the brother. Why?"

"The nigga is coming over to the crib tonight."

Keeta looked shocked. "And?"

"What you mean *and*? I don't know how that shit
came about."

"Yo' ass invited him, that's how it came about." Keeta
started laughing. "Bitch, go home and dust the coochie
off. I know the bad boy got cobwebs on it," she snickered. "It's unnatural to go as long as you have without
any dick."

"Bitch, you got me fucked up. I don't know this nigga
like that," Karin defended herself. "You done lost your
mind."

"Then why the fuck you invite him over?"

Karin revved up her engine, rolled her eyes at Keeta and said, "Damn if I know."

Later that night . . .

"Oh . . . Peanut. Oh God, that feels good." Karin buried her face in the pillow and bit down.

Peanut had her bent over the sofa. Her purse was still over her shoulder, he had her dress up over her ass and her legs spread wide and was slowly stroking her. His dick was brick-hard as he watched the action, pulling it all the way out until just the head was barely in her. Then he would thrust it all the way back in. *This bitch got me fucked up.*

His legs were getting weak. Not only was the pussy good but it was tight as a drum. He started pumping faster, holding on to her hips as she began throwing the pussy at him.

"Oh, shit!" she screamed out. Her body turned stiff as a board and then she nutted, shaking as he pounded into her. Then he pulled out, shooting his babies all over her bare ass.

CHAPTER NINE

Born, Slim, Teraney and Jo Jo were all standing downstairs in front of the hospital with long faces. Shadee's condition was still touch and go. The doctors were keeping him in a medically induced coma so that his body had a better chance to heal from the multiple surgeries performed in a week's time. Sha no longer had a police officer by his bedside even though they still hadn't gotten the 411 on why he had one in the first place. Everyone was relieved to at least be allowed to see him and assess the extent of his injuries but was fucked up in the head after everything was explained to them. Especially when the doctor said he was now waiting for the next of kin to inform them of Shadee's prognosis, the extent of his injuries and what surgeries had been done. They were now all thinking to themselves that they couldn't wait to get the punk mofos who did this shit to their homey.

If they tried to remove the bullet in his head, the doctors were sure that there would be an 80 percent chance that it would kill him. They were successful at removing the bullet that entered his cheek and traveled until it stopped under his right eye. However, they were unable to save his eye. The third bullet put a hole through the top part of his ear and lodged itself in the side of his head. They were able to remove that one as well as the two in his thighs. His anus was ruptured, damaging his colon. It needed sixty-eight stitches and he would have to wear a colostomy bag, also known as a shit bag, until he was able to go through additional surgery.

"You gonna be all right, maine?" Slim asked Born.

"Yeah, I'ma hang out here until his pops gets here. Plus, I don't wanna be around when y'all get wit Doc. I ain't feelin' that nigga like that no more. Dude livin' foul," Born stated matter-of-factly. "That nigga don't even deserve a chance to explain what went down."

"Chill out, lil' nigga. You always quick to jump to conclusions," Teraney teased him.

"Whatever man, I'll check y'all later."

Born turned and went back into the hospital. When he got back to Shadee's bedside he said, "Unc, everything gonna be all right. Just fight. I need you to get well. I didn't tell nobody about that tape. I almost did, but I didn't. When I find that fat freaky fuck, they better hope the Grim Reaper gets to him before me. 'Cause I'ma take care of him. Believe that."

Everyone except for Born was seated in Doc's living room. The tension in the room was at an all-time high. Everyone's angry glare locked in on Doc. Before he got jacked everyone had been kind of scared of him. But since that L of seventy g's there were no more punks in the camp. Every nigga in the room was now loudly singing a different tune.

Doc had grabbed a chair out of the kitchen, placed it in the middle of the floor and straddled it. He had a smirk on his face. "What? Y'all niggas here to bring me up on charges or some shit like that?"

"Yeah. As a matter fact niggas can't afford to take no L at a time like this. So yeah, you gonna have to come up offa that bread," Slim announced. "We also lettin' you know that we gonna re-up with Janay."

"What!" Doc snapped.

"Nigga, you the one responsible for us taking a loss of seventy g's," Jo Jo added.

"Man, I took a loss too!" Doc spat. "Plus, the nigga took fifty thou from my stash spot. And what the fuck y'all comin' at me like this for? That could have been any one of us who got jacked."

"Nigga, if you would have stuck to the program and came straight in, right now we would be gettin' money instead of having this sit-down," Slim barked.

"So whatchu saying? You want me to pay the shit back?" Doc was pissed and sneezing. Being under that cold shower for over an hour had given him just that... a cold.

"That's exactly what we're saying!" Teraney spat.

"Hold up, niggas, we haven't decided how we gonna do this yet." Slim let those words sink in before continuing. "But money is money. And right now, like I said, we gonna eat with Janay and Big Choppa and we want you to step down for a minute until we figure out our next move," Slim announced.

"Ain't this some shit! So it's like this?" Doc hissed as he grilled each and every one of the niggas in the room.

"You don't have any idea who did this? I mean shit, maine, the streets ain't even sayin' nothing." Jo Jo couldn't even hide the fact that he was suspicious.

"Man, fuck you!" Doc stood up, pushing the chair over, slamming it into the floor. "Y'all in my muhfuckin' crib!"

"What the fuck's that got to do with anything?" Jo Jo was now up and in Doc's face. "You got jacked, right here in your own *muhfuckin' crib.*"

Teraney jumped up and stood between them. "Both of y'all fools need to chill the fuck out."

"No, what y'all niggas need to do *is* get the fuck out. Like I said, y'all in my crib disrespectin' me on some suspicious shit."

"Nigga, we ain't takin' no L. So let us know something before tonight is out," Teraney threatened. Doc went to the door and yanked it open, grilling each of his boys as they walked out, one by one.

Jo Jo turned back to him, forming his fingers into a pistol, and aimed at him.

Janay had refused, against Big Choppa's orders, to leave her house. Once her father saw that it was a no-win situation he and Crystal had the living room remodeled. They had it painted and re-carpeted and installed all brand-new furniture, and this was only her second night there in the house since everything went down with Shadee and Brianna.

The doorbell rang and she jumped. *Who in the hell could that be? If it's the fucking police again . . .* She peeked out the window. "Doc? What the fuck do this nigga want?" she mumbled. She tied her robe shut, unlocked the door and cracked it. "What could you possibly want?" Her face looked as if she were smelling a rotten corpse.

He stood there looking her up and down before pulling out a couple of stacks. "Whether you like it or not, I gave my word that I would always look out for you and Marquis. Can I come in for a few minutes? I got a few things I need to fill you in on."

"First off, let me enlighten your punk ass. Me and Marquis is tight. We don't need shit from yo' gump ass. And lastly, why should I let you in? Whatever you got to say, you can fill me in right here. You got all of sixty seconds. Fifty-eight." *The nerve of this muthafucka.*

"Sha would want you to have this." He held out the loot, which she didn't take. "Plus I got some business to discuss; it will only take a minute."

"Nigga, if it'll only take a minute, like I said you got all of fifty seconds."

"Aiight, fine. But listen up. Wit Sha out the way, I've stepped up to the plate to handle business. Money ain't gonna stop. So let me lay the spiel down. I got them thangs for thirteen a whop. Now, I just recently got a connect. He's family so we don't have to worry about no foul shit poppin' off. Dig, you need to get wit me when you're ready to cop or re-up. You can't beat thirteen—"

"Hold up, fun boy." She cut him off and opened the door. "First off, I'm good. And lastly, I wouldn't dare get money with your faggot ass. What I look like workin' with my man's bitch?" She went to slam the door but he stuck his foot out and grabbed the doorknob.

"Get the fuck off my door, Doc."

"Girl, I don't know why you trippin'. I'm just doin' what Sha would want me to do. Now, you either gonna do shit my way or—"

"Or what?" Big Choppa's voice boomed as the door flew open and he came charging at Doc, and the both of them went pummeling down the steps. "Or what? You punk muthafucka!" Big Choppa tried to crush Doc's nose with his fist.

"Daddy! Don't get any blood on you." Janay ran off the porch. "Let him go! Plus, we don't need any more heat at this address."

They were rolling around the grass, rumbling. Janay ran back into the house.

Big Choppa was raining blows all over Doc's face. "Punk...bitch...stay away from my daugh— Fuck!" Doc had kneed him in the nuts and was now on top of Big Choppa, raining blows on his face.

"I ain't gonna be too many of yo' punks," Doc gritted as Big Choppa grabbed a brick. As he raised his arm to hurl it at him, Doc pulled out his heater and cocked it. Big Choppa stood frozen with his arm held high and the brick up in the air.

"Drop the fuckin' heat, Doc!" Janay was running down the steps with her pistol. When he turned to look at her that's when he felt the brick smash against his skull. That's the last thing he remembered.

"Daddy, are you okay?"

Big Choppa was breathing hard and was bent over with his hands on his knees. "Baby girl…" He gulped some air into his lungs. "That was a workout. These young niggas think I can't go toe-to-toe with dem." She grabbed his arm, stood him up. He looked over at Doc. "Nigga, I'm comin' after yo' ass for disrespectin' me like this. Put that on yo' punk-ass daddy's grave."

Janay walked her father into the house and locked the door. Janay immediately got on the phone and called Slim.

Teraney answered, "What it do?"

"Who is this?" She couldn't make out the voice but she knew it wasn't Slim.

"Who dis is?" he asked again.

"It's Janay."

"Girl, we've been hittin' you up for days. Where the fuck you been? You aiight?"

"I know, I had to get my head straight. But listen, Doc came over to my house trying to strong-arm me. My dad was here and they got into it. Come get your man. He's laid out on my grass. Y'all need to come get him before the po-po does."

"What you mean he laid out?" She heard the panic in his voice.

"He got knocked the fuck out," Janay said, mimicking Chris Tucker from the movie *Friday*.

"Damn, this nigga just got out of some shit. Aiight. I'll be over there. But we need to talk business."

"That's cool. Hurry up and get this nigga off my lawn before them boys be over here. Make sure Slim is with you."

CHAPTER TEN

"Mommy, the phone is ringing," Tameerah sang as Nyla juggled the bags of groceries while fumbling with the keys to open the door.

"Okay. Okay."

"Mommy, hurry up, it's still ringing." Tameerah was bouncing up and down.

"I hear it, Tameerah." As soon as the lock turned, Tameerah pushed the door open and ran for the phone. Nyla rushed for the kitchen table to set the heavy bags down.

"Mommy, it's Daddy. It's Daddy!"

"Nooo, Tameerah!" Nyla yelled as she hurried into the living room to make Tameerah hang up the phone. But when she reached her it was too late.

"Hi, Daddy." Tameerah beamed. "Fine. Yes. Yes. Uh-huh. From the store. I miss you too. Yeah, she here. Okay, Daddy. I love you too. Here go my mommy!" She held out the phone for Nyla.

Damn, why did I teach her how to press five? "Go wash

your hands so you can help me put the groceries away."
She then said to Forever, "Hey."

"Hey? I haven't seen or talked to my wife or daughter in weeks and that's all you got to say is hey?"

"What you want me to say, Forever?"

"That nigga must be fuckin' you real good."

"I ain't trying to hear that stupid shit. I've been running all day, I just stepped into the house and I got groceries to put away. So what's up?"

"Fuck you mean what's up?" *This bitch done lost her fuckin' mind.* "I'm not about to clock out on yo' ass over the phone. Just bring my daughter to see me, first thing in the morning."

"How you know I don't have something to do, Forever?"

"Just be here in the morning." Forever hung up, pissed off and feeling as if his happy home was now crumbling to pieces. He was trying to ignore it, hoping that Nyla's antics would stop and everything would go back to normal. But with each unanswered phone call, empty visiting day, mail call with his name not mentioned he had to face it: shit was coming to a close.

How foolish was he to think that he had Nyla that open to where she wouldn't trip over him getting Shan pregnant? Then on top of that his money wasn't rolling in like it used to. He'd been hearing several cats give Zeke mad props and saying how he was doing big thangs and was now the man to see. He didn't want to believe that. But he also knew that there usually is a little truth to all rumors. And since his cash flow was slowing down something had to be up.

"Nigga, take your head outta them clouds. What the fuck is up with you?" Zeke stood in front of Forever.

"Boy, where you been?" Forever asked his cousin.

"I told you, I'm working the midnight-to-seven shifts now. That's why we been missing each other."

"Damn, yo, come take this walk with me." Zeke shrugged as he fell into step beside Forever. "Man, shit has been crazy on the home front."

"What's up?" Zeke asked.

"Nyla really been trippin'. I ain't exaggerating neither, yo. She stopped answering the phone. I don't get any more letters. I ain't had a visit in almost a month. One night I called and she was on the phone with this nigga. The next time I called I had JB's cell phone and it was after midnight. She was just gettin' to her sister's to pick up my daughter. Her attitude done changed, man." Then he mumbled, "I'm losing her."

"You paranoid, boy." Zeke's face was twisted up, not really giving a damn and not wanting to hear the bullshit. His focus was on gettin' that paper. Plus, he wasn't feelin' his cousin like that no more.

"Sheeit, nigga, you been through it already," Forever reminded him. "So you know it ain't paranoia."

"They say all's fair in love and war. But hell, when wifey starts acting like she cuttin' out…I can't even explain how I was feelin', shit was scary fo'real." Zeke wished he could forget the shit.

"Tell me about it, she'll be down here tomorrow and I don't even know—"

"Yo, Zeke, I need to holla at you, man. I need—" Bing, his most loyal runner, interrupted.

"Hold that thought," Zeke cut his runner off, not wanting Forever in his business. Then he turned to Forever. "Ever, let me go holla at this youngin."

"Man, how you just gonna bounce in the middle of my crisis?" Forever snapped.

"Chill, nigga, I'll get wit you later."

He left Forever standing there with a look of disbelief on his face and shocked that Zeke wasn't really paying him any attention. Plus, lately Zeke was giving him the cold shoulder.

"What's up, big pimpin'? Everythang cool?" Skye asked Forever. "I was wondering when you was gonna check in. Y'all niggas keep them contraband-ass cell phones. What's really good?"

"Shit, I was hopin' you had somethin' good for me. Make my day."

"I don't know about making your day and all that. But check it. I been watchin' and ya boy is shinin'. You know he got that from his sister, right?"

Forever took a minute to decipher what Skye had just told him. So it was official that the money and dope that Shan jacked from Forever she gave to Peanut to get him up and running. And now he was quickly becoming the man to see.

"Yo, good lookin', dawg." Forever hung up, feeling some kind of way, and went to get ready for tomorrow's visit.

"Hey, you," Peanut said to Nyla.

"Hey back, what's up?"

"You don't sound too good. Everything cool?"

How does he always know when to call?

"Yo, Nyla, everything aiight?" He heard her sigh.

"Everything's fine, Peanut. Just a little stressed. What's good with you?"

"I got something for you."

"Do you?" Her curiosity got the best of her. "What is it?"

"It's an outing. A trip to the spa. It'll be right on time and just what you need. I'ma come scoop you up in about an hour."

"In an hour? Peanut, how am I supposed to jump up and go to a spa?"

"How? Easy. Just do it. It ain't like you gotta pack a bag. Get your sister to watch the baby. It's my treat." He could feel her crack a smile through the phone. "So you game or what?"

"I'll see you in an hour." She hung up the phone and yelled, "Tameerah, you want to go over to Auntie Lisha's?"

Exactly an hour later, Peanut was pulling up into her driveway. She locked her front door and walked around to the driver's side of his ride.

"Do you want me to follow you?" she innocently asked Peanut. That was another thing he liked about her.

"Girl, you better get your fine ass into this truck." He leaned over and opened the door for her. She jumped in and slammed it shut. "I'ma ask you to relax, shawty." He could see the tension all over her face.

"You have no idea how I'm feelin' right now."

"I still want you to relax, I got you. I got just what you need."

Her eyebrows shot up. "And what is that supposed to mean?"

"Now see, there you go, I'ma ask you to get your mind out of the gutter! I ain't even on that." He watched her crack a smile.

"Mmm-hmm," was all she muttered as she leaned back, got comfortable in the seat and closed her eyes.

"Now see, was that so hard?"

"Believe it or not, I know how to relax," she mumbled with her eyes still closed. "So where are we going?"

"Now you just said that you know how to relax, so convince me." He looked over at this woman. And once again reasons ran across his mind as to why he was diggin' her so much. Was it because she belonged to someone else? Maybe it was because she's so petite and he was willing to put money down and bet that her pussy was real tight and always hot. Whatever the case, he was anxious to see where they would end up. He knew that he liked how she always looked as if she had just come from the beauty salon and today was no exception. She had on a white-on-white Baby Phat sweat suit, sneakers to match, diamond studs, Cartier watch and no wedding ring.

"What?" She felt him observing her.

"I said relax, not fall asleep on me."

"Relax, sleep, it's all the same to me." She smirked. "So what were you thinking as you were checking me out with your microscope? And don't lie."

"How I'm feelin' your steelo."

"And what else?" Her eyes were still closed.

"I can't tell you that."

"Umm-hmm, mind in the gutter. Just as I thought."

"No it wasn't...well maybe a little," he confessed.

"How much longer until we reach our destination?"

"About forty-five minutes; you wanna blaze this up?"

Her eyes popped open and he was holding up a big fat joint. "Why not?"

Almost an hour and two joints later they pulled into an office complex and got out. Nyla curiously checked out her surroundings. He grabbed her hand and smiled at her. "Don't worry, I'm not going to let nothing happen to you. You're gonna like what I got planned." He held the door open for her and they stepped inside and followed the signs for Crystal Waters Health Spa.

"Oooh." Nyla giggled. "You were serious, weren't you?" He held open another door for her and the scent of vanilla enveloped her. There were water fountains strategically placed as well as white candles.

"Of course. What did you think?"

"Do you have a reservation, sir?" the young lady at the desk asked. Her nametag read Danita.

Nyla had slipped away to investigate the variety of bowls of white chocolate candies. She was looking around in awe, impressed with the layout of the spa.

"Nyla." Peanut waved her over. "This is Danita. Whatever you want Danita will take care of you."

Danita held out her hand. "Pleased to meet you, Ms. Nyla." She shook Nyla's hand. "Come with me and we can get you started on the Crystal Waters' experience."

She grabbed her elbow, leading her away from Peanut, and the gentleman who appeared behind the desk. She immediately started hyping up the Crystal Waters Spa. Peanut winked at her and Nyla waved back at him.

By the end of the day Nyla had indeed experienced the works: a full-body massage, a mud wrap, which she didn't like because it felt icky, a facial, bikini wax, manicure and pedicure. She had to admit that she was feeling like…a brand-new woman.

"Yo, am I that nigga or what? Damn! You look like you're floating," Peanut greeted her as she sauntered through the double doors with a huge grin plastered on her face. And indeed she did look rejuvenated.

"Thank you, Peanut. I feel like I'm floating." She gave him a hug.

"It's not over yet."

"It's not?" She grinned up at him, excitement evident in her voice.

He grabbed her hand and they headed for the car.

"Got another stop to make but you gotta promise me

you won't trip and get the wrong idea. You gotta trust me on this one. Can you do that?"

"Where are we going?" He helped her into the front seat and shut the door. Before he could get around to the other side she had the door open for him. "Peanut, answer me. Where are we going?"

"You gonna trust me or what?" He jumped in and started the truck.

Her mouth turned from a smile to a pout. "What's the 'or what' part?"

Peanut couldn't help but laugh at her skepticism.

"Trust you or what, Peanut?" she prodded. "And stop laughing." She punched his arm.

"I'm taking your ass home right now, or you're going to enjoy the second part of your evening. So what's the deal?"

She sucked her teeth and was still pouting. "Take me home."

"Aiight then. The choice is yours."

"Siiike! Spark up and give me the rest of my evening."

"You sure? 'Cause ain't no turning back and I don't want no opposition for the rest of the evening. Deal?"

"Deal." Nyla was practically jumping out of her seat.

"We're not gonna spark up until we get to where we're going."

They drove another forty-five minutes before pulling up to the Ritz-Carlton. He turned and looked at Nyla, whose mouth had fallen open. "Uh-uh-uh," he sang as he wagged his finger. "Remember our deal." She started to say something but he held up his finger, motioning for her to be quiet. The valet opened their doors and they both got out. He grabbed Nyla's hand and tried not to laugh as he practically dragged her into the hotel and to the front desk. Less than five minutes later he was leading her to the elevators. "Chill out, girl, you aren't even enjoying the scenery of the hotel. This is a brand-new spot, first class!" Peanut teased her. He had the upper hand and he was really enjoying it.

She was shaking her head no. She turned to him and started to say something but instead turned her back on him.

He leaned over and pressed twelve, then put his mouth to her ear and whispered, "Don't panic. We ain't gonna do nothing that you don't want to do."

Shit. She ran her hand through her hair.

Peanut watched and was enjoying the fact that he had her squirming. When the elevator doors opened Peanut waved his arm and smirked. "After you, madam. We will be occupying suite 1204," he said in a concierge's voice.

"Oh, so the concierge has plenty of jokes," she mumbled as her eyes scanned the room numbers. She stopped and took a deep breath in front of room 1204.

"Why you acting like I'm leading you to jump off a cliff or something?" Peanut chuckled as he stuck the card key into the slot. When the door popped open he led the way and closed it after stepping inside.

"Awwww, Peanut." She covered her mouth. The room

was decorated with red-and-white balloons and red-and-white rose petals. The table was lit by candles and the waiter, who was already inside, pulled Peanut to the side, whispered something in his ear and then left.

"You had this all planned out? What if I would have said take me home?"

"It would have been your loss. Go freshen up or whatever you need to do. He'll be back with dinner."

She was already off and inspecting the suite, no longer nervous or feeling guilty. When she finally made it back into the dining area Peanut was tipping a different waiter and was holding a bouquet of red-and-white roses. The entire setup had her feeling special...and very sexy.

After Peanut saw the waiter out, she walked over to him, got on her tippy-toes and kissed him lightly on the cheek and then on the lips. "Thank you, Peanut. Thank you for taking my mind off of...everything."

"The pleasure's all mine." He handed her the roses, and she kissed him again. "Let's eat, I'm hungry as hell."

"What do we have?" She was eyeing the beautiful table spread. He held out the chair for her to sit down. Then he lifted the silver lid. A huge grin spread across her face. "Slick. Real slick! That's why you had Danita ask me all of those questions about if I had my choice of a dream meal for right now."

"How else could I have planned your perfect dinner? You wanted filet mignon; you got filet mignon. Here is your Caesar salad with cherry tomatoes and artichokes."

He frowned. "And here is your steamed glazed carrots, baked potato and sesame rolls."

"Don't hate, Peanut. This *is* my meal, remember? Where is my fruit tart? And the extra sour cream for my twice-baked potato?" She lifted another lid. Another smile crept over her face. "Nigga, you got mad cool points from this sista."

"Enjoy, Nyla."

After the meal and the downing of a whole bottle of Krüg they found themselves in the Jacuzzi splashing and taking turns dunking each other under the water. Peanut had just let Nyla up for air and she was coughing and laughing at the same time.

"Okay, okay. You win!" She scooted back and leaned her head back. "I'm dizzy, boy." He was standing over her, ready to dunk her again. "Peanut, stop."

"Who tha man?" He reached down and grabbed her foot.

"I told you! Seriously. Stop playing. You tha man." When he let her foot go she waited for him to sit down and then grabbed him around his neck and pulled him down. He grabbed her head and pulled her down with him. They both went under. Water was all over the floor as if they were having a pool party.

Their heads bobbed up at the same time, splashing more water on the floor, and both of them were laughing. Nyla jumped out, ran to the toilet and began hurling. Peanut laughed even harder.

"You're drunk, girl. You told me you didn't get drunk and you knew how to hold your liquor."

"I'm...dizzy, not drunk."

"You're drunk." He stepped out of the Jacuzzi, wet a washcloth with cold water and handed it to her.

She slowly stood up and started giggling. "It...hurts... to...laugh." She wiped her mouth and then leaned over and hurled again.

"You need to lay your drunken ass down." This time he took another damp cloth and wiped her face. "That shit was fun, wasn't it?"

She nodded yes as he dabbed her face as if she were a little kid. He then wrapped a towel around her. She had on her bra and panties. He still had on his boxers.

"Lay down. And I'll see about getting us some dry shit."

She tore off the towel and came out of the wet bra and panties as Peanut stood there watching her and licking his lips. She grabbed one of the hotel robes. "Wake me in an hour."

That's the last thing Nyla remembered as she opened one eye and then the other, realizing where she was. She sat straight up and looked over at Peanut, who was knocked out. Her heartbeat sped up as she slowly turned to look at the clock. It read 8:57 a.m.

"Oh. My. God," she gasped, covering her mouth with both hands.

"Yo, Watkins," Forever greeted the officer. "Can you call the visiting room and see if I have a visit? It's almost ten and you know my wife is always one of the first ones here."

Watkins picked up the phone and dialed. Forever stood impatiently, hands in his pockets, rocking back and forth on his heels.

"This is Watkins. Yeah, uh, does Forever Thompson have a visitor?" Watkins twirled a pen in the air as he listened to the visiting officer on the other end. "Uh-huh, uh-huh. Not yet, Thompson." He kicked back in his chair and engaged in a private conversation. "You don't say?"

Forever cursed under his breath and stepped away...angry. "I know this bitch didn't front on me like this!"

CHAPTER ELEVEN

"Who is it?" Keke, Peanut's ex, yelled out from behind the door.

"Peanut."

Keke stood there. She glanced at the clock, it was 1:45. *Why didn't I leave at one as I planned?* Then she looked over at the calendar. Peanut had been home for a month; at least that's what she heard. And now he decided to stop by. Just like him to try and make her sweat.

"Open the muthafuckin' door, Keke!" he snapped.

He finally heard her unlock the dead bolt and turn the lock. Keke slowly pulled the door open and stood there looking Peanut up and down. He had on a LRG hoody and a pair of Sean John jeans and was rockin' some Adidas Top Tens. She looked past him to see what he was driving but was damn near knocked over as he brushed past her.

"Come in, have a seat." Her voice dripped with sarcasm.

He reached back and snatched her up by her throat. "Bitch, you got me fucked up! You don't wanna push me over the edge!" Spittle was flying out of his mouth as her eyes were getting watery. "Or do you?" He squeezed tighter. Her face began to change colors. He tossed her back onto the couch, where she lay gasping for air. He calmly sat down across from her. He went into his back pocket, pulled out some weed and a pack of Backwoods and started rolling up. When Keke went to get up, he barked, "Sit your ass down and stay the fuck down!"

"Why I—"

"And shut the fuck up!"

She sucked her teeth and rolled her eyes. But at the same time she was trembling. Even though he hadn't come home when he first got out, she had known she wasn't in the clear. She had known she was eventually going to get a visit. Hell, the house was just as much his as it was hers. And he still had a lot of shit there, even though she had packed it away.

Her gaze followed him as he went into the kitchen and came back with two Coronas. He sat back down, fired up his blunt, and started taking swigs out of the bottle. He sat there and just looked in her eyes as he got high. For twenty minutes the only sounds were of him puffing on his weed and guzzling down the Coronas.

Damn. This nigga gonna hold me hostage or what?

"I thought you were smarter than that, Keke." Peanut finally decided to break the silence.

"Who you talkin' to, nigga? I'm about as smart as yo' dumb ass. I ain't the one who was getting fuck—"

Before she could finish her sentence Peanut was up and across the room and had slapped her clean off the couch. Then he kicked her in the stomach. "Bitch, you must have forgot!" He glared at her. "But check it. Your name on my tongue tastes like shit. Fuck being loyal. What, it's been four years we been down for each other?" He answered his own question, "Yeah. And I've been nothing but good to you. I was only gone for a minute and you turned on me with the quickness. I thought your ass had some brains and a little bit of loyalty."

She lay there as Peanut went upstairs. She looked at the phone, wondering who she should call, if she should lay there or make a fast getaway.

"Don't move, Keke," he yelled down the steps as if he heard what she was thinking.

Well that answers that question, she said to herself. *I hope he hurries the fuck up.* She was now getting mad. *Shit. Yeah I left. So the fuck what? Niggas go to jail and get left all the time. Nigga actin' like he's been locked up for ten years. Shit, the nigga ain't do a day over sixty. So now he's mad and kicks me in my fuckin' stomach. I'ma get his bitch ass back.*

"Yo, Ke." Peanut smirked as he came down the stairs. "I'm glad I came by. You know why? Now I gotta change of heart. Since you had niggas all up in and out of my shit, I said fuck it. She can keep this shit. I'ma boss. I was just gonna burn the muthafucka down to the ground. But since you got my shit all packed the fuck up you know what? I changed my mind. *You* gonna get the fuck out!" Keke's mouth opened in shock. She was getting ready to plead her case but he stopped her. "If you want to keep all thirty-twos in your mouth, I suggest you close that bitch. I don't give a fuck where you go but by tomorrow this time all of your shit needs to be gone. Are we clear?"

She wouldn't answer.

"Keke, do we have an understanding?"

"Peanut, you can't expect me to be up and out of here tomorrow. I don't even have anywhere to go," she pleaded.

"That's not my problem. I'm sure you got at least one nigga or bitch willing to put up with your funky ass." He headed for the door.

"Can't you give me until the weekend, Peanut, damn! It's not like you don't have a place to go." She was now up and on the porch with him.

"Yeah. That's the problem. I'm holed up in some gotdamned apartment while you all up in my house, trickin' my money away." He stepped off the porch.

"You're in an apartment because you want to be. You got enough bread to have a house."

"Just be outta here by tomorrow night, bitch."

"Peanut, I—"

"I ain't got shit else to say. Instead of following behind me, you need to be in there packin' ya shit."

Just then a navy blue Chevy Impala screeched to a halt. When Peanut saw the window ease down and tip of the Glock pointed at them he yelled, "Ke, get the fuck down!" *Splat! Splat!* The shots rang out. Peanut pulled out his heater.

"Take that to the bank, ho-ass nigga!" The unfamiliar voice rang out and the Impala's engine roared as it took off down the street. The neighbors were already pouring out of their houses.

"Ke," he mumbled as he went over to her. "Keke." That's when he saw it...her face. It was covered in blood. Her forehead sported a gaping hole and her eyes were staring at him. "Ke...damn...son of a bitch!" he spat as he listened to sirens in the distance.

Forever was ironing his prison fit, getting ready for his visit, when Zeke walked past. "You just gettin' off yo' good government job?" Forever teased him.

Zeke nodded and stepped into the laundry room and leaned up against one of the dryers. "You ironing yo' good government gear?" Zeke teased back.

"Hell yeah," Forever responded without shame.

"So Nyla finally comin'?"

"Supposed to be. I haven't spoken to the bitch, she won't answer the phone but had the nerve to leave a message with her sister."

"That's fucked up," Zeke stated matter-of-factly. "Let me know how shit turned out. Wake me up when you get off the visit. I'm tired as hell."

"I don't know why you working like a Hebrew slave. You don't need the loot from what I'm hearing. They say you that nigga to see, and the one who cats tryna be." Forever smirked.

Zeke took that comment in stride. "Hey, a nigga gots ta eat."

"So what you sayin', man? You wasn't eatin' when we was gettin' money together? You *was* family, nigga, and I treated you like family. I always had your back," Forever told him.

"*Was* family?"

"Yeah, *was.* You cut the fuck off. Family don't go behind family's back. You couldn't man the fuck up and step to me? You had to act like a bitch and go behind my back? I heard about your visit with my brother. I'm waiting and waiting, thinking you was going to get at me." Forever laughed. "But that never happened. You pulled a punk-ass move nigga. Just tell me why, man? You been on some ole funny-type shit."

An older white man with huge black-rimmed glasses came in carrying a bag of laundry. "Get the fuck outta here, we talking!" Zeke yelled. The guy backed out quietly.

"Nigga, go 'head with that weak-ass bullshit," Forever spat.

"Man, fuck you." Zeke ranted, "You the muthafucka that's weak. Allowing your woman to turn you into a snitch."

Forever smirked. "Snitch? I know yo' punk ass snitched on me! But you don't know what the fuck I did. All I know is I made you, nigga. All you was doin' was ridin' my coattail. If it wasn't for me, you wouldn't have shit. You wouldn't be shit. All I got to do is say the word and you'll be back to being a runner for one of these small-time, petty-ass knuckleheads."

"Never that, Cousin. So don't get it twisted. This is a new day." And quickly Zeke left out.

Forever unplugged the iron and remembered that he had clothes in the dryer. He began folding them up and thinking about how shit goes down in the joint, and then his mind went to how fast Zeke had left out.

"Forever." Fat Louie stuck his head in the door. He was out of breath and sweating. "I was looking all over for you."

"What's up, maine?" Forever didn't even bother to look up as he continued to press his pants.

"Fool, why you chillin' like it's nothing? Zeke and 'em on their way up here. Y'all got serious beef or sumthin'? 'Cause word is, he strapped up. I told Tops and them to be ready, but shit, Z is on his way."

"Fuck!" Forever spat. "I ain't got nuttin' on me."

"Hold up, I'll be right back! I got you."

"Nigga, I'll be dead by the time you get your fat ass back!"

Fat Louie had already disappeared.

Aws hell to the naw. He went back and plugged in the iron. It sounded as if Zeke was in the hall. He grabbed a shirt and a pair of pants out of the dryer, turned the iron up high and went to press the pants.

Not two minutes later and just as he was expecting,

Zeke came to the door. "Ever, come here, man, let me holla at you."

"Nigga, you come to me. Ain't nobody else in here." Forever gripped the iron firmly, still ironing but not taking his eyes off Zeke.

"Cool." Zeke closed the door behind him, and when he got up on Forever he went for his shank. Forever swung the iron, slapping Zeke across the jaw.

"Fuck!" Zeke gritted as the hot iron ate his flesh.

Zeke went for Forever's throat with the shank, but Forever ducked and it landed on the back of his shoulder. Zeke dug it deeper, twisted it and Forever yelled, "Aw damn. Make sure you kill me."

The door flew open. "Yo, the po-po," one of Zeke's runners said. Zeke smoothly tossed him the shank. He caught it, and then Zeke felt the iron hit the back of his head.

The next day Zeke and Forever were still in the hole. Zeke's head was bandaged and he had second-degree burns on the back of his head and neck. Forever's shoulder was bandaged up and he had forty-two stitches.

"Thompson." The officer kicked the bars. "You have a visit. I'll be back in ten."

Forever's eyes popped open as he looked up at the ceiling. "Now the bitch decides to show up," he mumbled as he slowly sat up and swung his feet to the floor. He was pissed that his right shoulder was fucked up. Luckily for him the guard came back twenty minutes later. That's how long it took him to get his self together, working with his left hand.

Nyla was watching Tameerah play with the baby sitting across from them. She was playing peekaboo and the baby wouldn't stop laughing.

The inmate visitors' door opened and the men filed out. Nyla's eyes got big as saucers and her mouth twisted into a frown at the sight of Forever bandaged up and in an orange jumpsuit. *This nigga is back in the hole.*

"Tameerah, here comes your father."

Tameerah looked around, spotted Forever and took off running. "Daddy! Daddy! I was playing with the baby. I want a baby. Can I have a little baby?"

He swooped her up, forgetting about his stitches, and grimaced as the pain traveled throughout the shoulder and down his arm. "I miss you, girl." He kissed her cheek. "Daddy loves you."

"I love you too, Daddy. You hurt yourself?"

"Yeah, baby, I did. But since you're here I feel much better."

"Good." She hugged him around his neck. "Can I have a baby?"

"What?"

"Can I have a baby?"

"You have to ask your mother that."

"Mommy, can I have a baby?" Tameerah peeked over at her mother.

"After you finish all of your schooling, and you're a big girl, yeah."

"Aww man, how big?" She pouted.

"Bigger than me."

Tameerah squirmed her way down from Forever's arms. "Daddy, you want some yogurt ice cream? I got money to buy you one!"

"Do you?"

"Um-hmm. Don't I, Mommy?" Nyla handed Tameerah her own little clear plastic purse that was full of coins. "C'mon, Daddy." She pulled Forever's hand, and they went over to the vending machines.

Nyla's hands were beginning to sweat. She was anxious to get their confrontation over and done with. Even though she wasn't sure what she wanted the outcome to be.

"Daddy, can I sit by the baby and eat my yogurt ice cream?"

"As long as you don't try to feed the baby you can."

"Thank you, Daddy." She puckered up her lips and Forever kissed her. He watched her take her yogurt, spoon and napkin and sit next to the baby.

After she got situated he turned his attention to Nyla. He looked her over. Looking to see what was different about her. Her hair was still fly, just the way he liked it. *What other nigga is likin' it more than I am?* She had on a pair of Parasuco hip-hugging jeans. *Who's grabbing on to those hips?* The crisp white blouse was caressing her breasts. *Damn, what nigga is running his tongue over her nipples?* And the pair of black stilettos she wore said, "Come fuck me." *Why the fuck am I torturing myself like this? I ain't seen a nigga that could hold on to a bitch while he's doin' a dime.* Finally he noticed that she didn't have on her usual perfume...his favorite.

"What kind of perfume are you wearing? What made you switch up?"

She sucked her teeth.

"I just wanted a change."

"Why are you doing this shit, Nyla? I'm at the end of my bid. Just because your little scheme didn't work, you just gonna cut out on me?" He was fighting to control his temper.

"Why are you blaming everything on me, Forever? Oh, so you forgot about that bitch Shan and y'alls little love child on the way? You forgot that you're getting ready to have a whole 'nother family?"

"Nyla, you and Tameerah are my only family, so stop with the bullshit. I told her to get rid of that baby and that she was only business and that I already had a family."

"So...you think a baby is just going to go away like that? She said she was keeping it, Forever. Remember?"

"Why the fuck are you stuck on that, Nyla? I told you it wasn't nothing. She was a nobody, damn."

Nyla laughed. "A nobody? That doesn't make the baby go away? What if I got pregnant by some nigga and told you it wasn't nothing? How would you be acting?"

Forever sighed.

"Yeah, that's what I thought. So when are they transferring you? They said if you got in trouble again, they were gonna transfer you, right?" she snapped.

"I'ma try to beat this one, Nyla. My man the lieutenant is handling it."

Nyla sucked her teeth and rolled her eyes.

"What's that all about, Nyla?"

"You're getting transferred, way across the fuckin' world somewhere. I told you, I'm tired, Forever."

"So if I don't come home real soon, and if I get transferred, you gone, huh?"

Nyla folded her hands across her chest and the look on her face said it all.

Forever was crushed. "Fuck it and fuck you. Tameerah, baby, come here and talk to Daddy. This is fucked up, Nyla," Forever gritted.

Tameerah jumped onto her daddy's lap. He spent the next hour explaining to his daughter that he probably was going to get moved and wouldn't be able to see her as often. He told her that they would talk on the phone and that he would be home in a minute to take her wherever she wanted to go and that he loved her very much.

When the visit was over, Forever said to Nyla, "I hope this nigga is worth it." He turned and walked away.

CHAPTER TWELVE

Shan heard a tap on the hotel door. She snatched up her robe, slid her feet into her slippers and yelled, "Wrong door." When no one responded she looked through the peephole and immediately her frown turned into a huge grin. She pulled off the scarf she had tied around her locks, peeked in the mirror and then opened the door.

"What a surprise! You said you wouldn't be here until the weekend." She stepped aside to let Briggen in and closed the door. His Armani scent filled the room. When she saw him set down the Louis Vuitton garment bag the kitty instantly perked up.

"You don't sound too excited to see me." He gave her that smile.

"Oooh, *we're* excited. I kinda miss you," she teased.

"Kinda?"

"Yeah, kinda." She walked seductively over to him and stood in front of him.

"Rewind back to the *we're* excited part."

She eased her hands up his chest and slid his jacket

off his shoulders. "You heard me, I said we're excited to see you."

"Who is the *we're?*"

She took his hand and pressed it up against her hot and slick pussy. "Me and her," she purred.

"I see," he mumbled as his middle finger slid back and forth across her goodies. A soft moan escaped her throat, and he eased that finger inside her slickness and it came back dripping with her juices. He leaned over and their mouths met as she hungrily devoured his lips. Both his hands slid over her ass and squeezed and massaged her cheeks. She groaned as her trembling hand grabbed his dick, squeezed and teased it. She then undid his belt buckle and unzipped his pants. His pipe sprung out greedily through the slit in the boxers.

"You finally ready for big daddy?"

She smeared the pre-cum all over the head and used her other hand to slide his clothes down over his ass. "I'm ready."

He slipped her robe off and she unbuttoned his shirt. He eased the negligee up over her head and stepped out of his pants and boxers. She eased him backward to the bed and laid him down. Seductively, she licked her lips at the sight of his big willie standing strong and tall, as she took off his shoes and socks and eased out of her slippers. She climbed on top of him, grabbed his pipe and slid the head up, down and around her dripping wet pussy.

"Oh shit!" he grunted as he slowly pulled her down

until his joint disappeared inside her heat. "That's it, baby. Can you still take all of this dick?" he groaned.

She grabbed two handfuls of her locks, bit down on her bottom lip and began to joyride the dick. Up, down, side to side, all around, faster and faster. Seeing her response, he said, "You forgot how good this dick was, didn't you?" and slapped her ass.

"Give it to me, daddy," she purred. "You know how I like it." She spread her legs wider, put her hands on his chest and was making that pussy pop. "Fuck me, baby, fuck me the way only you can!" she screamed. Her clit was pressing hard against his dick, which was thrusting hard, up and down, digging deeper and deeper. "That's it, baby. Fuck this pussy! Oh please...don't stop...please," she begged as her eyes rolled back up into her head and she felt a surge of heat sear from her toes up to her nipples and her pussy tightened and clamped around his dick, causing him to jerk. "Oh shit, Brig...I'm cum—"

"Fuck!" Briggen yelled as he pumped her harder and harder and his body went stiff and his nut burst through and met hers. She slumped over him and he slumped backward. Both sweaty, fulfilled and out of breath.

"Yo, I need you to get out," Born hissed.

"What?" Zoie, his suburban jump-off, snapped her neck back.

"Hurry up." He pulled over to the curb. "I gotta do something," he snarled, not taking his eyes off the black Pathfinder with the license plate that read DAWGZ.

Zoie looked around at her surroundings. "Where in the world am I, Born? You want me to get—" Born hit the gas, causing Zoie to jerk back and forth. "What the hell is the matter with you? Aaaaaah!" she screeched. "You are trying to kill me!" Born turned the corner, almost leaning on two wheels, in hot pursuit of the Pathfinder. "Booornnn!" Zoie screamed as she put her seat belt on.

"Shut the fuck up or get out!"

"Let me out!" Her trembling hands released the seat belt and grabbed her purse. She was obviously pissed off.

Born could care less because his gaze was firmly locked on the Pathfinder, which was pulling into a KFC.

Born finally slowed down. "Get out." He grabbed his gloves out of the glove compartment, focus still locked on the Pathfinder. "Zoie, forget this ever happened."

"Son of a bitch!" she mumbled as she jumped out of Born's truck and wanted to slam the door but he pulled off too fast and it barely closed. "Crazy fool!" she yelled as she looked around. Her anger turned to embarrassment when she noticed that all eyes were on her.

The Pathfinder sat behind a Corolla with a loud muffler before pulling up to the pickup window. Born ended up following the Pathfinder for twenty more minutes, until it pulled into a gas-station-slash–liquor store. It *was* him. Big Freddie stepped out of the store with an armful of KFC trash. He had a big afro and reminded you of the rapper Bone Crusher. After he tossed the trash in the can he headed to the side bathroom. He had a Doberman in the back who was barking. Born cocked his burner, twisted a silencer on the barrel, pulled his cap down low, got out and headed for his mark. He posted up in front of the bathroom door…and waited. Born looked around and hoped that everybody would stay away. However, he was willing to lay down anybody that got in his way and who thought they could stop him from deading Big Freddie.

Knock, knock.

"Hold up!" Big Freddie yelled.

Born heard the toilet flush, then the door flew open.

Splat! A bullet ripped through the fat of Freddie's stomach.

Freddie let out a yelp. "What the fuck?" Freddie looked down at his gut, ran his hand over some blood and fell back against the sink. "Oww, man! Shit!" He was stunned.

"Shut the fuck up, before I put another one in your fat ass. You probably can't even feel it."

"I'm shot," Freddie whined. "Take the money, man."

"Give me your wallet."

"I'm shot!" he kept repeating in disbelief. "I can't believe you shot me."

"Nigga, I'm trying not to split yo' wig. Just give me your fuckin' wallet."

Freddie reached for the wallet, grimacing in pain as he held it out to Born.

"Now take out your cell phone, call up your man Blue and tell him to pull all of them DVDs with your dogs and Shadee."

"Who?"

"Shadee, nigga! You know who the fuck I'm talkin' 'bout. Do it now or I'm going after your family, starting with your wife. Hurry up! Tell him to do it now and I betta not see another one of these bitches resurface anywhere. As a matter of fact you betta get them back from everybody you sold them to," Born threatened.

Freddie was gasping for breath as he hit the speed-dial button. Born held up his wallet and kissed Freddie's forehead with the barrel of the Glock. Born stiffened up and listened intently when he heard a vehicle approaching. *Damn.* He exhaled slowly when it kept going.

"Just do it, Blue," Freddie screamed and was barely breathing as he told Blue what to do about the DVDs. He had slid down to the floor.

"Hang up now," Born gritted as he backed up. Freddie was still on the floor, looking up at Born with begging eyes.

"Shadee was my uncle, nigga, you fucked him up. You didn't have to do that."

"How was I supposed to know, man? I try to give the client what they want. C'mon, man, I'ma take care of the situation. Don't kill me, man," Big Freddie pleaded. "You see I got a family, man. Please don't kill me. I did what you asked me to."

Born backed up against the door and let off two more shots. He cracked the door, peeked out and pulled his cap down low. He sprinted to his truck, jumped in and pulled off.

* * *

An hour and a half later Born was knocking on Janay's door. When she opened it up she was greeted by the barrel of his Glock. She slowly stepped back as Born came in and kicked the door shut with his foot.

"Who else is here with you?" he barked.

"Nobody. What the fuck is your problem, Born? If you're here to rob me, you know you gonna have to kill me, right?"

"Shut the fuck up, Janay! You helped that bitch set up Sha, didn't you?"

"What?" she snapped.

"Them fucking dogs and my uncle. You was in on that shit, wasn't you?" he yelled.

"Boy, if that's what this is about you better check yo'self." She turned and walked away. "Who the fuck told you some bullshit like that, Born?"

"The DVD. How all that shit go down right here in your crib, Janay? I swear you better get to singing and it better sound good."

Janay sat down on the couch and glared at Born. "Nigga, I wasn't in on no sick shit like that. I was mad at him but I didn't take part in that bullshit."

"You was wifey, Janay. Sha loved you more than anything. Why was you mad at him? Why did you have that bitch Brianna over here?"

She just stared at him and wouldn't say anything.

"Janay, I'm not here for a social visit. Believe me, I'm trying not to peel your dome back."

"You can't handle the truth, Born."

"Maine, come on with all this bullshit. Yo' ass better get to talking."

"I walked in on Shadee and Doc fucking." She smirked while not taking her gaze off Born. She wanted him to feel it and to get sick and throw up as she had. She needed for someone to know exactly how she was feeling. She wanted to replay the horror for him.

The arm with the gun slowly lowered. "Bitch!" he spat and was looking crazy. Before she knew it his Glock was kissing her forehead for the second time.

She began talking for her life. "Them niggas was fucking, Born! I told you you couldn't handle the truth. Sha had the nigga givin' him brain and before he was about to bust he bent Doc over like a bitch and raw-dogged him in the ass. They are like a man and a bitch...two lovers. Oh yeah and they both got that shit. HIV," she said with a smirk on her face, and the tears wet her cheeks for the hundredth time.

"You bitch. I—"

"I loved him so much, Born. I was even willing to stay with him and work it out. But then Brianna came over and she said that Sha proposed to her. Born, that nigga never even proposed to *me* and I have his son. That shit hurt, it hurt real bad. That's when I left. Left her ass right here with him. Like I said, she was infected too. I went to my father's house. She had to have the shit planned. So there, you got the whole true story."

Born was just standing there. His face had turned into stone.

CHAPTER THIRTEEN

Peanut spotted Prissy's white-on-white Infiniti Q45 in the parking lot of the corner grocery and liquor store and made a U-turn. Prissy had been running one of his spots for almost two years and they had been fucking for half that time. But as soon as he got locked up and Shan went to get some money from her she got funky on him. He assumed that she thought she had it like that.

He parked two spaces down from the Q, got out and sat on the hood of her ride. He lit a Newport as he finally caught a glimpse of her. Her dark skin was still creamy chocolate. Her hair was in a ponytail and her ass wasn't as big as he remembered. When she turned around Peanut gagged off his Newport. "Damn! What the fuck happened to her?" She had a black eye and her jaw was lumped up. She looked like she had been in a rumble with De La Hoya. The two chicks walking past him heard his outburst and craned their necks to see who he was talking about.

"Let me hit that square!" the white chick called out

to him. He looked her over, passed her the cancer stick and waved her off. *Just like a white hood chick to ask for a square out of a stranger's mouth.* "Good lookin' out. I appreciate it." She hurried off and caught up with her friend.

When Prissy came out of the store and saw Peanut, she momentarily froze in place but tried to play it off. "Damn, Peanut. I—"

"Later for that shit, Prissy." Peanut started laughing. "Bitch, you done changed addresses and phone numbers on me. You ain't tried to get in touch with me so cut the bullshit. Just give me my money so that I can keep it movin'."

"I tried to get in touch with you." She did her best to control the tremble in her voice as she walked around him without even looking his way.

"I said I don't want to hear that bullshit!" Peanut snapped. "So shut the fuck up."

She did just that as she felt him watching her place the two bags in the backseat. She fumbled around for a minute, but when she finished she handed him a wad of bills.

"What the fuck is this, Pristina?"

"It's a stack, Peanut."

"You about eight more short, don't you think? Give me the keys to this car."

"C'mon, Peanut. Not my ride." When she saw that he was dead serious she sighed and reluctantly said, "Follow me to the house."

"You got the rest of my money there?"

"Most of it."

"Most of it? Don't make me fuck up your other eye. I want all my shit."

He went and jumped into his truck. He tagged closely behind her for about twenty minutes before pulling into a complex called Willow Wyck. They parked in front of the third house and got out.

"How long you been here?" Peanut wanted to know.

"It's only temporary. This is CoCo's spot."

"CoCo!" Peanut yelled in surprise. "Y'all couldn't stand each other, now you tellin' me y'all living together? Damn, that much shit can change in three months?" Peanut shook his head in disbelief. There were so many times that when he was with CoCo, Prissy would wild out on the both of them, and vice versa. They fought like cats and dogs, he reminisced as he checked out his surroundings.

"People change, all right?"

"Bitches like you and CoCo don't. I can't believe y'all hoes tried to play me like this. Something's up. What, y'all set up shop out here?"

"No."

"Where at then?" Prissy wouldn't answer as she unlocked the door and stepped inside.

Peanut patted the forty-five he had in his waistband as his eyes adjusted to the dim living room. "So where y'all hustlin' at?" he pressed as he looked around the newly furnished living room and started walking toward the kitchen, with Prissy on his heels. He flicked on the kitchen light. The furniture in here looked new as well.

"I'm not hustlin' anymore."

Peanut chuckled and then his eyes turned ice-cold. He got up on her and punched her in the mouth, knocking her up against the refrigerator. "Bitch, why the fuck you tryna play me for a busta?"

Prissy was wide-eyed and had both hands over her mouth. She immediately went to explaining. "I serve the people at my job and CoCo be at this house on Poplar. Damn Peanut, you didn't have to hit me."

"That's all you had to say from the jump. So both y'all bitches can pay up. Where she at?"

"Upstairs. The room at the end of the hallway."

"Where's the rest of my money?"

"Upstairs."

"Who else is here?"

"Nobody."

"Stay right here for a minute."

Her eyes bored a hole into Peanut's back. She was confused as hell. Why was she mad at him? He was a ballin' nigga that fucked around...a lot. What else was new? He always treated her right. Shit, she had her own place, she was happy and he never put his hands on her...until today. Why did she let CoCo talk her into this bullshit? Lately she had been so stressed her hair was falling out.

Peanut placed his ear to the door to confirm what he

knew he heard. Somebody was on the other side fuck-ing. He pulled out his gat and slowly turned the knob, cracking the door about an inch. His eyes lit up and he stiffened as CoCo had her face between another broad's thighs, eating her pussy. He opened the door wider and the chick getting ate out had arched her back and had both of her hands palming CoCo's head. He was all the way in the room and they were so busy fucking they didn't even notice him.

"Yo, Prissy, come here," he yelled out.

They both jumped and grabbed on to the sheets and blankets, trying to cover themselves up. CoCo wiped her mouth with the back of her hand, looking as if she had seen a ghost. The other girl was still breathing hard and obviously pissed since her nut had been interrupted.

"Who the fuck is you? Who is that, CoCo?" she barely managed to get out.

"You fine as hell, who the fuck is you?" Peanut teased. "Who am I? Sheeit, I'm that nigga that's right on time. Can I join in?"

Prissy was in tears when she stuck her head in the bedroom. She glared at CoCo, then her voice quivered the girl's name. "Reeva? Reeva, you sneaky backstabbin' bitch!" she snarled as she almost knocked Peanut over and charged over to where Reeva was.

"Prissy, no!" CoCo yelled as Prissy went to beating Reeva's ass as if she had stolen something.

"Ain't this a bitch!" Peanut mumbled as he watched the three of them go at it. "Girls gone wild fo'sho." And two of them were naked and Prissy's blouse had just gotten ripped. Since CoCo was trying to pull Prissy off of Reeva, she was getting the best blows in.

"Coco, I hate you!" Prissy screamed out as she tried to whip both of their asses at the same time.

"Aiight! Aiight!" Peanut tore in among the trio and snatched Reeva up. "Get yo' shit and get the fuck out."

"Get your hands off of me!" she yelled. "CoCo, tell him," she said with attitude while looking at Peanut as if he was the scum of the earth.

CoCo refused to look at Prissy but kept her focus on Peanut.

"CoCo, tell him!" Reeva ordered. Seeing that CoCo wasn't going to check this nigga, she gritted, "You bitch!"

"Your mammy is a bitch!" Prissy yelled.

Reeva yanked away from Peanut and began scrambling around for her clothes.

The room was quiet as they watched Reeva hastily throw something on. "How am I going to get home, CoCo?"

Prissy put her hand on her hip and glared at CoCo, who was in a daze but was throwing a robe on.

"You know what? Fuck you, CoCo! You is so wrong for this weak-ass-nigga shit!" Reeva screamed before storming past Peanut and stomping down the stairs. They waited until they heard her open and slam the front door.

Peanut leaned up against the dresser and smirked. "So

this is how y'all get down, huh? Y'all partners for real, on some Thelma-and-Louise-type shit."

"I'm sorry, Prissy," CoCo pleaded, finally looking at her. "I—"

Slap! Prissy slapped her so hard she fell on the bed.

"All right then," Peanut mumbled. "Look." He stood up. "I see that I interrupted some serious girl-on-girl shit. Y'all dirty bitches owe me some money. I just came to collect." *And I'ma get y'all bitches for tryna play me.* "Prissy, you owe me eight grand; CoCo you owe me forty-five hunned. Pay the fuck up and there will be no love lost." They both stood there. Prissy was looking down at the floor and kept running her hands through her hair.

"Umm, Pea—"

"Umm, Peanut, my ass!" he cut CoCo off as he pulled out his pistol, pointing back and forth between the both of them. He walked up on CoCo. "Y'all hustlin', so give me my fuckin' money." He slapped her in the head with the burner and grabbed Prissy by her hair. "I'll blow this bitch's brains out, CoCo. Give me my fuckin' money."

"Okay, okay." She was trembling. "I have to go—"

"Stop playin'!" Prissy screamed. "Give him his money. I told you this was going to happen. Go in the safe and give him his damn money," Prissy gritted.

"Oh, I see. CoCo got a lot of game with her. Aiight, it's like that, huh, CoCo?" He tossed Prissy aside and then lunged at CoCo. He busted her in the mouth and then slammed her up against the wall, causing Prissy to let out a panicked scream. CoCo refused to cry as he shoved her toward the closet, blood dripping from her mouth.

Peanut turned to Prissy. "So you a follower, huh? First you let this bitch turn you out. Then you let her talk you into taking my loot. And what is she doing? Shittin' on you, beatin' on you just like a nigga. Shit, you might as well had stayed with me." Peanut smirked.

"Here, Peanut." CoCo had bundles of cash in Ziploc storage bags. "It's all there."

"Bitch, you got blood all over it. Dump this shit out." He pushed Prissy away from him. As he counted the stacks, he stuffed them inside every pocket he had.

"Who y'all working for?" he decided to throw out there.

"I work for myself," CoCo snapped.

"Woo," Prissy blurted out.

CoCo cut her a look to kill.

"Well, good luck, y'all dirty bitches." He left out.

"You can't stay?" Shan was massaging Briggen's dick through his sweatpants. "She's bringing the keys over to the house in the morning. Just one more night?" Shan whined.

He kissed her forehead. "Naw, baby. Something important came up that I gots to handle. But I'll be back." He slid her hand off his johnson. "Yo, girl, you trying to tempt me?"

"Yeah," she answered innocently. "I know I had you held hostage for the last three days, I would like one more day. I had fun." She pulled him to her and pecked his chin.

"I enjoyed being held hostage. You took real good care of Daddy. You need anything?"

She rose up and kissed his lips. "I just need for you to hurry up back."

"I'll do that."

The Realtor Karin picked up Markeeta and they headed over to the hotel to pick up Shan. "Markeeta, I should have let you hook me up with your cousin Briggen when you tried to. This nigga is getting ready to put this broad out in Bloomfield. Swan Lake at that." Karin shook her head in disbelief.

"Bitch, stop being so fuckin' greedy, ain't you fuckin' her brother? I thought you was trickin' with him?" When she didn't respond, Keeta snapped, "Well are you?"

"Trick?" Karin looked at Keeta as if she were crazy. "Please, you could never associate that with me," Karin snapped back.

"Umm-hmm, you gettin' ready to work that nigga." Keeta giggled.

"Do you think Shan is workin' your cousin Briggen?"

"Hell naw! Brig got about four bitches that *he's* workin'. She don't know it yet but she gettin' ready to help run the hair salon."

"Shit, I can't tell. He gettin' ready to move that ho into a 350,000-dollar condo. She look like she gonna be livin' lovely to me," Karin stated, not able to hide her jealousy.

"Believe me, that 350,000-dollar condo only means

that she gettin' ready to help him make double that. My cuz is all about his paper."

"I see." Karin was still like, *Damn. This bitch is about to live real lovely. I need to be in on that.*

"Boy, where the hell you been at? I've been trying to reach you." Shan spoke as if she were Peanut's mother.

"I just called you. Where the hell have you been?" Peanut asked his baby sister.

"I went to look at my new residence. Karin brought the keys over earlier. I am so excited. And oh, she asked about you."

"I'm sure she did," he stated with arrogance.

"What's that supposed to mean?"

"I told you about stayin' out of grown folks' business."

"Whatever, boy."

"Now can you tell me when is it that you are planning to move into this house?"

"By the end of the week. I'm not moving into that big-ass house until the lights, gas, phone and cable is on. Plus, I gotta get some furniture," she rattled off. When Peanut didn't respond she asked, "You got something to say?"

"This cat you movin' in with, I haven't even met him. You puttin' a lot of trust in this nigga. What happens if one day he wakes up and decides that he's tired of you? Then what? *Technically* it is his house."

"I know that, Peanut. I still have my forty-five-hundred-dollar check that my job gave me for relocating. I do have a job and I do have a big brother. So *technically*

I'm just enjoying the ride. He'll be back and forth so it's like I'm house-sitting and living for free. I'm not stupid, Peanut." He was making Shan feel like a teenage girl moving out on her own for the very first time.

"I didn't say you were. I just wanted to make sure you had a plan as well as a backup plan. When do you start work?"

"Next week I start orientation. That gives me a little time to get situated in the new house and learn my way around town."

"How do you like the D?"

"I don't know yet. The only thing I do know is I like my new house. How soon are you coming back to spend the night with me? And where are you?"

"I'll probably be there sooner than you think. Keke got killed."

"What?" Shan shrieked.

"She got shot. And the crazy thing is, the bullets were meant for me."

"What? Oh my God...Peanut. When? How? Why didn't you tell me?" She fired off the questions, not wanting to believe what she was hearing.

"Last Tuesday. I went over there just to look that bitch in the face. I was on some GP shit. When I got there she had my shit all packed up. I had to remind her that it was my crib and told her to pack her shit and get the fuck out. When I left, she was following me talking shit. We were barely off the porch. That's when they rolled up and got the shots off. The po-po is on my ass so I have been layin' low."

"Where are you now?"

"I'm over a friend's house."

"My house is your house...so come whenever you're ready. I'ma hook you up a room."

Peanut smiled. "I'll be up there. I got to see a few more people first."

"I hope it ain't no more of your ex-chicks. I told you to chalk them up as an L, boy."

"Listen to you. Trying to tell a grown man what to do." He chuckled to himself. "And for your info I already went to pay Prissy and CoCo a visit, and guess what?"

"What?" *Beep.*

"Let me take this call, baby sis. I'll call you back later on."

"I want to continue this conversation. But in the meantime, I'm sorry about Keke. Be safe and I love you."

"Love you too." He checked the caller ID and saw that it was Nyla and smiled. He clicked over. "What up? You aiight?"

"What's up with you? What you gettin' ready to get into?" she asked seductively.

Peanut perked up at the words *get into.* "What you want to get into?"

"You want to come over a little later?"

"I can make that happen. I need to tie up a few things. I'll swing through around ten. I'll call when I'm on my way."

"Bye." Nyla exhaled after she hung up the phone.

Lisha looked at her and shook her head in disbelief. "So you going all out now, huh? You gettin' ready to give up the goodies and everything. I'm in shock. I know Mr. Forever is turning over in his grave."

"Bitch, turning over in his grave? He ain't dead."

"You killed his spirit. Trust me, the nigga is dead."

"Lisha, stop it please. You are beginning to scare me."

"All right, all right. I'ma stop making you feel guilty."

"I need you to help me plan something nice. I haven't done this in a very long time."

"Oh my God! You're gonna fuck him in Forever's bed?"

"Bitch, this is my bed; it's been my bed for the last six years."

Lisha twisted her mouth up. She honestly didn't know how to deal with her sister on this level. She had always admired and respected her trueness and dedication to Forever throughout his bid.

"Sis, bear with me here. I gots to get used to seeing you like this," Lisha explained.

"Trick, are you gonna help me or what? Shit, I'm nervous and this shit is new to me as well. But hey, this is the choice that I've decided to make. And I'm feelin' this nigga. And I'm going for it, with or without your approval."

Lisha ran her hands over her face. "Okay." She looked her sister over. "Let's do it."

They spent the next few hours selecting the music,

fixing dinner and getting the candles, bubble bath and bedroom nice and sexy. They saved her selection of negligees for last.

Nyla had just released the drain in the tub when the phone rang. She snatched a towel off the rack and shot out of the bathroom. She slapped the speaker button. "Hello."

"Yo, it's me. I'm pullin' in your driveway."

"What?" She glanced at the clock. "It's only nine-thirty. You're early."

Peanut found that funny. "What, you want me to go and ride around for a half hour and come back?" He chuckled. "Girl, open the door." She heard the engine turn off. And he hung up.

She ran and peeked out of the window. There he was walking up the driveway, carrying a shopping bag and some roses.

Ding, dong.

She took a deep breath, tied the towel firmly across her chest and went to open the door.

"I thought you—" Peanut smirked.

"Mmm-hmm, you thought wrong. I just got out of the tub. That's why I said you were early."

Peanut gave her a sly grin. "That's cool. Where's your daughter? I brought her something, and these are for you." He handed her the roses and the shopping bag.

"Tameerah is next door at my neighbor's. Thank you for the roses." She peeked inside the shopping bag and set it on the table. He followed her into the kitchen, and was right on her heels. She inhaled his cologne as she pulled out the bottles of Alizé, Patrón, and Grey Goose vodka.

"All righty then!" He smiled at the sight of the Goose. And not one to be outdone, he dug into the shopping bag and pulled out a big box of chocolates, a medium-sized teddy bear for Nyla, and small box of chocolates and a miniature teddy bear for Tameerah.

"Aww." She sighed. "How cute. Here, make yourself comfortable and useful. Put these on ice while I rewind and get ready for our night. You threw it off, Peanut."

"You already look ready for the kind of night I got in mind." He leaned over and kissed her lips, wasting no time. She greedily sucked on his tongue, which tasted like an Altoid. She felt his hand ease to her waist and glide around to her ass. He pulled her close enough to feel his hard-on and she let out a sexy sigh.

"You like that, don't you?" he whispered.

"Mmm-hmm," she purred not turning his lips or tongue loose.

He eased his hand between her thighs. "I bet you are nice and tight." He slid a finger up inside her, and yes, it was tight, and caused his erection to grow harder. "Your lips . . ." he mumbled, "are so soft . . . so sweet." He ran two fingers over her clit and felt her fingers dig into his back. "I bet these lips are soft and sweet as well."

"Ooooh," she purred.

He kept playing with her clit as his lips slid over to her ear. "When was the last time you had some dick? When is the last time you been fucked in a bed? You deserve this, Nyla, don't you?" He stuck two fingers inside her warmth. "Don't hold back, baby," he whispered as he continued to put her at ease. "This is your night. You wanted this... hell, you needed this and Daddy's gonna take real good care of you." He felt a tremor run through her as she began grinding on his fingers. He loosened the towel and it fell to the floor. His hand moved across her cheek, down her chin to her shoulder and then his hot mouth went to her breast.

"Peanut," she gritted, "oh . . ."

He swooped her up and she fell into his embrace and melted.

"Where is the bedroom?"

"Just go," the words softly escaped her throat. She was ready to fuck.

He carried her up the stairs and went right to her bedroom. She pushed the door open and he laid her down on the bed. She immediately sat up and began unbuckling his pants as he took off his jacket and T-shirt.

She lay back and grabbed the Magnum from under her pillow as he continued to get naked. She opened it with her teeth, not taking her eyes off his big, thick-ass johnson.

He saw her eyes stretch and smirked. "You knew it was big but not this big, right?"

"Don't talk shit until you show me that you can work it," she teased as she rolled the condom on. She was on her knees at the edge of the bed.

He leaned forward to kiss her again, hands framing her face. Her mouth opened for him as she hungrily devoured him while her fingers slid up and down his massive thighs and over his strong, firm ass. She was on fire and soaking wet as she broke the kiss and lay on her back and spread her legs sexily.

Peanut licked his lips as he crawled in between her pretty brown thighs.

"No," she pleaded, "I want you inside me right now."

He kissed her belly button and ran his tongue around it. "Peanut...please. Fuck m-me."

She felt his hot breath on her stomach as his mouth found her breasts and sucked them both, his teeth nibbling and tugging on her nipples. He felt her feet glide up and down his thighs as she raised her ass. He grabbed her hips as her small hand wrapped around his dick and put it to her opening.

Peanut thrust hard as if he was going to ram all ten inches in but instead only gave her a measly inch. "Oh, Gooood," she groaned. Her slick cream oozed from her sweltering pussy as she tried to get more of his dick. "Pea—"

He put another inch in and her hips started grinding, around and around. "Ssssss, ooooh yeah." She was getting her fuck on with just two inches. He gave her another one and she started grinding faster. She grabbed his ass cheeks and tried to pull him all the way into her but he once again gave her only an inch at a time. "Give it to me," she begged, "I need this."

She shrieked when she felt all of him as he held it in deep.

"You want me to fuck you? Fuck this tight pussy?" She nodded her head yes. "Like this?" He began a stroking, pounding rhythm. In and out, in, out. "Like this?"

"Y-yess." She was writhing underneath him, lifting her hips, trying to make sure she was getting all ten inches.

"Oh, baby. I knew this pussy was going to be tight and good," he whispered in her ear, not skipping a stroke. He was digging around in her thick hot juicy pussy, which was now contracting around his dick. *Fuck.*

Her pussy muscles clamped down on his dick as she screamed, "I'm cumming," causing him to drive faster and deeper, feeling as if he were losing his mind. The pussy was so hot, tight, juicy and good. He soon lost control, his body stiffening, and he began shooting full force into the Magnum.

"Oh shit," she gasped, trying to catch her breath. "I gotta have more. I gotta have more." She trembled beneath him.

Peanut's face was buried into the pillow. "Give me a minute." He was trying to catch his breath.

She pushed him over and pulled the condom off and got into position for a sixty-nine.

Ding, dong. Ding, dong.

"What?" Nyla asked in disbelief.

"Who are you expectin'?" Peanut was still out of breath.

"Nobody." She got up and snatched her robe and put it on. "I'll be right back."

Peanut eased up and reached for his jacket. He put his

gat on the bed, threw on his boxers and went to the top of the stairs.

"Who is it?" Nyla hollered.

"It's me. Diane."

Nyla unlocked the door and Diane was standing there with Tameerah. "Nyla, girl, I gotta get Tracey to the ER. She broke out into what looks to be hives. Her tongue is swollen. I don't know what the hell is going on. I'm sorry, girl. I'll call you when I get back."

"It's okay. I hope she'll be okay."

"Me too. I gotta run."

"Mommy, I'm hungry. Can I eat a TV dinner and watch TV in your room? And can I sleep with you tonight?" Tameerah ran past Nyla, heading straight for her mother's bedroom.

CHAPTER FOURTEEN

Zeke stood outside Lieutenant Scott's door waiting to go in. He had been in the hole for almost two weeks, all burned up and shit with hardly any medical attention. Forever had gotten his ass real good with the iron. But Zeke had known that at some point there would be confrontation and was glad to get it over. He just didn't think he would be the one to initiate it. Zeke knew that all good things must eventually come to an end. Shit, he wasn't stupid. Forever was family, so niggas were already yappin' about he was going against tha grain in gettin' that money. Yeah, blood is thicker than water, but if ya gonna stay in the race you need water to survive. So Zeke took advantage of business while the gettin' was good. Fuck the iron burns, they would heal up. He was still the man and still on top. Zeke had heard Forever was in for a transfer so he wasn't gonna trip about bumpin' heads with him again on a combat level.

Zeke was running all of this through his mind while spittin' the lyrics from Young Jeezy's "I Luv It." "I count hundreds on the table, twenties on the floor, fresh outta work," but he switched the words at the end saying, "I'ma go to the lieutenant's office and call my people for some more, and I luv it!" He had to laugh to himself as he dusted the dust off his shoulder and kept it movin'.

The door to Lieutenant Scott's office opened up and Scott's main flunky and partner in crime, Lieutenant Marion, stuck his head out.

"C'mon in, homey." He waved Zeke in. Lieutenant Marion was six feet six inches and skinny as a rail. Zeke suspected that he was smoking but wasn't positive. He was dark-skinned with big eyes and had an unmistakable gapped smile. Zeke followed him into the lieutenant's office and was surprised to see that they didn't have Forever in there. Lieutenant Scott knew that they were a team but Zeke knew that Scott always indicated that he would roll exclusively with Zeke and he was ready to wheel and deal. Lieutenant Scott would soon be working for him, if things went his way.

"Have a seat." Lieutenant Scott pointed to the chair next to Lieutenant Marion. Lieutenant Scott was a short brown-skinned brother with wavy hair, light brown eyes and baby-smooth skin. The ladies and the punks loved him. "Man, you put me in a very compromising position." He was leaning back in his chair, vigorously rolling a pen between his palms while staring at Zeke. Zeke glanced over at Lieutenant Marion. "You can talk in front of him," Scott assured him.

"Compromising? Man, you run this shit, so stop playin'. Ain't nothing compromising to you, so cut the bullshit and go ahead and say what's on your mind." Zeke leaned forward, anxious to hear what Scott was going to propose.

"I'ma leave the decision-making to you. Shit, I've come to the conclusion that we need each other. We all gots to eat. And now since this shit happened, more mouths are open, so you need to consider opening your pockets a little wider."

"How wide you talkin'?"

"Sixty-forty."

"Sixty-forty!" Zeke leaned back into his chair, not taking his eyes off Scott. He, Forever and Scott had all gone to school together. "Is this after profits or before?" Zeke smirked. "Nigga, you think I'ma ho-type nigga? I know y'all didn't take this bullshit offer to Forever, did you?"

"Yeah, we did, but he got to talking crazy so now you're sitting here."

"Sixty-forty, Scott? You fuckin' me with no Vaseline, nigga. I'm the one with the fuckin' connect and I'm the one doing all the work. I see why Forever ain't go for this bullshit. Y'all muhfuckas just got mad greedy."

"Greedy?" Marion interjected but shut up when Scott held up his hand.

"Zeke, man, you may have hooked up the business and got the connect, but we taking the most risk." He paused to let his words sink in. "You're not looking at the big picture. Let's say that we can do business and we get Forever out of here and any other competition off the compound...this will be all *yours*, baby boy."

Zeke straightened up at that comment. Marion smirked and said, "Yeah, that's what I thought."

"Look." Scott continued to pitch his spiel. "Sixty-forty sounds like a lot but you'll still be making almost double what you and Forever was pullin' in. You'll have more clientele than you can handle. Nigga, you gettin' ready to get paid up in this bitch. But I need to know because we gotta move fast before Forever makes his move. We ain't the only muhfuckas in uniform up in here tryna eat, we just smarter and a little higher up on the food chain."

"It's a win-win situation, man." Marion tried to appease Zeke.

"Let me make a phone call first," Zeke requested. "But I need to know how much can y'all move?"

"I told you, double what you and Forever was doing. I'm serious, man. I gotta get on my grind. My girl left me a copy of the latest issue of *Robb Report* on my dresser. The shit they got up in there is sickening. Nothing that can be indulged in on a lieutenant's salary. That's fo'sho'. Just say you in and you know I got you, dude," Scott said.

"I need to make that call now and y'all niggas need to step the fuck out," Zeke ordered.

Scott sighed and looked over at Marion.

"Let him use that wall jack," Marion suggested. "That would be better."

"Hell naw, I want to use this desk phone right here. The same one y'all make your personal calls on."

"So we got a deal?" Scott asked, with Marion hanging on to their every word.

"Let me make this call and I'll let you know."

"I can give you five minutes." Scott and Marion stood up at the same time. Scott handed Zeke the phone, then he followed Marion out the door.

Shan stood in line, waiting patiently for her turn to go through the metal detector. She was here at the Federal Correctional Institution (FCI) in Milan, Michigan. This was the first day of orientation and she counted a total of eleven new jacks, including herself. She still had butterflies in her stomach and knew it was because she was far away from home, living with Briggen of all people and getting ready to start a new job at yet another prison. She had been up to her shoulders in shit at the last prison but was determined to do it right this go-round. And definitely no more Forevers. He was the biggest mistake of all.

It was finally her turn to go through the metal detector.

"Good morning, can I help you?" the brother asked flirtatiously, licking his lips while looking her in the eyes and flashing a million-dollar smile.

Oh God. Temptation everywhere I go. Maybe I need to work at an elementary school instead of a prison. Niggas galore. "I'm here for orientation."

"Well, I'm Officer Hooks." He was looking at her as if she were a biscuit and he was ready to sop her up.

She couldn't deny it. He was a cutie at around six feet two, two hundred thirty pounds, rich caramel complexion with a low fade. And a wonderful body.

"You don't strike me as the officer type," he mused.

"Actually, I'm in education. I'll be teaching the computer classes."

He grinned. "Okay, but you still don't strike me as the prison type."

Damn, what a smile that dude has. It reminded her of the last time she was going through a *F.E.D.S.* magazine and she read that article on Alpo, the snitch. Hooks was giving Alpo a run for his money with that smile.

"What's your name?"

"I'm Shan. Shan McKee."

"Is that Miss or Mrs.?" He was looking for a ring.

"It's Ms. McKee."

"Well, Ms. McKee, I'm Rob Hooks and if you ever need anything, anything at all, just holla. This quarter I'm on first shift. Aiight?"

"Okay, thanks."

"Good, we need a beautiful sista like you around here. You might be able to tame some of these wild-ass men in here. You know they always act calm and smooth around a pretty sista such as yourself."

"Oh, you're really piling it on, aren't you? Anyways, what's the first day of orientation like here? What can I expect?" she asked to change the subject.

He flashed that beautiful smile again. "A pretty lady that's not afraid to change the direction of a conversation. I like that. You want to keep it business, right? I got you. All of y'all are going to get a physical and the rest depends on who's scheduled to lead the orientation for the day. Let me warn you now. They're not consistent around here. So just go with the flow."

"I see, and thanks for your welcoming speech." Shan grinned at him and went to catch up with the rest of the group.

"I told you, anytime."

By 3:45 Shan was walking to her car like a zombie. After the physical examination the rest of the orientation was a total blur. When her physical examination revealed that she was pregnant she felt as if she had been slammed by a Mack truck.

"Why they tryna stick me for my paper?" Skye and his baby brother, Melky, spat along with the Notorious B.I.G. It was Saturday night and they were chillin' in Melky's Range Rover. It was handicapped-equipped and he was handlin' the wheel. Skye was ridin' shotgun, enjoying downtime with his little brother. The music went low as the car phone started ringing. Melky hit the speaker button. "Who dat?"

"It's me, boy, whatchu up to?" the sultry voice asked. She had that country accent. Melky was lovin' the country girls.

"Who is this?" Melky winked at Skye.

"Damn, you got that many bitches, nigga?" She smacked her lips and was very much offended.

"You know I got hoes for days," he jokingly stated.

"Oh, so you got jokes now, huh? You sound like you in your truck. You by yo'self?"

"Look, what's up? And I need to know who this is. And what can a nigga do you for?"

She smacked her lips again. "Nigga, you wasn't askin' who is this when you was eatin' my pussy or after I had to damn near practically carry yo' drunk ass in the house and up the stairs!" she snapped.

That piece of info jogged his memory. "Oh, my bad, Taylor, what's up, boo?"

"You have that many bitches over that shit is just one big fucking blur, huh?"

"C'mon, Miss Lady, it's not even like that." He looked over at Skye, who appeared to be enjoying watching his brother, the crippled mack daddy, squirm. He recalled Melky talking about this chick Taylor and how bad she was. Just then he looked up and saw something.

"Yo, follow that Denali right there," Skye ordered, the smirk leaving his face.

"Taylor, let me get with you later. You caught me in the middle of something."

"Fall back a little, man." Skye was now wishing that he were driving.

"I got this, nigga," Melky assured him.

She heard Skye's voice and freaked. "Oh my God! I thought you was by yo'self. Oh my God! I'm so embarrassed. You just put me out there like that?"

"Damn, all of these buttons, nigga, I thought you hung up on that bitch," Skye said.

"Who you callin' a bitch?" she snapped.

"Girl, I'll holla back. That ain't nobody but my brother." Melky tried to smooth things over.

"What's up, Taylor? Don't act like that, Ma." Skye wanted to make her feel even more embarrassed. *Click.* The dial tone was loud and clear.

Both of the brothers started laughing.

"Who is the mark?" Melky was getting excited. It had been a while since he had some action. Melky automatically reached under the seat and placed his burner on his lap.

"Chill out, baby bruh. It ain't that kinda party." The Denali pulled into an Applebee's on Union as Melky rode into the Chili's next door to it and turned around.

"You want me to pull into the Applebee's?"

"Yeah."

"Good lookin', bruh. I thought we was going to get our party on, not do some work. This is like old times." Melky was hyped, still not learning from the incident that put him in the wheelchair.

Skye pulled out a spliff and passed it to his brother. "The plan was to just kick it. But this cat is wanted by a couple of peoples and I need to have first dibs."

"Who is he?"

"This cat named Peanut." Melky swiftly pulled into the Applebee's lot. He parked and shut the engine off.

"Well what the fuck is he doing? Counting his money?"

"He probably blazin' up just like we about to do," Skye stated.

"Nah, nigga. He got a shorty in there he all up on, where your glasses, yo?" Melky teased.

"Nigga, I don't need glasses. I was mainly keeping an eye on the truck. Fuck the shorty. I'm after the nigga."

"Here they go now."

Melky sparked up the spliff as they watched Peanut get out and then go around to the passenger's side, where he opened the door. Out stepped Nyla.

"Aww hell nah. Hell to the muthafuckin' nah. Ain't this some shit!" Skye was beside himself.

"Nigga, what the fuck is yo' problem? You trippin' real hard." Melky took another pull on the spliff.

"Forever, man. That's Forever's wife. This shit is real ugly, yo."

Melky looked at the happy couple as they disappeared into the restaurant. "Ugly? This shit is downright grimey. Same ole story. Peanut done came up off Forever's package and now he came up off of wifey too. Umph umph umph. That's some fucked-up shit dude. Ever gonna flip the fuck out. So what's next? What we gonna do?"

"I gotta be one hunned. We gonna stay on the nigga until it's just that." Skye leaned back and got comfortable in his seat.

"Damn, what if I gotta go to the bathroom?"

"Man, you still got a dick. Piss in that bottle and just shut up and chill. As a matter of fact, smoke on this." He handed him a freshly rolled spliff.

* * *

Peanut and Nyla were having a conversation over a sea-food platter appetizer. "So has Tameerah questioned you any further about the strange man that isn't her father coming around?"

"You know she has, every chance she gets. So far she likes you but I think that's only because you keep buy-ing her toys."

Just then his celly must have vibrated because he pulled it out and looked at the caller ID. "I've been wait-ing on this call. Excuse me, I need a few minutes."

"Go right ahead." Nyla smiled at him.

Peanut got up and took the call. While he was talk-ing he had his eyes on Nyla. She was obviously in deep thought as her gaze was fixed straight ahead. When he sat back down she gave him a weak grin as she twirled a straw and kept circling it around in a tall glass of iced tea.

"A penny for your thoughts, baby girl." The concern and sincerity in his voice were unmistakable.

"I'm just thinking about us...me...Tameerah." She looked up at him and couldn't help but think about the cards that were on the table and the two times that they had gotten busy. Their first time was a straight fuck...and that's exactly how she'd wanted it. After five long years of very little dick, hell, she needed it, and it was damned good. But the second time they took their time and it felt as if they were really making love. Shit, Nyla was now engaging in a mental battle about the entire situation. She didn't want to put herself out there, and for what?

He reached over and slid his fingers down her cheek and ran his thumb lightly across her bottom lip. She liked it when he did that. "Talk to me, boo. I'm all ears. What's up? Finish your train of thought. I need to hear what's on your mind."

"Where are we going with this, Peanut?"

He could hear the nervousness in her voice. "I think that's up to you, Nyla. I'm sure that there is no doubt in your mind that I'm really diggin' you. You're the one who's holding back." He stroked the side of her face.

"How is it up to me? I'm walking away from a nigga that I've been with for the past seven years. Am I just a fuck to you or are you ready to make a commitment?" She moved his hand away from her cheek.

"The ball is in your court. I've been checkin' you for a minute now. I know you've got a difficult decision at hand. But check it. I'm not about to be a fill-in while you wait on that nigga to come home."

"Oh, so it's all about some temporary pussy, huh? And since you didn't respond to my question on commitment, I surmise that it's out of the question. Damn." She frowned up. "I fucked up a near-perfect relationship for this? What the fuck was I thinking?"

"Naw. It ain't even like that. Let me hip you to some shit. I know you still love dude. And you're right, I don't want a commitment from you. For all I know, that nigga could come home tomorrow and you would leave me hangin'." Nyla's face tensed up. "Exactly. Look at your face. All distorted and shit. I'ma roll witchu, shawty. But

182

if you want to fuck with me on the next level, ain't no turning back. I play for keeps."

Just as the conversation was getting heated, the waitress appeared with their meals. Peanut canceled his and decided on drinking instead. Just like a good drunk, he always told a sober story. Peanut did not hold back. He ended up telling Nyla his heart's story, revealing details about all the bitches he went through and how they left him for dead when they thought he was on his way to the joint. But during the entire time he was in jail all he could think about was her. That won Nyla over. Before they knew it they lost track of time and were closing down the restaurant along with the employees.

Melky tapped Skye on the leg. "Here goes your man." Melky started up the car, ready to tail them.

After Applebee's they had followed Peanut's Denali all the way to Nyla's house where they parked in the cut and waited...and waited.

Skye glanced at his watch.

"It's 3:27," Melky answered for him.

They watched as Peanut and Nyla indulged in many goodbye hugs, kisses and feels. For a minute it looked as if they were gonna fuck standing right there in the doorway.

"I seen enough of this shit. C'mon, nigga," Skye was mumbling in an attempt to will Peanut to hurry the fuck up. He didn't want to leave and miss something. Finally Nyla closed the door and Peanut got in his truck and pulled off, with Skye wanting to follow him but it would have been too obvious to do so at four in the morning. "Another time," he promised. "Another time."

Melky started up his Range Rover and pulled off.

Peanut had circled around the block and ended up following *them* home. "Y'all niggas don't know who the fuck I am or who y'all fuckin' wit!" Peanut said as he watched them go inside *their* crib.

CHAPTER FIFTEEN

Briggen and Shan were lying in their king-size bed in their new home. Briggen had just retired from fucking her brains out and now the only sounds in the room were the rain and branches pounding against the windowpanes mixed with Briggen's light snores.

Shan's gaze was locked on the branches tapping against the window. *What the fuck am I doing?* she kept asking herself. *Am I insane? This is the second time I did this shit. I know Peanut is going to quirk out. And what is Briggen going to do? None of them hoes he got is pregnant. Maybe he had himself un-fixed.* She started giggling at the choice of her new word.

"What's so funny?" Briggen sleepily asked while startling her at the same time.

"I thought you were asleep."

"Naw, you busted. What's so funny?"

"Do you really want to know?"

"Yeah," he grunted, eyes still closed and groggy.

"I was thinking that you had a vasectomy and then got it undone."

"A vasectomy? Where did you get that shit from?" he asked, becoming fully awake.

"Because of all them bitches you fuckin'. Why don't you have any babies?"

Briggen's eyes darted over to the bedroom clock and it read 2:21 a.m. He closed his eyes. "It's three in the morning and you worrying about who I'm fucking and why they don't have any babies? Go to sleep, Shan," he calmly nixed her off.

She remained lying on her stomach staring out the window. "So . . . why don't you have any babies?" she kept prodding. "Briggen, answer me, please. I need to know."

"Naw, baby, I'm not shooting blanks."

"So, how come there aren't any little Briggens running around?"

"Ain't nobody tryna give me no little Briggens. The bitches I fucks with is only concerned with gettin' paid. That's how I like it and how I pick 'em. Why you trippin' on babies? You tryna give Daddy a little Briggen?" he teased. As soon as he thought about what he had said his eyes popped wide open. He slowly slid the sheet off him, turned over and scooted close to Shan. "What? You tryna give me a little Briggen?" He brushed his lips over her shoulder. She wouldn't say anything so this time he nibbled slightly on her back. "We can start working on it right now." Briggen was now very much wide awake and ready to fuck. "You feel that?" He tossed one of his legs across her and began grinding against her ass.

"Briggen, stop," Shan whined.

"I thought you was ready to give me a little Briggen." He ran his hand down to her thigh and raised her ass up. He easily and slowly slid his dick inside her. "Yeah, you ready," he whispered. "Look how wet you are." He stroked her pussy long and slow. "Ahhh...shit this feels good. I'm glad you woke me up. You wanna carry Big Daddy's son?" he groaned as he pumped a little faster. "Whoa, baby." His dick grew harder as her sweltering juices caused his knees to buck. He thrust into her deeper but when he looked down at her she was crying.

"Fuck!" he grunted as he pulled out of her, and was out of breath. "Was I hurting you?" She buried her face in the pillow. "Shan, what's the matter? Talk to me, baby," he pleaded as she continued crying into the pillow. *What the fuck is wrong with her?* "Shan." He rolled her over onto her back and she covered her face with both hands. "What I do, baby?" He pulled her hands from over her face.

"I-I—I'm p-pregnant," she sobbed.

He leaned back on his knees and scanned her body, especially her stomach. "You're pregnant?" he whispered, still looking at her stomach. "Damn." He remained frozen in place. Finally, he drew a line from her chest down over her stomach. "You got pregnant quick, girl. When did you find out?" He was talking more to himself than to her. He was very much surprised by this revelation and felt as if he was going into shock.

"Let me up, Briggen." She wouldn't look him in the face.

"When did you find out?"

"My first day of my orientation. They gave us all a physical."

"So... why are you crying, Shan?"

"*Why* am I crying, Briggen?" she asked incredulously.

"Yeah, why are you crying?" he wanted to know. In his eyes he saw no reason that she should be shedding tears because she was pregnant by him. Shit, after all he was Briggen.

"This is embarrassing for me. Now get from over me, Briggen. Let me up."

She pushed him off her, got up, stormed into the bathroom and locked the door. She grabbed his robe off the hook and put it on. She stood in front of the mirror and was not happy with the person staring back at her. The person in the mirror looked a mess. Her eyes were red and swollen, her nose was runny and puffy. The person in the mirror was asking, "How could you do this again?" She turned on the cold water and splashed it onto her face. The person in the mirror was extremely disappointed. This was a replay of the drama that she had just weeks ago narrowly escaped.

She squeezed her eyes tight when she heard Briggen tap on the door.

"Shan, open the door." He turned the doorknob. She wet a washcloth and dabbed at her face.

"Give me a minute, Briggen."

He turned the doorknob loose and repeatedly beat his forehead against the door. "Pregnant," he mumbled.

This was all-new territory for him. None of the chicks he was with were trying to get pregnant. Their focus was on stacking that dough and he was cool with that. Children? As far as he was concerned, a child wasn't supposed to come until later on. Now he could truly forget about fixing his relationship with Forever. Even if Forever didn't want Shan anymore, with him getting her pregnant, he knew that Forever would be like it's the principle of the whole thing. He was kicking himself for not being more careful. This would be the first and the last time that he would slip up like this.

He heard the lock release and backed up. The door came open and Shan walked right past him and headed over to the window. The heavy rains were still pounding against them. She hugged herself as she tried to formulate her words.

Briggen stepped up behind her, sliding his arms around her waist. His gaze was fixed on the rain as well.

"What have I gotten myself into? I didn't plan this. How—"

"Shhhh. Listen to me, baby, let's just take this one day at a time. Can we do that?" He placed a soft kiss on her neck. "One day at a time. I know this caught you off guard, hell it caught me off guard too. This is very, very new to me."

"I don't know what to do, Briggen."

"We'll figure it out. It's no rush. Let's get some more sleep and maybe we can start hashing it out tomorrow. Plus, I'm supposed to go look at this spot that Markeeta found for a beauty salon. I want you to come with me. I want the shop to be yours."

"You what?"

"I'm offering you a business, Shan. A chance to stack some dough."

"Oh, so now you're revealing your true motives. You're ready to lure me in and lump me in with the rest of your bitches! What's in it for you?"

"You know what's in it for me. I gotta wash my money. It ain't like you won't be eating nice off the arrangement."

"I'm not like the rest of them hoes, money is not my number one motivator." She waved him off. "I'm going to bed. I'll be in the guest room." He stood there and watched her storm out.

What? No she didn't just storm out like she's starring on one of them damn soap operas. Shit, this is going to be harder than I thought. And hell, money motivates all them other hoes. Why she gotta be different? Briggen was talking to himself.

Peanut had memorized the license plate of the Range Rover. He lay back for a half hour before driving off and remembering the address where the Range Rover had pulled up into the driveway and parked.

"Nigga, where the fuck you been?" Skye snapped at Forever.

"I'm in transit. I'm out here in redneck Oklahoma City."

"In transit! They movin' you? I thought you had pull up in that muhfucka. What happened yo?"

"It's a long story. I just found out that they sendin' me to Milan, Michigan. As soon as I get situated you gotta come through; it's important. I'll be in touch. And keep this line open."

"Yo, nigga, hold up. I got some shit you need to hear."

"Make it quick. They gettin' ready to count."

"Your boy, Peanut, I've been watching him and he been fuckin' wifey, man."

As Forever's heart unraveled it felt as if it were going to pound through his chest. He was finally getting the news that he had been dreading. "Is this fact or rumor, maine?"

"Nigga you know I ain't one to come at you with no fuckin' bitch-ass rumors. I told you I've been watchin' the nigga. I caught them out at Applebee's and I followed them home and he left the crib about three. I thought they was going to fuck in the doorway, the way they were all over one another."

"Aiight, man." Forever had heard enough. He was crushed.

Skye hung up feeling some kinda way because he had had to break that news to Forever. He couldn't imagine what it felt like to be locked up and have your shorty walk away from you and leave you for dead. Forever definitely had drama, but Forever was no longer his focus as he zoned in on the honey getting out of the candy-apple-red Corvette. Skye and every other male in the detail shop were drooling. Some were being slick, while others were just outright lusting and making loud and lewd remarks.

The honey apparently had heard enough. "Y'all niggas act like y'all never seen a beautiful lady before," Janay snapped as she made her way into the shop.

"Aww, bitch! You ain't all of that. Take yo' black ass on in there," a tall lanky, freckle-faced thug yelled out. The two guys with him folded over in laughter.

Janay stuck her head back out the door and said, "If you see a bitch, then smack a bitch, you yellow-ass punk."

That got a series of oohs and aahs from the customers and workers standing around.

"Youngin, leave that lady alone. She come here all the time," said the bald old-timer who kept the front of the shop cleaned up and presentable.

"Fuck you, old man! Mind yo' business," the freckle-faced thug spat before he hawked up a wad of phlegm and spit it on him.

"That's a damn shame," a lady with a McDonald's uniform sighed as she watched the old man wipe the phlegm off his shirt while mumbling obscenities. The only ones laughing were Freckles and his two boys. Everyone else was looking on in disgust.

Skye lay in the cut with his cap down low, checking out everything as he fingered his Glock. He watched as the men shined up his Vette and wiped Armor All on the tires.

"I'ma make that bitch swallow my nutsack, watch," Freckles taunted.

The attendant who was working on freckle-face's ride whistled and held up his keys. "Here you go, maine."

"Rus, go park my shit. I'ma wait on this bitch," Freckles ordered. "And tip that nigga. I'ma get you back," he lied.

"Maine, fuck that bitch! Sharonda and 'em waiting on us," Rus reminded him.

"Nigga, this shit ain't gonna take long." Freckle-face went to the front door and peeked in. "See, here she come now."

Everyone's attention, especially Skye's, went to the tall, fine, bodacious and chocolate Janay coming out the door. The attendant was calling Skye but he brushed him off.

Freckles hauled off and smacked her dead across the face. "I see a bitch so I'm smackin' a bitch," he gritted on a stunned Janay. "Now whatchu got to say?" he based up, as he got all up in her face.

"I ain't got shit to say. I let my pistol do the mutha-fuckin' talkin'." She whipped out her pistol and aimed it at his face.

"Nooooo!" Skye yelled out, and a shot rang as he pounced on Janay. Everyone in the parking lot ran and ducked for cover.

"That bitch aimed at me," Freckles cried in disbelief.

"Aimed? She shot at you!" Rus yelled. "C'mon, man, let's get the fuck outta here."

DunDee, the owner, came running out.

"Y'all got five minutes before the po-leece get here. I told y'all hoodlums before, don't bring dem guns 'round my 'stablishment. This a place of bidness. If anybody gonna be shootin' it's gonna be me!" his southern baritone voice bellowed throughout the parking lot.

"You all right?" Skye looked Janay over.

"Hell no. Thanks to you, I missed," she seethed.

"Put your piece away and get outta here. Is that punk-ass nigga worth you takin' residency in the penitentiary? You got any kids? Trust me, my girl is in the penitentiary. You don't want to be there. Especially for no bullshit." Skye was trying to get her to think logically.

"That punk muthafucka put his hands on me! My damn daddy don't even do that." She was so mad her face was feeling hot as the tears streamed down her cheeks.

He took her by her elbow and led her to her ride. "C'mon, we need to get out of here."

"Damn it! I didn't even get his license plate. I gotta go after him." She was now shaking. The attendant gave her the keys and they fell to the ground.

"Calm down, Miss Lady. You ain't in no shape to go after nobody. Don't worry about them. I can find them for you. Get in." He helped her into the car. "We need to get out of here before the po-po comes." He could have sworn that he saw steam come out of her nose.

He jogged over to his ride and noticed that all eyes were on them. He jumped in and pulled off behind her. He followed behind her until she pulled into a mini shopping complex. She parked her ride and rolled down the window and watched him get out. He was driving a Vette exactly like hers, except his was money-green.

"Yo, you gonna have me catch a case. We drivin' the same whips and shit. I know they think we are partners in crime," he joked as he checked her out.

"I'm Janay. Who are you? And you're not from here. New York?"

"Yeah, that's who I be and where I'm from." *Big Choppa's other daughter. Damn, I'm the shit when it comes to being at the right place at the right time. Melky ain't gonna believe this one.*

"Well, New York, I wish you would have let me pop that nigga."

Damn this bitch is gangsta. "You need to chill out, Ma. You're allowing anger to overcome any and all rational thoughts." He went around to the passenger's side, and she unlocked then opened the door. He got in and pulled out a blunt.

"Who are you? The po-po?" she asked.

"The po-po?"

"Yeah, I mean you just appeared out of nowhere. Like you were following me."

"Hell nah, I'm not five-o! I was there getting my car detailed before you pulled up. Plus don't you think I would have locked yo' ass up for possession of a firearm or for tryna kill somebody or some shit like that?"

She giggled. "Okay, nigga, I get your point. So since you ain't the po-po, fire that up then. I think I need a drink too. I still can't believe that nigga violated me like that," Janay vented and was still shocked as they sat in the car, smoking and talking for the next hour. New York was her kind of nigga.

Nyla was curled up on her love seat with the phone pressed to her ear. She was waiting on the operator to put the call from Forever through. Peanut was stretched out on the sofa across from her, snoring. She was actually feelin' him. He was slowly but surely winning her heart.

"Hey, Forever, how are you?"

"Hey, Forever, how are you?" he mocked. "Bitch, you got a lot of fuckin' nerve. You fuckin' that nigga all up in my house? You got my daughter around this nigga? I never thought you would go out like this. I ain't gonna lie, you hurt me, Nyla." Forever felt that he had totally lost control of everything.

"Hold up. I know you didn't call me a bitch!"

"Nyla, I didn't stutter."

"You the bitch! Okay, yeah, I'm a bitch. But it's Ms. Bitch to you, nigga. Anyway, what yo' punk ass want callin' my house? You want to dish out the bullshit, but I bet you can't take it."

Forever laughed like a madman. "Bitch, I'ma talk real calm. What? You bumped your head on that nigga's balls while you were sucking his dick? Because all of a sudden you talkin' real greasy to a nigga. And what house do *you* have? That's my fuckin' house you're in, bitch!"

"Punk nigga, please! I earned every brick, nook and

cranny in this muthafucka. Just because you ain't got no in-house prison pussy you call yourself checkin' me? What, you can't get no dick neither?" They went back and forth.

"Real talk. I ain't even tryna go there with you. Do you. 'Cause I'ma shine when I get home."

"Good for you. However, you need to keep in mind that I am not your enemy. We still have a daughter together. Just because I've decided to move on doesn't mean that we have to be enemies and disrespect each other." Nyla couldn't believe he had called her out of her name and was talking to her as if she wasn't shit. That hurt. He was losing his fuckin' mind as far as she was concerned.

"And as far as the enemy is concerned, you dumb ho, you sleepin' with the enemy! So keep fuckin' that lame-ass nigga, Peanut. I'll be to see both of y'all when I touch down. Oh, cat got your tongue? Yeah, you fuckin' the enemy. I know all about Peanut. Obviously you don't. But I ain't mad at you for keepin' it in the family. Shan's baby will be a part of our family, bitch. And since you are fuckin' her brother that makes you auntie." He started laughing.

Nyla's mouth was wide open. She had jumped off the love seat and headed upstairs. She couldn't chance Peanut hearing this conversation.

"What did you just say?"

"You heard me. Shan and Peanut are brother and sister."

"Who?"

"The bitch who says she's pregnant by me and the lame-ass nigga that you are fuckin' all up in my house are sister and brother."

"What?" Her head started spinning.

"You keepin' the shit all in the family," he brazenly stated.

Nyla fell to her knees.

CHAPTER SIXTEEN

Born quietly opened the door to Shadee's hospital room. He was pissy drunk, and even though he had a visitor's pass he was sneaking in. Shadee was still in the ICU and remained hooked up to a breathing machine. Along with the heart monitor those were the only sounds in the room. Born, in his drunkenness, leaned up against the rolling tray table beside the bed. His weight caused it to roll away from the bed, and Born fell backward onto his ass.

Several seconds later a nurse rushed in and alarm was evident on her face. She was confused when she saw Born struggling to get up off the floor.

"Are you okay? What happened?" The nurse grabbed Born by the arm and helped him up.

"Why y'all makin' my uncle suffer like this?" he slurred. "He's already dead, why y'all doin' him like this?"

She could see his fiery red eyes tearing up. "Sir, I can't answer that but if you would like for me to page the on-call resident I will."

"Nah, nah." He waved her off. "Just leave me alone with my uncle, yo."

She checked Shadee's IV and the rest of the equipment before slipping out.

Born clumsily managed to get seated in a chair next to the bed. "Yo, Unc, we gotta talk. I don't even know how to bring this up. Fuck it!" He pounded his chest. "You hurt me, man. I saw some shit and I heard some shit and it fucked me up. You was never on no homo shit. That wasn't you, maine. But Janay . . ." He choked up and tried to continue. "Janay said she caught you and Doc . . . ungh." He jumped up, ran into the bathroom and threw up, almost missing the toilet. He grabbed some paper towels, wet them with cold water, wiped his face and then rinsed out his mouth. "Fuck!" He punched the wall.

He made it back to the chair, falling into it. "Why you go out like this, Unc? And you got that package? Why you ain't go out like a real G? You was like a father to me. I looked up to you. You fooled me, nigga. I thought you practiced what you preached. You was supposed to be a man of your word. You still my uncle though. Yeah, fag, AIDS-infected and all. I got your back. I took care of Big Freddie's sick ass and made them muhfuckas pull all them DVDs. Nobody will see you with the dogs, so don't worry. That nigga is toast. I'll catch him in hell. But not before I catch up with Doc's bitch ass. Ya girlfriend or boyfriend, whatever the fuck he is, I don't want him spreading the word that y'all was doin' that thang thang. Plus he done fucked us out of seven birds. So you already know he was canceled. Trust me, he gettin' ready to lay with the worms. I'ma make sure of that."

Born took a good look at Shadee. He actually looked like a dead mummy to him.

The nurse who had helped him up earlier stuck her head in and said, "Visiting hours are over, young man."

Born stood up, looked down at his uncle and said, "I can't front no more. Just the sight of you makes me sick to my stomach." He then pulled out a syringe and stuck the needle in between Shadee's big toe and the one next to it. "I wasn't going to do this, but I changed my mind. Ain't no sense in chancing you getting better and walking around here like a dead man. I figured I might as well take you outta ya misery." Born stumbled out of the room.

Janay and Crystal were in Big Choppa's kitchen cooking their father's dinner. They were making sure to talk low enough that Big Choppa couldn't hear them. They were acting like schoolgirls. Crystal was still seeing Skye, and Skye and Janay would kick it over the phone except that he told her that his name was New York.

"I can't believe you seeing somebody and didn't even tell me," Janay said in a chastising tone. "What does he look like? Where does he live?"

"It's only been a few weeks. And it's not serious or anything. I don't know where he lives. We went out a couple of times, we fucked and we still talk. We doin' it like that. I ain't trippin'. Plus the nigga dropped a few grand on a sista. I ain't tryna marry the nigga or no shit like that. Sis, you know how I do. So, now that I told you all of my business, what's up with you? And turn that fire down."

Janay lowered the flame under the chicken and went and stood in front of her sister. "I've been talking to someone," she whispered.

"Who is he?" Crystal whispered back and they both broke into giggles.

"His name is New York and—"

"New York?" Crystal cut her off. "What's his real name?"

"I don't know."

"And you call yourself checkin' me?" Crystal flipped the script.

"I'm the oldest, bitch! You can't be questioning me. I'm supposed to be looking out for you," Janay snapped as she went to turn over the chicken. "I'm feelin' his conversation," she continued. "This nigga is either a boss or he frontin'. I haven't been able to put my finger on it yet but it's something about him."

"Well introduce me to him and I'll let you know what's up."

"All right, I'll see what can be arranged. And why don't you get with Skye, and I'll check him out for you. You know how we do when it comes to these niggas."

"It's a done deal then," Crystal said. The sisters were in agreement for a change.

Briggen and Woo were chillin' in Woo's living room. Briggen was checking out Woo as he dumped the ounce of weed onto the plate. Briggen had grabbed some hydro from a Detroit nigga from P. Rock, Plymouth or whatever they call it. The nigga had all different kinds of weed. This was far beyond Briggen's knowledge. All he had smoked was purps. But dude introduced him to some weed with white hairs on the end of the leaves. You needed scissors to cut them off the bud. Briggen was laid back as Woo was cutting it up.

"Nigga, why you so quiet?" Woo asked, full of suspicion.

"Shan is pregnant."

Woo kept cutting the weed until what Briggen said registered. Woo leaned back into his chair, cocked his head to the side and ran his hands over his beard. "Word? I thought you wasn't tryna get none of these hoes pregnant." He sat up and began rolling up the weed.

"I wasn't." Briggen shrugged. "But sometimes shit happens."

"So let me get this straight. Your original plan was to expand to the D. First get a house, put this broad up in it so that you can run shit in comfort. Then, open the beauty salon and have Shan and your cousin run it, set up a couple of traps and run the dough through the business. But...now you feelin' this broad and since you knocked her up the game plan has changed."

Briggen reached for one of the blunts, fired it up and immediately began choking. As he held the weed in his lungs he looked at Woo, who had a look on his face that said, "You dummy!"

"So what's the game plan now?" Woo prodded.

"I don't know why you trippin', ain't nothin' changed, nigga. I want Silk and Tee Tee to come down. Let Jay and Donny-Boy step up. I need to get with them tonight."

"All four of 'em?"

"Yeah."

"Aiight, cool. Wanna meet at the club?"

"That'll work." Briggen stood up. "Just hit me up later when all of y'all are there."

"Sit yo' ass down, nigga. I ain't lettin' you off the hook that easy."

"Maine, go 'head with that."

"When Mia and them find out, shit's gonna be crazy."

"What? So you sayin' you don't got my back?"

"I got you, dawg. I'm just surprised at this whole scenario. But hey, big pimpin', you dat nigga."

"I got this." Briggen took another pull off his blunt, opened the door and left.

"Let me find out big pimpin' ready to settle down and be a family man!" Woo yelled out.

Briggen smiled and headed for his ride. "Nah, never that!"

"Did you get that info for me?" Janay sweetly asked Skye.

"Yeah, I got it," Skye cockily answered.

"I appreciate it. Give it to me so I can write it down."

"Whoa, whoa, hold up, shawty. I still think that you need to rethink this."

"Oh, so now you gonna flip the script on me?"

"Naw, it ain't that. I just don't want to see you get caught up in no unnecessary bullshit."

"The nigga put his hands on me! Or did you forget?" Janay was getting pissed all over again as she paced back and forth, replaying the scene at the detail shop.

"You not thinking clearly and that's not good." Skye swerved around a wooden plank in the middle of the road.

"You shouldn't have gotten the info if you never had intentions on giving it to me," Janay snapped. She listened to him chuckle.

"Whoa, little snapper. I ain't the enemy."

"You know what? I'm straight. I'll put somebody else on the job. Believe that. Ole boy will get dealt with."

"Okay, Billy Bad-Ass, but you still need to eat. Every good soldier needs to eat for strength to be ready for war. So can a nigga take you out?"

"Who said anything about a war? That peon-ass nigga just didn't know who he was fuckin' with. I plan on teaching him some manners. That's all. No need for a war."

"Yeah, all right, but you still didn't answer my question."

"Where?" She still couldn't believe he had asked her that. "Where do you want to take me?"

"I don't know. Give me a time to pick you up and by then I'll have it all together."

"I don't know you like that to be inviting you to my crib."

"Aww, that's low."

"Well I don't."

"I can respect that. We'll just arrange to meet somewhere."

"Yeah, we can do that if I decide to go out with you."

"You want that info, right?" When she didn't respond he said, "Then you'll be going out with me."

"This is bullshit."

"What?" Skye asked, acting as if he didn't know what she was referring to.

Janay and Skye continued to kick it on the phone and Skye wasn't even aware of the beige Impala tailing him. The streets had finally coughed up Skye's name. Doc couldn't believe that this out-of-towner had the balls to come on their land, set up shop and eat lovely off their hard-earned sweat, blood and loot. But Doc swore to himself that this nigga wouldn't live to see daybreak.

At the light Doc did two more lines. His boys were right. That recent loss was all his fault. If he hadn't been pillow-talking while laying up with this bitch-ass nigga Greg, Skye wouldn't have known about his move. Doc had been trying to catch up with Greg but it was obvious that dude was ducking him out. But he knew he'd eventually catch up with him. Greg couldn't stay away from the ass. And for now, he just needed to know where Skye laid his head.

Doc was so focused on Skye he failed to see the Caddy tailing him. Born had borrowed the ride from a friend, and going against his orders from Slim, here he was anxious to put Doc to sleep. He refused to have him around to tarnish Shadee's reputation. His anger was sharpening his focus because he noticed that Doc seemed to be following that money-green Corvette.

When the Corvette pulled into a Hampton Inn, so did the Impala and the Caddy.

When Skye got out of his Vette, the Impala came to an abrupt stop and a figure jumped out and pointed a burner at his face. That's when he realized that he had been followed and hadn't even peeped it.

Splat! The impact from the bullet penetrated his shoulder, causing Skye to jerk back. "Ahg!" he screamed and noticed that the shooter was the nigga he had jacked and tied up in the shower. "Fuck!" he gritted as he dropped down and crawled around to the other side to seek cover.

"Who you gonna jack now, pussy?" Doc yelled out.

Skye heard more shots pop off and wondered what the fuck was Doc shooting because it damn sure wasn't him. Then he heard an unfamiliar voice yell, "You the pussy, nigga. And this here is for my uncle." Skye heard four more shots fired, someone scream out, footsteps running followed by a car pulling off.

Then it got quiet.

Born smiled as he lit his blunt. He replayed in his mind that beautiful shot to Doc's dome. It was no way in hell he'd survive the shot that split his wig, literally, in two.

"Meet me at the crossroads," he sang along with Bone Thugs-N-Harmony.

Skye peeked over the hood and didn't see anyone...not even his shooter, the nigga he had jacked. He wasted no time getting in his ride and pulling off. He fumbled with his cell phone and finally got the call through.

"Hello," a familiar voice answered.

"Tommy."

"Who is this?"

"Skye, man," he gritted as he tried to drive and apply pressure on his shoulder at the same time.

"Skye? Long time no hear from. What's up, dude?"

"I need to see you. I got one in me and I can't stop the bleeding."

"Whoa, whoa, dude. I got company."

"C'mon, man, you know I can't go to the hospital. It's only one. Let me come over there."

"Aww hell naw, you know the rules. Where you at?"

"I'm in my car."

"Well park that muhfucka and I'll come to you."

Skye frowned as he looked around and noticed that he wasn't too far from Crystal's house. "I'm close to this broad's house. You can meet me there." He gave Tommy the address. "I owe you one."

"Nigga owe? Have my paper when I get there. You know how I do it."

"Nigga, just hurry up. I ain't ready to die," Skye teased.

"Punk, you ain't gonna die from one in the shoulder. One."

Skye heard the dial tone, and called Crystal.

"So you and New York going out tonight?" Crystal was on the phone talking to Janay. "Where y'all going? He's coming over there?" Crystal was very surprised at that.

"I'm not sure where we are going. He just told me to be ready. I'm gonna meet him somewhere."

"Oh, I was gettin' ready to say. You invitin' a nigga over to the crib, what's really good? This y'all's first real date, right?"

"Umm-hmm. You'll be able to watch Marquis, right?"

"Sure, but I ain't cooking. Can you stop and get some Pizza Hut first?"

"When do you ever cook?"

Crystal was getting ready to say something smart but someone clicking on her line stopped her. "Oh, that's my line, I'll see y'all later." Crystal clicked over. "Hello."

"Hey, it's me. I was hoping that you was home. Mind if I stop by? I'm in a little bit of a jam. I'm right around the corner. You don't have company, do you?"

"No, I don't. C'mon on." As soon as Crystal hung up, she pumped her fist and hurried into her bedroom to change into something sexy and freshen up.

Before she could apply some makeup her doorbell was ringing...and ringing. "I know that Skye is not ring-ing my bell like that!" She hurried up to the door and peeked out the curtain. She unlocked it with a puzzled look on her face. She opened the door prepared to cuss him out. "Why are you—" She closed her mouth as Skye pushed by her and she saw that his left shoulder and his shirt were a bloody mess. She closed the door and locked it.

"Sorry about this but I was in the area when this shit happened."

She didn't know what to say as she grabbed his elbow and led him to the kitchen. She was not going to allow him to bloody up her furniture or her carpet.

"I got somebody coming here to meet me and take care of this. You got a few clean towels? I'll replace them." He began to take off his jacket and the rest of his things.

She went to get some towels. When she came back, his jacket was on the floor and he was struggling to take off his T-shirt.

"Let me help you." Together they managed to get it off. "Eeeew, that's pretty deep." She stared at the gunshot wound. "Aren't you in pain?"

"I've endured worse." The doorbell rang.

"Is that your people?"

"I hope so."

Crystal went to the door and yelled, "Who is it?"

"It's Tommy."

She looked over at Skye.

"Yeah, that's him."

She opened the door and a scrawny brown-skinned

dude with hazel eyes, dressed in G-Unit from head to toe, waltzed in. He quickly began unloading his backpack.

"What's up?" He nodded at Crystal and went over to Skye. He immediately began laying out his supplies on top of the kitchen table and going to work.

"Damn, dude, what you do, fly over here?"

"Don't worry about it, punk. Just know that I'm here. You know how I do it. Plus I didn't want yo' punk ass to die on me."

"Fuck you, nigga. And hurry up, this shit hurt."

An hour later Crystal was sitting on her couch with her legs curled under her as she watched Tommy clean up his mess.

Skye came out of the kitchen and sat next to her on the couch. His bare chest was glistening and Tommy had removed the bullet and bandaged up his shoulder. His sweatpants were dirty and had blood on them. "I appreciate this."

"It's cool. You just caught me by surprise."

"The shit caught me by surprise too." He looked her over and noticed that her hair was on point and that she had on a pair of hip-hugging Parasuco jeans, a blouse showing her belly button and a pair of cute little Nike sneakers. "Is that one of the outfits I brought?" he teased.

"No. I'm afraid not."

Tommy came out of the kitchen. "Aiight, dude, that shot I gave you is going to have you feeling drowsy so don't try to drive for a couple of hours. Other than that, yo' punk ass will be aiight. But come see me or go to a hospital in a couple of days so that somebody can make sure you're healing okay. I wouldn't want you to die from an infection."

"Gee thanks," Skye said with much sarcasm.

Tommy tossed him a mesh bag. "Keep your dressing cleaned. That's enough to last for a week. I'm out."

"Thanks, man," Skye said.

Crystal got up and saw Tommy out.

"Yo, I need another favor." Skye hated to do this to her.

Crystal locked the door and folded her arms over her chest. "I'm listening."

"Do you think you can run to a store and pick me out an outfit? I gotta take care of something." He was determined to keep his date with the thug missus, Janay.

"I thought he said for you not to drive?"

"I ain't thinking about that pussy. I just need an hour for a nap, some dro and I'll be straight."

"Y'all niggas are so hardheaded."

"Can you help a brother out or what?" He went into his back pocket and pulled out a wad of bills. "Here you go. I owe you big-time."

You sure do. Especially since I planned on getting some of that dick. And now you're leaving?

She grabbed her purse, tossing the money inside. "Don't die on my couch. If you start to feel like you're getting ready to cash out, call me," she teased.

He laid his head back onto the headrest. "Oh, so you're

a comedian now? I told you, all I need is an hour and I'll be good."

Crystal grabbed her cell phone and left. After she got into her car and started it up, her cell phone rang. It was her sister.

"Hello." She turned down her radio.

"Bitch, you sound like you're in the car! Your ass is supposed to be home. I know you're not reneging on me."

"Janay, shut the hell up. You got a key and I just need to make a quick run."

"Where to?"

"To get this nigga something to wear."

"What nigga?"

"Skye, girl. He got shot. Don't ask me shit because I don't know shit. But check it out. He's at the crib and now is your chance to meet him. Where are you?"

"I just placed the order at Pizza Hut, then I'll be headed over there. Bitch, don't keep me waiting because I still need to go back and get dressed."

"I won't. Check him out and let me know what you think."

"So he got shot?"

"Yeah."

"And he came to your house? What kind of nigga is that? You need to find out something on this...Skye person."

"Just wait for me at the house. We can run a background check on his dick if you want to."

"Bitch, whatever! Just hurry yo' ass up."

CHAPTER SEVENTEEN

Shan was standing on mainline with the gentleman who was her boss as well as the head of education, ·Gordon Wright. She had spent all morning with him and now here they were inside the FCI's huge dining hall. Mainline in the federal prisons is where all the department heads, unit managers, counselors, warden, assistant warden and lieutenants stand around making themselves available for the inmates. If the inmates have any questions, concerns or problems they can come to mainline and address the appropriate staff member.

Gordon was also using this opportunity to introduce Shan to other staff members. She was anxious for Gordon to go on about his business because his bad breath was killing her.

She looked around the huge dining hall at the sea of khaki-clad men, labeled as inmates.

"What else do we have on the agenda for today, Mr. Wright?" Shan wanted to know.

"After we leave here, we'll go to my office. I need to make sure we covered everything and then we're done."

"Mr. Wright, don't be talking this pretty young lady to death. What's wrong with you, man? And did you pop a breath mint?"

Shan and Mr. Wright both turned around. Mr. Wright broke into a wide grin. "Jackson, don't try and show off just because you see me standing next to a pretty young lady. Ms. McKee, this is one of your workers. He sort of fits in wherever the education department needs him. He's a GED tutor, computer tutor, floor waxer, librarian, errand runner, you name it. Jackson, meet Ms. McKee. Ms. McKee, this is Derick Jackson." Jackson was a big, husky, brown-skinned, teddy-bear-looking brother.

The color drained from Shan's face. "Hello, Mr. Jackson."

"Nice to meet you, Ms. McKee. I'm at your service. Whenever and whatever you need, if I'm not around have them send for me or just page me, and I'll come running."

"I'll do that," she responded like a robot.

"Just don't change my days off," he joked. He turned to Mr. Wright. "Look, man, I want to introduce you to somebody who may be able to take my place if Unicor decides to give me that position I put in for. I'll vouch for this guy here. Forever Thompson, this is Mr. Wright. We call him Professor Smurf behind his back. Mr. Wright, this is Forever Thompson. He just got here from FCI Memphis."

"Good to meet you, Mr. Thompson. When you get a chance, look for my open-house hours and come and see me. We'll talk then."

As Mr. Wright continued to talk with Forever and Derick Jackson, Shan's head was spinning. Out of the corner of her eye she felt Forever's gaze piercing right through her. *How did this happen? Why the fuck is this nigga following me?*

"Um, Ms. McKee," Mr. Wright interrupted her thoughts. "Mr. Thompson here said he's from FCI Memphis; you were there, weren't you?"

"Yes, I was. I worked there for less than a year. However, his name rings a bell, like all the other troublemakers." Shan wasted no time in putting him on blast. "I hope that won't be the case here, Mr. Thompson."

She looked at Forever and he had this beaming smirk on his face. She wanted to reach over and smack it off.

"I'm going to grab a bite to eat. I'll catch you in your office, Mr. Wright." Shan had to get out of there...ASAP. If she didn't, she imagined herself turning into the Incredible Hulk and whipping Forever's ass.

Back in her office with trembling hands she found some Tylenol and quickly popped two of them. What she really wanted was a drink. She picked up the phone and dialed Peanut.

"Who is this?" he barked into the phone.

"It's me. You got a few minutes?" she groaned.

"Always for baby sis. What's up?"

Shan sighed. "You are not going to believe this."

"Try me."

"Guess who I saw today?"

"Who?"

"The nigga who I ran away from."

A few seconds of silence went by before Peanut said, "You mean the nigga you got pregnant by?"

"Yes," she snapped. "I swear I wanted to fuck his ass up."

"Damn. Too late for that, baby sis. So now what?"

"I don't have the slightest idea. But I'm not quitting or running away."

"He said something to you?"

"Not with his mouth, no."

"You want me to arrange something?"

"No," she snapped. "And watch what you say over these phones. I'll call you tonight." She immediately hung up.

Later that night Shan sat up in bed waiting on Briggen to come in. He had said he would be there by nine and it was now after eleven. Shan turned off the light and got under the covers and fell into a deep slumber.

Light, tingly kisses on her shoulder and down her arm woke Shan up. She opened her eyes and sleepily mumbled, "I tried to wait up for you."

"I got tied up, got here fast as I could. How was your first real day of work?"

"When was the last time you spoke to your brother?"

"It's been a minute. Why?"

"So you mean to tell me it's no coincidence that you wanted me to move to Detroit and now all of a sudden he gets transferred here?"

"What are you talking about he got transferred?"

She sat up and turned the light on so that she could read his face. "He's here, Briggen. He's at the prison. I saw him today."

"What did he say to you? You sure it was him?"

"Of course I'm sure it was him. He was talking to my boss," she snapped.

"Hold up. Who you using that tone with? I didn't get him moved here. I don't know why you would even think that. You sure *you* didn't get him moved here?"

"You know what? Fuck you, Briggen." She got up out of bed, and he grabbed her arm, pulling her back down.

"I didn't mean it like that, but you see how stupid that sounds? That's all I wanted you to recognize. Quit that job. Fuck him and that prison. You don't need to be around him or that environment." As far as Briggen was concerned, Forever had come right on time. He didn't want Shan working at the prison...period.

"Is that why you got him sent here, so that I could quit? So that I'll be more inclined to run your beauty salon?"

"You trippin' now. I'm just saying you don't need to work. Yeah, I would like for you to run the beauty salon. You said you would give me an answer and I'm patiently waiting for it."

"Briggen, let me go." She snatched away from him. "I need some time to figure out just what the hell I'm doing here. Because right now, I don't even know."

* * *

218

Janay finally picked up the pizza and was on her way to KFC when her phone rang. She looked at the caller ID and recognized Skye's—or rather New York's—number.

"What's up?" She couldn't help but smile.

"You going out with me or not?"

"Yeah, I'm game," she said.

"Is ten o'clock cool?" Now it was his turn to smile.

"That's perfect."

"So where are we going to meet?"

"Hold on a minute."

Skye listened as she placed a food order. When she came back on the line he said, "We are going out to eat. I would suggest that you save your appetite."

"Oh, I am. This is for my son and my sister. She's baby-sitting and she doesn't like to cook. So in order to get her to babysit I had to stop at Pizza Hut and KFC. Then I'ma head over to her house, drop my son and the food off and I'll get back home to get ready. You want to meet at DunDee's?"

Skye was still stuck on the part of the conversation where she said she was on her way over to her sister's.

"New York, are you still there?"

"Yeah, yeah, I'm here. I'll call you at nine to let you know the meeting spot."

"Just be sure you got that info for me."

"I got you, Ma."

"Bye."

"I'm out." He ended the call. "Fuck!" Skye was feeling drowsy but he got up and got his bloody jacket out of the trash and put it on.

When Janay, Marquis and Crystal arrived at the house, Skye or Mr. New York was gone.

Shan was on edge and was hoping that Briggen was going back to Memphis for the weekend. But he was still here and Peanut was on his way over. Finally they were going to meet up and Shan felt like a teenager bringing her boyfriend home for a very strict and old-fashioned father to meet.

Briggen got tired of Shan's inability to sit still, her walking back and forth, constantly straightening up shit that didn't need straightening up. "Why are you so nervous, girl? You act like your brother is gonna whip yo' ass or something," he teased.

"He can be an asshole. And I told you he didn't want me to move out here. Plus, what if he doesn't like you?"

"What's not to like about me?" Briggen cheesed. "You like me. Isn't that the only thing that matters?"

Before she could answer, Peanut was pulling up into the driveway. She jumped up and ran to the door and was very surprised to see Peanut accompanied by Karin, the real estate agent.

Shan stepped out onto the porch, "Hey, big brother. Karin." Peanut smiled at her as he got out of the car.

"Hey, girl." Karin beamed as she looked around at the forty-eight-hundred-square-foot property that she had sold. "It's looking good, girl. The landscapers did an excellent job. I see y'all bossed up with the gingerbread roof and y'all had Pella Windows come through."

Peanut came up the steps and gave his sister a bear hug. "How are you?"

She hugged him back. "Tired. Confused. It's like I'm just going through the motions. But I'll be all right."

"Is this nigga inside who you've been trying to keep hidden from me? If not, you know I'ma camp out until he shows up."

"Yeah, he's in there."

"You stay in trouble. Now do you see why I didn't want you to move away?"

"I was in trouble and I was living right up under your nose, so what difference does it make? Trouble seems to come looking for me."

They both turned around when Karin cleared her throat to get their attention that she was still standing there.

"C'mon in, Karin." She grabbed her brother's hand and led them both into the house. "Welcome to our humble abode." She took them to the family room, where Briggen was seated, engrossed in a college basketball game.

When they stepped into the room he stood up, went over to Peanut and offered him a pound. "Peanut, I feel like I already know you, maine. I'm Briggen."

"Briggen, I wish I could say the same. My sister has been keeping you a *big* secret, even down to your name."

"Oh, has she?" Briggen peeked over at Shan.

"Calvin, you already know Karin. Boys, I gotta give Karin a tour, show her what the decorator did."

"How come your brother doesn't know about me,

Shan?" Briggen wanted to see her squirm. But she acted as if she didn't hear him, practically dragging Karin behind her.

"See how she do?" he hollered after her.

"We'll be back," Shan yelled, anxious to show off the house to Karin and to get away from being put on the spot.

Right away Karin noticed that once you got inside Briggen and Shan's domain you would have thought you were inside *Metro Home*, the exclusive magazine for decorated homes. The vaulted ceiling commanded your attention with the open skylight that could have served for the home's drop top, considering how large it was. The slate flooring that ran throughout the lower level led you into what Shan referred to as Briggen's Chef's Palace. The kitchen was like no other with glass cabinets and a built-in wine cooler that held twenty bottles of champagne and fifty bottles of wine and stayed fully stocked. The Sub-Zero refrigerator, flat grill stove with pancake griddle and granite countertops all had track lighting. All Karin could say was, "When do we eat?" causing Shan to burst into laughter.

Since Briggen was so private, Karin wasn't allowed a full tour of the home. She thought that was ridiculous, especially since she was the one who had sold it to him. But Shan snuck her to the master bedroom, which spoke volumes about femininity and masculinity. How the two had been combined was beyond Karin. The bedroom was like a mini-apartment, the size of the room well over a thousand square feet. Karin's mouth fell open when she saw that gold leaf marble covered every inch of the room. The only thing that did not have the marble floors was the walk-in his-and-hers closets that could have been a small boutique. They were covered with Berber carpeting, and the shelves were the same gold leaf marble that was on the bedroom floor. In the center of the room held the largest bed she had ever seen. It was a California extended king, where twelve people could sleep in comfort. She had to ask Shan: where in the hell do you buy sheets for that thing and how much do they cost? Another thing that she thought was absolutely fabulous was what she mistook for an armoire built into the wall was a minibar with a kitchen sink in it. But what blew her mind and had her green with envy was that once the bedroom was completely dim, the huge painting of a black man with a woman on his back lit up the room. *Gorgeous*...she had never seen anything like it. Whoever Shan hired to decorate...did the damn thang.

Briggen turned to Peanut. "Have a seat, man. What you drinking?"

"You got any Coronas?"

"I believe that we do." He handed Peanut an ashtray with several blunts in it. "I'll be right back."

Briggen came back carrying four Coronas in a bucket of ice. "You got it smellin' good up in here."

"This that purp?"

"You know it."

"How much a pound go fo' down here?"

"Sheeit, 'bout forty-two hunned."

Peanut nodded as he continued to blaze it up. He kept his eyes on Briggen, trying to size him up, and ready to cut from the bullshit formalities.

"Let's talk, maine; that's the real reason I'm here. Let's start with how you was able to get my sister to come to Detroit?"

Briggen took a swig of his Corona and opened another bottle for Peanut. *Uh-oh, here it goes, time for the interrogation.* "You probably didn't know that we used to kick it before she got that job at the prison."

"Yeah, maine, I just didn't know who you were. I try to keep up with my sister. We all we got."

"I saw her parked in front of my store and she was crying. I hadn't seen her in a while. I didn't even know that her girl had split her own wig. Anyways, I talked her into coming to my crib and just chill until she got her mind together. I even left her there by herself for a few days. I was always diggin' her, so I was amped that she came to the crib. She told me that you really didn't want her to go so far away, so I too started suggesting that she don't go all the way to Cali. I was already looking at this area since I got a few cousins out here. So—"

"A few cousins, huh? You can be straight up with me. This is my sister we talkin' about. I hustle. You hustle. You plannin' on settin' up shop out here? I heard muthafuckas out here be gettin' that bread and not on no small scale."

Briggen took a couple more swigs from his bottle of Corona. Now it was his turn to size Peanut up. It was obvious that Peanut did a little homework. But just what and how much he wanted to share with this total stranger, he didn't know.

"I'm not settin' up shop," Briggen said with a straight face.

"So what's up with my sister runnin' one of your businesses? You puttin' the shit in her name. I don't want her to get caught up on no conspiracy bullshit."

"I'm doing all I can to protect her but you know how shit can go."

Peanut shook his head. "Wrong answer, nigga. She carryin' your seed, and she's the only family I got. Let her go."

"Come again." Briggen needed to be sure he heard him right.

"Let her go, man. You throwin' bricks at the penitentiary for you and for her. If I'm gonna do my dirt and keep her out of harm's way, you think I'ma let some outsider put her out there? Naw, bruh. And what about all of them chicks you got? What happens when they find out Shan is pregnant? My sister gonna be caught up in the middle of that bullshit. They already disrespected her once before. Shit, you ain't even got them in check."

"Hold up, my man. I let you speak real greasy to a nigga out of respect for Shan. I see you really did your homework. You got a small layout of me but please don't disrespect me and try to tell me how to run my shit. First off, young blood, I've been in this game for years. My paper is real long. Selling drugs and doin' anything else illegal for that matter is…well, you know what time it is. However, I'm a businessman about my bread. I am also a man in every sense of the word. What kind of nigga would I be to jeopardize my future child's mother's freedom?"

"Yo, but this is my family we talkin' about." They both pulled on the purple-filled blunts in silence. Peanut's original intention for this visit did not include him being so overprotective of Shan. But once he got in Briggen's presence the vibe that he gave off screamed, "Get your sister away from this nigga." "I suggest you let her go, and I'm trying to be as nice about it as I possibly can."

"I feel your concern and I can't blame you. You kicked it to Shan about your feelings?" Briggen smirked.

"Naw, ain't no need to. The last nigga she fucked with, fucked her over and now you think you gonna put her in harm's way? I mean, give the sister a break. Like I said, I *suggest* you do me this one, tell her it ain't going to work out and let her go."

"Why don't we let her make the final decision? Because you know if and when she finds out that you are trying to run her life she's going to fuck with me just because, and end up hating you."

"Look, nigga, I'm her brother and it's obvious she can't make her own decisions."

"Hold up. Just because my brother Forever put—"

"Hey, y'all, how's it going?" Shan asked as she and

226

Karin stood in front of the TV. Karin sat down next to Peanut and Shan sat next to Briggen.

"What about your brother, Forever?" Karin asked, clueless as to what was going down. "How is he? I bet you he won't even remember me. He'll be getting out soon, right? Let him know I got something real nice set up for him."

Everyone else in the room got quiet. Peanut was the first to try and smooth things out and hide the fact that shit was getting ready to get ugly.

"Briggen here is getting ready to show me some flicks of his *brother*, Forever." He glanced over at Shan. She wanted to shrink to the size of a bug and crawl up under a rock. All this time she had been able to keep from him the fact that Forever and Briggen were brothers.

Briggen, as if on cue, pulled out his wallet and started flipping through it. Shan sank back into the chair. She was busted.

"Excuse me, I'ma run to the ladies' room," Karin said, getting up.

"This is Ma Dukes and Pops." Briggen began explaining who everybody was. "This is Markeeta's parents. Her moms and my pops is sister and brother." He skipped over one of the flicks. "This is Forever's daughter, Tameerah. This one is his wife and daughter together. This is—"

"Wait a minute. Go back to his wife," Peanut's voice cracked.

"Boy, go 'head," Shan snapped, thinking that Peanut wanted to try and get with her.

Peanut slid the picture out. "This is Nyla," he blurted out.

"Aw hell no!" Peanut stood up and began pacing the floor. Then he burst out laughing. Briggen and Shan were looking at him as if he were crazy. "Ain't this a bitch?" He stopped and looked at the both of them. "Ain't this a muthafuckin' bitch!"

"You want to fill us in, bruh." Shan was trying to figure out what the hell just happened.

"You know her?" Briggen asked.

"Know her? I'm fuckin' her."

"You what?" Briggen and Shan said together.

CHAPTER EIGHTEEN

Woo," Tami moaned as her fingernails dug deep into his muscled shoulders. Her legs were wrapped around his waist, her thong pushed aside, and her skirt was up over her ass.

Woo had her back against the front door, pounding his nine-inch rod into her wet, hot pussy. His jeans were down around his ankles and both of his palms were gripping her firm, ripe ass as he thrust harder, wishing he could knock her back out. Her eyes rolled back into her head as she felt his dick stiffen and as each thrust got deeper and faster while grinding into her G-spot.

"Babeeee," she stammered as the dick was feeling so good she wasn't sure if she was talking in tongues or a foreign language.

But it was too late. "Uugghh." Woo gritted his teeth as his knees buckled and the cum filled his dick up and then shot out like a high-speed power hose.

"You muthafucka!" she panted as she tried to clamp onto his dick. "I was gettin' ready to cum again." She wanted to scream as she felt his limp dick slide out. "You could have held on a little longer." She unwrapped her legs from around his waist. He went to kiss her and she mushed him in the face.

"What the fuck is wrong with you? Why can't I get a kiss?"

"Kiss my pussy, nigga. How you gonna cum before me?" She wanted to knee him in his balls.

"Unh-unh. I'm not kissin' the set of lips that you want me to." He pulled up his pants and boxers and slapped her on the ass.

"Why not?" she asked with an attitude saying that she was insulted.

"I told you. I don't get down like that."

"Nigga, please, why not?"

"Because…I ain't gotta explain nothing to you, and plus you ain't my bitch." He began to back away from her.

"Shit, that ain't never stopped you from hittin' this pussy before. But I'm glad you said that. If I would have known how you was feelin', I would have never let things go this far," she snapped as she stormed past him and headed for the bathroom. They hadn't been fucking for more than a month and each time they had to sneak and make it quick. They both worked for Briggen. Tami was Briggen's main dope trafficker, and had been his girl for almost two and a half years.

"It's a little too late to be talking about things going too far," he yelled after her. "We done already crossed that line."

When Woo first started flirting with Tami he was only

trying to see how far she would let him go. Even though she was Briggen's dope broad her style of hustling and how she dealt with niggas completely turned him on, and actually Woo had seen her first and pointed her out to Briggen. But as always when Briggen saw something beneficial to him he had to have it. Fuck what anybody else wanted or who he had to knock over to get it.

Tami played hard to get at first. But since she and Woo would work together every so often, shit happened and the attraction seemed to be there. They both knew that they were playing a deadly game, but that made shit more intense, the fucking that much better, the stakes that much higher and they both accepted that it was all a part of the game.

She burst out of the bathroom crying. "I swear I think he's watching us." She held her phone out to show him the caller ID. "This is the third time he did this."

"Answer the phone next time. You actin' all guilty and shit."

"What if—"

Woo's celly started ringing. He held up his finger to hush her up as he picked it up. "Yo, Brig, what's up? Where you at?" He looked over at Tami.

"I'm at the club. Tami came through yet? I've been trying to reach her."

"She left about an hour ago," Woo lied easily. "She handled that and broke out."

"She didn't say to where?" Briggen wanted to know.

"Naw, maine, not to me she didn't."

"What time you want me to come through?" It was obvious to Woo that Briggen was agitated.

"Let me hit you up around four."

"Aiight, dawg," Briggen agreed and they both hung up.

"Tami, you gotta stay ahead of the game while you're handling his business. You can't be ignoring the man's calls."

"Woo, mind your business. He knows that I'm pissed at him. I can handle my business without him clockin' my every move. Plus I'm not even fuckin' with him on that level no more."

"Then why was you just all spooked up and crying, talkin' about he watching us? Why all of a sudden you're so angry with him?"

"He's foul, that's all. He did some foul shit."

"Oh, so you know about ole girl being pregnant?"

"What? Who's pregnant?" The room grew dead quiet.

"Fuck," Woo mumbled, kicking himself for allowing that to slip out.

She was now up in his face, yelling, "Who's pregnant, Woo?"

"If you don't know it ain't my business to be telling you." He turned away from her.

"Bullshit!" she screamed as she pushed him with both hands. "Who is pregnant?"

"What the fuck do you care? You just stood here and fucked me, then you tell me that you ain't fuckin' with him no more, that it's all business. So why the fuck do you even care?"

"You know what? Fuck you, Woo. I'ma find out on my own. And this little fling me and you had going on is over! Revenge feels good, but I'm slippin', fuckin' around with you and now you tell me my nigga has put his seed in some other ho?" She started out the door and stopped. "Oh, if any of this ever gets back to Briggen"—her eyes turned into slits—"I'ma kill yo' ass."

He chuckled. "Bitch, you got me fucked up, talkin' to me like I'm a lame-ass nigga. Just because you got a couple of bodies on your hands I'm supposed to be scared? You better get the fuck outta my face talkin' stupid. Better yet, get the fuck outta my house. You stupid bitch!"

After she slammed the door, Woo locked it and headed for the shower. "She better be glad that I know that she's just talkin' out the side of her neck."

Peanut was parked in a hooptie on Skye's block watching his house. A Range Rover finally came out of the garage with Skye and the nigga that had been with him the other night. He lit a Newport and mentally went over his next move. After he was satisfied he cranked up the hooptie and pulled off.

"Can you send the next person in please?" Shan said to the inmate who was just leaving her office. It was her open-house hours and it seemed as if that line kept getting longer.

"Excuse me, Ms. McKee." This was a young brother

who looked to be no more than eighteen. "I've been on the waiting list for the computer class for almost six months now. Can you check and let me know how far down am I?"

"What's your name?"

"Baron Pritchard."

"Mr. Pritchard, I can't even lie. The last teacher left things in a mess. And I've been here for almost three weeks and still haven't put a dent in getting it all organized. As far as the waiting list is concerned, on Friday a new one will be posted. So look out for it. I did my best at piecing it back together."

He frowned as if to say that wasn't what he wanted to hear.

"How many more people are waiting to see me?"

He backed away toward the door. "It was only one left when I came in."

"Thank goodness. I'll see that one and that will be it for today." She leaned back into her chair and stretched until she heard her door shut. She quickly straightened up then a scowl covered her face. "Open my door please." Shan's blood began to boil but her voice was very calm.

"I know I can talk to my jump-off in private."

"Jump-off? Nigga, you got it twisted."

"Do I? I thought the definition of a jump-off was a bitch that you fucked whenever you wanted to." He smirked as he sat down and made himself comfortable.

"What? Am I supposed to cry? I don't give a fuck what you call me. Because you were just a big ole bitch-ass trick to me. I got exactly what I wanted from you. Money and a good fuck. You served your purpose. My brother is out of jail and is on his feet, thanks to you. And know that your brother wifed me. My life couldn't be better."

"A jump-off that likes to be tossed around. I ain't mad at that. So what's up with the pregnancy? I don't see no stomach so my guess is you got rid of it, which was all you had to do in the first place. Wifey will be glad to hear about that."

Shan went into her purse and pulled out a bottle of prenatal vitamins and iron pills. She shook them in his face. "That's where you got it wrong. I'm very much pregnant. It just so happens that I carry just like my mother. Mostly in my ass, hips, and thighs." She set the vitamins on top of her desk directly in front of him, stood up and showed him the little bulge in her stomach. "So tell wifey she might as well welcome us to the family," Shan said with a straight face. She was not about to let Forever off the hook that easy by letting him feel that the stress of getting the other woman pregnant was behind him. She wanted to remain a nag in the back of his mind and mess up his happy home just as he had messed up her happy life.

"That's sad since I won't claim the little bastard."

"You don't have to claim him. Your brother already has."

"You would stoop so low as to make my brother believe that it's his. But that's typical of a jump-off. You haven't even noticed that none of them bitches he fucks with have any kids? Did he tell you why?" He started laughing.

"You know what? You are a pain in the ass. I wouldn't care if they had babies or didn't have babies. They handle his business. He keeps me happy so I don't care about what another bitch is doing. Besides, they all work for him."

Forever broke into laughter again. "Damn. You dumber than I thought." He stood up to leave, and she had a puzzled look on her face, which he was enjoying. When he got to the door he stopped and said, "And oh, I will get my money back that you took from me. I put that shit on our seed." He winked at her and left out.

Peanut was worn out mentally and physically. Between the trip to his sister's house, him not feeling Briggen and Shan being pregnant by this nigga. And what were the odds of his fucking Forever's wife and Forever being Briggen's brother? Then when he got back into town he had to go deliver and collect because his main runner was locked up. And plus, he had to see what Skye was up to. He owed that nigga some payback for the role he played in teaming up with Brianna and getting him locked up. Now he was sitting up in Nyla's crib trying to decide how he was going to play this bitch.

Nyla looked over at him and could tell that something was on his mind. But then she was wondering if she was just paranoid. Forever had dropped a bomb on her and she had been in a fog ever since. She didn't know what to do or what to say.

"Are you all right?" She began lightly massaging his neck.

Fuck it, he said to himself. *I might as well get the shit over.* Then he thought about it and decided to get dirty.

"Naw, I'm real tensed. Suck my dick."

"What?" She snapped her neck back. He had never used that tone with her before.

"Suck my dick." He unzipped his pants and pulled them down, along with his boxers. He gave her a chilling look that caused her to not ask any questions and just get down on her knees with the quickness. She looked up at him then quickly averted her eyes. "C'mon, give Daddy some head."

She grabbed his dick at the base and slowly began slobbing the head. Peanut watched her with a smirk on his face. After watching it get harder he placed both hands on her head and began fucking her face. "Suck Daddy harder," he ordered. He was pumping her mouth lightly, feeling his dick hit the back of her throat. "I know you can swallow more than that." He pumped faster. "Suck Daddy harder. Don't get tired now." He could tell that she was trying not to gag. "Breathe for Daddy," he told her as his dick was now down her throat. He tried to push his balls in her mouth.

Tears were streaming down her cheeks as he fucked

her mouth as if he had no respect or love for her. She was very glad when he pulled out.

"Look at this boy." His dick was hard as steel. The veins were popping out and pre-cum was oozing out the head. "You did Daddy real good. Now stand up."

She stood up slowly, looking at him, not knowing what to expect. This Peanut here was tripping. He slid her baby tee up over her head and motioned for her to take off her panties and lean over the couch. He spread her legs while admiring her ass. He grabbed his dick and rubbed it up and down her pussy. "You want this?" he teased.

"All of it," she purred. Her nipples and pussy felt as if she had struck a match to them and it all went into flames. "Baby, put it in please," Nyla begged. He kept rubbing it against her pussy as she tried to get on the head. "Put it...oh shit!" She moaned as she felt the wood bang up against her pussy walls. "Oh m-my gosh," she kept chanting as he stroked and fucked the pussy until her body seemed as if it was going into convulsions. He pulled out, spread her ass cheeks and began to penetrate her back door.

"No! Wait!" She tried to stand up but he pulled her ass back onto his dick. "Ooow, Peanut, please wait, oh God." He kept pushing. "You're...not using...Vaseline, oh my God!" she screamed. "You're hurting me."

"You didn't use Vaseline when you and that nigga fucked my sister in the ass, did you?"

"Peanut, nooo let...me...explain."

He took that last thrust and rammed it the rest of the

way in, causing her once again to scream out in agonizing pain.

"Just like with my sister the hard part is over now." He gripped her hips tighter and was thrusting so hard he was lifting her feet off the floor.

Even though she was sobbing loudly he kept punishing her asshole. He wouldn't let up. On top of that, her ass to his surprise was wet and juicy. "How does it feel to you? I feel a nut c-comin' on." He pounded into her ass and pulled out, nuttin' all over her ass cheeks and back.

He stood there, grabbed up her baby tee and as her body was wracked by sobs he wiped his dick off.

"Peanut, I'm sorry. I was vulnerable and desperate. I didn't know what else to do. Please listen to me, dammit!" she pleaded. "I gave up so much to be with you." She could barely stand up, but she wanted desperately to stop him from leaving. She needed him to listen to her. But her steps were slowed down from the pain of that horrific ass-fucking. She glanced over at the mirror and her face was smeared with black streaks of makeup. Her eyes and nose were so red and puffy from crying that she could barely keep them open. Her hair was all over her head. She could feel the bruises beginning to form on the inside of her thighs.

She grabbed his arm and he turned and looked at her in disgust.

He grabbed his jacket without saying a word.

"I gave up a lot to be with you." She stood up slowly and in pain, looking a whole mess.

"So what you're basically trying to tell me is that all of this is karma? Bitch, fuck you."

"Peanut wait...don't go," she screamed. "Please. Don't leave me like this."

Peanut turned and walked away, slamming the door behind him. She knew he was walking out of her life.

CHAPTER NINETEEN

Unh, unh, unh, unh! Man, I don't even know how to break this to you."

Melky had been watching Tami for the past three days, and he was now sitting down the street watching Woo's house. Briggen's gut instincts were telling him that Tami was up to something, but he didn't know exactly what.

Briggen had taken a liking to Melky when Melky pulled his coattail about one of his workers being grimey. Before Briggen could take care of the situation, Melky had already disposed of the worker. From that point on, Melky had been on his team.

Both Briggen and Forever had taken a liking to Melky and his brother Skye. And instead of Brig and Ever opening themselves up to be robbed by them, they would use them or put them to work. Skye was all right with it because he could unload the dope that he would jack and Melky thought their arrangement was a lovely thing. It made him feel part of the streets again even with him being paralyzed from the waist down.

"What it do, Melk?" Briggen was impatient.

"This bitch just came out of the house crying and screaming, 'I never should have fucked with that nigga.'" Melky did his best imitation of a girl's voice. "Now what nigga she talkin' about I don't know but she been in there for the last two hours."

"In where?" Briggen was now rattled.

"In Woo's, nigga."

"Woo's? I just spoke to that nigga." *No wonder that bitch wasn't answering her phone. Dirty bitch. Ain't this some shit! And they think they playin' me?*

"Man, I'm telling you she been in there for the last couple of hours. I'm sittin' on his block right now. She still sittin' in her car. You want me to roll up on her ass?"

"Naw, man." He knew Melky wouldn't hesitate to roll up on her and split her wig back. "You did good, lil' nigga. I'll handle it from here."

"Anytime, dawg. Hit me up. You know I'm about my bread and I'll put in work."

Briggen hung up, leaned back into his chair and burst into laughter. He laughed long and hard for a good while. He couldn't even tell anybody this newest chain of events because they would think he was making the shit up, or even better, they would say he was gettin' what he deserved. Haters! *Niggas needed to learn to hate the game and not the player.*

He was sitting in his office at the club going over some of the videotapes. He liked to stay up on who was par-laying at his club. With who, how often and what they were doing. He had several disguised cameras through-out the club. The majority of them only he knew about and only he could access with a special code.

His mind was still on Woo and Tami's betrayal. He was half watching the videotape but he became totally focused when he caught a glimpse of two people. He stopped the tape, hit rewind and let the tape roll. He was glued to the screen and couldn't blink. What he saw on the camera that covered the stockroom sealed the deal that he was about to make with the devil. Sharia was leaning up against cases of liquor; her head was rolling side to side as Woo was on his knees eating her pussy as if his life depended on it. She was serving up the same sexy moans and grinds that she gave him. *Bitches!* He shut his eyes tight. He refused to watch it go any further. He turned the recorder off and chuckled. *That nigga always talkin' about he don't eat pussy. Leave it to Sharia to turn his bitch ass out.*

Damn. He hadn't even seen that shit coming. He remembered Forever telling him that Woo wanted to be him, wanted what he had, and for Briggen to watch his back. *And now look. The nigga is fuckin' two of my bitches? Don't muthafuckas know that I'm not to be fucked with? They must have forgot. I guess it's time to remind them who I am. They want to play? We can play but there can only be one winner...me!*

"You mad at me?" Shan was holding her breath as she twirled one of her locks around her finger mercilessly.

"What you think, Shan?" Peanut growled. "Go ahead. Tell me what the fuck you think! You doin' some reckless shit. Here I am doing all I can to protect you and for what?"

"Protect me from what, Peanut?"

"These damn streets, girl. What the fuck you think?"

"You trippin'. I made a mistake."

"Girl, shut. The. Fuck. Up, with that bullshit. A mistake is when you accidentally dent a car or step on somebody's toe. This shit is beyond a fuckin' mistake."

"What you want me to say? Damn. I'm sorry."

"Uh-uh. Sorry ain't gonna cut it. Naw, it's what I want you to *do*, gotdammit."

"Okay, but why you gotta talk to me like that? What you want me to do, Peanut?" She was feeling bad for letting her brother down. She had always felt obligated to do the things that would make him proud of her. "Can you calm down a little bit?"

"Hell no! Because when a nigga calm down with yo' ass you go and do dumb shit. Like all this sneaking around, lying, hidin' shit like you ten or something." Peanut was heated and there was no mistake about it. She knew that he was about to blow his lid. "Look, Shan, we a team, baby girl. I ain't the enemy. But you got to get rid of this cat Briggen. Something ain't right. Leave the nigga alone."

"Hold up, Peanut. What does he have to do with this?"

"You gonna make me beat yo' ass, girl. What the fuck is the matter with you? Don't make me come up there and drag yo' ass back to Memphis. I'll do it and won't think twice about it," he threatened.

"I done had it with all this chastising you call yourself doing. You are not my daddy and I am not a fuckin' child. I'm grown as hell."

"Shit, you don't act like it. Look, I'm just trying to look out for you. All Briggen is doing is using you just like the rest of his hoes."

"Is that what you think? You talkin' about some shit you don't even know anything about. All of them hoes work for him. It's just business."

"Business! You big dummy!" He shut up to allow his words to sink in. "Business? If you call fuckin' them business, then I'm in the wrong one. Listen, do you know what comes with the territory of being a hustler's wife? Do you?" he yelled at her. "You see the outcome every time you go to work, or pass a funeral home. You couldn't possibly be that fuckin' blind."

"Boy, I suggest that you calm the fuck down. I done told you I am grown. You think I'm actually listening to you with all this hollering you're doing?"

"You so grown but yet you're fuckin' your life up! Leaving that nigga alone, now that's being grown." It got quiet. "Hello, hello!" Then he heard the dial tone. "I know her ass didn't just hang up on me." Peanut slammed the phone down.

"Tami, why the fuck you ain't answering your phone!" Woo snapped.

"Why you sweatin' me, Woo? I told you shit ain't happening with us no more. It's over."

"Bitch, please. Don't flatter yourself. I hit it and quit it...next!" Woo said laughing. "No, fo'real, I was callin' to reason with you. You should think about what is going to happen once you tell that nigga about us fuckin'. It's going to fuck everything up. And I can't let you do that."

"Nigga, your dick game ain't all of that, so don't flatter yourself. And who you think you're talkin' to? You Benson-ass nigga. I admit that this shit is my own fault. I played myself, fuckin' with the help. I ain't worried about what Briggen gone say or do. He don't own me. I was fuckin' both of y'all. I got what I wanted and needed. You've already been dissed and dismissed."

"The help? Bitch, you got me fucked up. Help? Woo ain't never been the help, I—" All he heard was dial tone. "I'ma fuck this bitch up!" Woo redialed her number only to get the voice mail. He hung up and began pacing the floor. Fifteen minutes later he was dialing Briggen.

Briggen checked his caller ID and saw that it was Woo and decided not to pick up. He wasn't ready to speak to him just yet. An hour later the phone rang again. He checked the caller ID and it was Tami.

"Look at these muhfuckas trying to cover their tracks," he sneered, still not answering. He wasn't ready to talk to her neither. They say that *Payback is a Mutha*, so he knew he needed to hit the both of them where it hurt.

The next time the phone rang, the caller ID read Silk.

Briggen, who was chillin' at what he and Shan called his city beach house, picked up the phone. "What up, dawg?" he greeted his family.

"Where you at, nigga? Woo been tryna reach you. He got some info for you. That info you been dyin' to get."

"Why he ain't tell you then?"

"He said you need to hear this shit, hot off the press and straight outta the donkey's mouth." Silk chuckled at his own attempt at a joke.

"Aiight, maine. I'll call him now." Briggen hung up and dialed Woo, who answered on the first ring.

"Yo, I've been trying to hit you up. Where you at? You spoke to Silk?"

"I'm chillin', what's the word?" Briggen braced himself for the bullshit as he leaned back massaging the Ben Wa balls.

"When is the last time you talked to Tami?" Woo tried to mask his excitement. "She on some bullshit and I didn't want you to get caught slippin'."

"Oh yeah? What's the deal?"

"Check it. The deal is that she and Sharia was behind that drive-by at the mall."

It took a minute before what Woo said sunk in. Till this day, he had never found out who was behind the hit that had him laid up in a hospital bed. That very same drive-by could have killed him and Shan. The thought of it put a nasty taste in his mouth. He was hoping this nigga was really going all out to cover his tracks. Because he knew firsthand how bad he wanted to know who was behind that drive-by. And here all of this time…Briggen had to admit this was a low blow. I mean accusing Tami and Sharia of trying to take him out? And what a coincidence that he's fucking both of them. The plot was definitely thickening.

"You still there? I know a nigga is shocked. Hell, so am I," Woo said.

"Where you get this info from and how accurate is it?"

Woo began breakin' it all down to him. He had way too many intimate details. So much so that he could have been in on it. For once, Briggen was absolutely speechless. After he hung up all he could do was sit there and stare into space and plot his next move.

Three days later…

Sharia was trying to figure out what she could get into for the day. She didn't have to be at the club until six so she wanted to chill out. She picked up her phone to check her voice mail. Thoughts of her and Briggen going on a nice cruise filled her head. She smiled but then immediately began to frown and the hair began to stand up on her neck when she heard Tami's voice.

"Hey girl, it's me. Just wanted to put you up on the latest. Somebody is *pregnant* and it ain't me. Is it you?" Sarcasm dripping throughout her voice. "If so…you did that!" Her tone far from sounding sincere.

Sharia immediately clicked out of voice mail and dialed Tami's number with trembling hands. *What the fuck is she talking about?*

"Pregnant? Who the fuck is pregnant? It ain't me. This nigga done got somebody pregnant?" Sharia was mumbling as well as getting pissed off because Tami wouldn't answer her phone. She decided to call Mia; she needed to get to the bottom of this immediately. Bad enough Briggen was fuckin' all of them. Now someone was pregnant and it wasn't her and it wasn't Tami. *It's that day care bitch. Her sneaky ass. All she wants to do is keep Briggen sniffin' up her ass. She needs to grow the fuck up and get this money like the rest of us.*

"Hello."

"Mia, this Sharia. I just got a message from Tami—"

"Look, I already heard." Mia wasted no time cutting Sharia off. "And like I told Tami's messy ass, it's none of y'alls business. And if I was pregnant, I wouldn't have told y'all no way. Y'all bitches worried about the wrong thing. Find something to do. Plus, you are callin' the wrong person because if y'all wanted to know so bad, call Briggen up and ask him." *Click.* She hung up on Sharia.

"That bitch!" Sharia ranted. "If she ain't pregnant and Tami ain't, then who the fuck is?" Sharia bounced up and began pacing back and forth across her brand-new carpet. "Damn it!" she spat. "This bitch done messed up my whole day." She went to the phone and tried to catch Tami again, but all she got was her voice mail. Still pacing back and forth, she almost jumped out of her skin when the front door popped open. When she saw him a snarl spread across her face. She wanted him to know that she was pissed off and wanted him to ask why, just so she could spaz out on him.

"I forgot you had a key. You haven't used it in God knows when." She folded her arms across her chest.

He didn't bother to respond, and she watched him head straight for the stairwell. She recalled the day when his handsome ass swooped her off her feet, rocked her world and loved her to death. But she had to admit that it was strange to her that she couldn't remember the day when he stopped loving her. Or the day that she felt he no longer loved her. Or the day that their relationship turned all business.

She watched him as he came down the stairs carrying a duffel bag and strolled into the kitchen. He came out carrying bottled water, staring at her. She could tell that there was something different about his demeanor. But as usual she didn't know what it was. She always had a hard time reading him. Then he sat the duffel bag on the couch next to him, tossed a folder on the coffee table, pulled out a pen and set it on top of the folder. "I need you to sign these papers."

"Who is she, Briggen?" She didn't pick up the pen but was glaring at him.

He picked up the pen for her, opened the folder and calmly pointed to the red Post-it arrow. "Sign right here." He held out the pen.

"Who is she?"

"Who is who?"

"The bitch you got pregnant, that's who, Briggen."

She signed her name and made an attempt to read his facial expression as he flipped to another page and pointed.

"Where you getting this information from?" He kept on his game face as he watched her sign and then turned to another page.

"So you're saying that you don't have a baby on the way?"

He flipped to another page. "Last one. What if I do, Sharia? What? You want to give Daddy a baby?" He had a cocky grin on his face.

She was speechless as she signed for the last time. *Give him a baby?* She looked at him to see if he was being funny or if he was being for real. Unable to figure him out, she swallowed hard and decided to look over the document, wanting to know what business he was putting into her name. She was making a killing off the club and was living lovely. She straightened up the folder and went to the first page. He leaned over and gently took it out of her hands.

"Don't I have a right to see what you're putting in my name?"

"You didn't answer me. You want to have my baby?"

"Briggen, what is this all about?"

She could now tell that something was up and it wasn't to her benefit. "What are you putting into my name?"

"Is he going to put something in your name?" He had this smug smirk on his face.

"W-what?"

"Did you think about that? You didn't even weigh your options before you fucked him? Did you?" He popped the top off the bottled water and took a huge swig. He watched as the color drained out of her beautiful caramel-colored skin. She reminded him of the actress Meagan Good.

She finally caught her bearings and sat upright. She was busted. "I know you ain't mad at me."

He shrugged. "Naw, I ain't mad, just hurt."

"Hurt, huh? I'm sure you heard that what's good for the goose is good for the gander?"

"Don't even try it. You know what the deal was from day one. But you chose to play."

"Oh well, *Payback is a Mutha*, ain't it?"

He laughed. "You killin' me with the cliché's, but you know what?" He pulled out his wallet and set two one-dollar bills on the coffee table.

"What?" she snapped, feelin' herself.

"I got the final payback. You just signed over a six-figure-a-year business to a nigga for just two dollars. I'm out."

CHAPTER TWENTY

"Boy, you better stop playing with me. You already on my bad side," Janay snapped.

"Hold up, how did I get on your bad side?" Skye was playing dumb.

"For standing me up the other night."

"Aww, man, I know you ain't gonna hold a nigga to that. My bad, baby girl. Tell Daddy how I can make it up to you."

"Daddy? Please, spare me. Just give me ole boy's address and I might let you make it up to me."

"All right, I'll give it to you, but I'm ridin' with you. You just can't roll up on dude tryin' to check him. He'll probably smack you again."

"Nah, nigga. I ain't gonna check him, but Ms. Pearl is."

"Who is Ms. Pearl?"

"My .380."

"I'm sure you nice with the hardware but even the best of 'em roll with somebody. You'll be a fool to roll dolo."

Janay released an exasperated sigh. All she wanted was the fuckin' address of the nigga who slapped her at the car wash. Her pride would not allow her to let him get away with it. Didn't he know who the fuck she was? If he didn't, he and everyone else would know by the time she finished with him. "Okay, Robin. You can go." She finally gave in.

"Who do you think you are? Batman?" Skye asked her.

"Yup, and you're my trusty sidekick. Ha. Ha. Ha."

"You want me to come scoop you up?"

"Naw, nigga, you know the routine. Meet me at our spot."

"Oh, how cute. We have a spot," he teased. "But seriously, we ridin' together. We can't ride up on these niggas in two cars."

"Don't underestimate me because I'm a girl," she scoffed.

"You think you are so damn tough. Show me what you workin' with."

"I'll see you later."

"Aiight then, it's on."

Shan and Briggen were in the driveway fogging up the windows of his truck. The driver's seat was pulled all the way back and Shan was straddling his lap, maneuvering so that all nine and a half inches were buried deep inside her. If any of their new neighbors were peeking out of their windows and saw the fog and the bouncing up and down of the truck, it wouldn't take a rocket scientist to figure out what was taking place.

"Mmmmm," Briggen groaned as he palmed both of

her ass cheeks and thrust his hips upward, causing his dick to hit that back wall.

"Ooooh," she purred, and shuddered at the same time. She wanted to tell him to make that move again but nothing escaped but moans. She felt as if she were floating. Her pussy and hips were winding in a slow rhythm, causing her clit to get all the friction that she could handle. She could feel her pussy driving him crazy as the tight small muscles gripped and grazed up and down the length of his dick.

"I-I-I'm done, baby, ah shit, I'm done." Briggen shut his eyes tight and gritted his teeth, and his dick swelled and his balls were ready to burst with semen.

"B-babeee," she squealed, tossing her head back, as his dick game drew out stream after stream of her juices. She jerked and twisted while he held her with all of his strength, wanting her to take all he had to give, until he fell limp. She lay motionless on top of him as they both enjoyed the aftershocks of that mind-blowing orgasm.

He ran his fingers through her hair.

"You tryna kill a nigga or what?"

A lazy grin spread across her lips. "Of course I'm not trying to kill you. I just want to remind you of what you're leaving here in Detroit each time you go back to Memphis."

"Aww that's cold. Especially since you know I'ma always come back to my baby. You know that, right?" His eyes locked intensely with hers.

"Yeah, I know that. But that doesn't stop me from missing you. Then on top of that you rush in and rush out."

"No I don't."

"Yes you do, Briggen. Look at us! We fuckin' in your car when we got all of them bedrooms up there."

"We already fucked in the bedroom. We wouldn't be fuckin' out here if you hadn't followed me out of the house."

"I couldn't help it. I don't want you to leave," she whined. "We barely even talk anymore," she whispered as she made circles on his chest with her fingers.

"Baby, what do you want to talk about? If something is on your mind, you know I'm only a phone call away."

"It's not the same, Briggen," she pouted.

"What made you start calling me Briggen? Especially since you were so adamant about calling me Calvin."

"See how long it took you to notice that? Just goes to show how you are in and right out."

"Don't even try it. I been noticed it. I just didn't mention it. So tell me, why am I Briggen all of a sudden?"

"When you step back and become the man I first met. That man was Calvin, and then I'll start back calling you him again," she stated with conviction.

"Oh, so it's like that?"

She shook her head yes. "Briggen?"

"Oh, so now you tryna be funny?"

"No. I want you to tell me a secret."

"A secret?"

"Yes, a secret." Her gaze was challenging him. He

let out a groan. "Briggen, stop being stubborn. Share a secret with me."

He chuckled. "Me stubborn? Not Briggen. Calvin maybe. But not Briggen." She punched him in his arm. "All right, all right. A secret. I have one but you can't tell anybody. And don't be judgmental."

"Stop playin', Briggen. And judgmental? I hope you're not getting ready to tell me you're gay." Her heart sank to her feet.

"Hell naw. Don't even try to play a nigga like that. It's my peeps. My peeps fuckin' around on me. I caught the shit on tape. I saw it with my own eyes."

They each needed a few minutes to see how the other one would respond to that piece of information.

Shan was the first to break the silence. "So...what are you going to do?"

He shrugged. "It ain't shit. I just thought I had some loyal muthafuckas around me. I'ma chalk that shit up. It's all a part of the game."

"Mmmhmmm. Easier said than done." She made sure to slip that in.

"Check it. These streets is like a jungle. I come across all types of breeds. Especially snakes and rats. You know snakes eat rats, and hawks eat snakes. And since I stay aboveground circling my prey, I have to honestly say that I saw it comin'. But being the cocky nigga that I am, I ignored it. But if you stay ready you'll never have to get prepared."

"Mmmm, that's deep." She ran what he had just said over again in her mind as he lit up a blunt.

257

"You ready to hear my secret?" Shan asked him.

"Spill it."

"Okay." She took a deep breath. "My secret is...my brother wants me to leave you alone."

"Umph," was all Briggen said as they lay there staring out into the night. "Sooo...what are you going to do? I hope you're gonna stay with me. I don't want you to leave me."

"Who is that talking?"

He was playing with her locks. "Calvin and Briggen. They both want you to stay. So tell me. What are you going to do?" Briggen threw her question right back at her.

"I'ma do me. Peanut is my brother, not my father. I know he is looking out for me, but my decision will be based upon how you play your cards."

"Shit, then charge it to the game."

Janay beeped the horn at Skye. He jumped out of his truck and jogged over to her.

"We goin' in my ride." When she looked at him as if he were crazy he said, "How you gonna do dirt in your own ride? C'mon, girl. I know where he at but I don't know how long he gonna be there."

Janay parked her ride and followed him to his car. It was a rusty Toyota Camry. She frowned, turning up her top lip. "Let's ride, gangsta," Skye teased.

They took off with Melky a few car lengths behind them. Janay didn't even know it. The only sound was when she checked Ms. Pearl for bullets. Skye was impressed. To him this was a gangsta broad for real. Skye blasted Dr. Dre's "Ain't Nuthin' but a G Thang" as they headed for the basketball court.

"Showtime," Skye sang as he pulled his hoodie over his head. Janay pulled her baseball cap down low. He slowed down as he looked for Freckles. "There yo' man go with the purple Nike T-shirt on."

"I see that punk." She pulled out some loot wrapped in a rubber band. She rolled her window down and stuck her head out. "Hey, cutie! You with the freckles, I know you got that strawberry." She waved her wad of cash at him. There was a ball game going on strong and Freckles was standing there watching, while nursing a forty and obviously trying to get his mack on with the bow-legged chick sportin' the hip-hugging jeans.

"Who dat?" he slurred.

"It's me, my nigga, Nay." She waved the loot once more. "You got dat strawberry or you gonna send me to who do got it?" Janay snapped as her other hand caressed the .380 sitting in her lap. He finally took the bait and began walking toward the rusty Camry. When he got close she took off her shades.

"What you workin' with, shawdy." He had no clue who she was.

"I wanna be workin' with an ounce of that strawberry," she said as she began counting her cash. When he got close enough and saw the burner in her lap she smiled at him.

"Why you strapped up, shawdy?"

In an instant she dropped the dough in her lap and had

the .380 at his neck and a grip on his T-shirt. "Why? Why am I strapped? Because of bitch-ass niggas like you who think they can put their hands on me. Remember when you smacked me at the detail shop? And you called me a bitch! So I gotta teach you a lesson."

"What? Wait! H-hold up. I know—" he stammered.

It was too late. *Block...Block.* She had pushed him back and since he was bent over when she let the .380 spit, the bullets hit him on the top of his head, literally splitting his wig. The Camry skidded off, and she let loose another one and it hit him in his stomach.

Skye was stunned. He looked over at her, and she was staring straight ahead. Beads of sweat were forming on her nose and top lip and light splashes of blood were decorating her face.

Damn, this bitch is gangsta all day long and she fuckin' strong. How she hold on to that nigga like that? He did the speed limit back to her car. He pulled up next to her ride. "You want me to get rid of that burner for you?"

"No, I got it." She stuffed it in her bag. "Thanks." She got out, jumped into her whip and pulled off. He watched as Melky pulled off after her.

Wise was from Brooklyn, New York, and a cousin of Skye's and Melky's. They sent for him every now and then when they needed an extra man. Wise was ridin' shotgun as Melky pushed his truck. Skye was in his truck following them.

"Once we get there, we gonna hit this nigga up on his

celly in exactly twenty?" Wise was going over the first part of the plan once more.

"Exactly twenty, then it's on from there," Melky confirmed.

"Aiight, cool."

They parked several doors down and Skye pulled up in the driveway and parked. He swooped up the bottle of Krüg and the box of chocolates and got out of the car. He confidently swaggered up her steps and rang the bell. The house was dark but there was a glare from the television. He saw the curtain move, then swing back into place. He smiled as he heard the locks turn and the door pop open.

"How did you find out where I lived?" Janay stood there with both hands on her hips. The screen door was separating them.

"Nowadays, you can find out anything you need to know. Just like I found out where ole dude hung, I just as easily found out where you rest yo' head."

"Oh, so you are planning on holding that over my head forever?"

"Nah. I ain't even cut like that. You seemed pretty shaken up earlier. I couldn't stop thinking about you so I decided to check up on you."

"You could have done that over the phone."

"It's not the same. I needed to see you face-to-face to be sure that you were all right. But excuse me, Miss Lady, I apologize for wanting to look out for you."

"Apology accepted." Janay didn't change the expression on her face.

261

They stood face-to-face. Skye looking her up and down, wanting to get under her silk short set, but reminding himself that this was actually business. She was eyeing the box of chocolates, the bottle of Krüg in his arm and the bag hanging off his shoulders. She deliberated on whether to let him in or not.

As if he could read her thoughts he said, "Throw on a jacket and bring a couple of glasses and we'll sit out here on the porch."

She was still undecided. "So...are the streets talking or what?"

"You know how the hood do. That was *one* of the highlights of the day," Skye said, causing Janay to smile. "Well you're smiling so I guess my work here is done. Check it. At least take this." He held out the Krüg and the chocolates. That got her.

She unlocked the screen door and motioned for him to come in. Melky and Wise, who had their eyes glued to the porch, blew out a sigh of relief. He was taking too long to execute Plan A.

"Have a seat," she said as she turned on a lamp.

She then disappeared and came back with two glasses. "So what's in that bag?" Janay craned her neck as he leaned over and zipped it open just enough to pull out an ounce of weed.

"Got some of dat fire, that's what's in the bag."

"I see. Why don't you roll up while I go change my clothes?"

"You look aiight to me."

262

"I feel naked. You're like one of the homies, not a nigga to be shaking my ass in front of." She smiled at him and then headed for the stairs.

"Real funny," he called after her. "You should get on at amateur night at the Apollo."

"Maybe I will," she yelled back down the steps. She headed to the guest bedroom where Crystal was and pounced on top of her.

"Bitch! What the fuck is the matter with you." Crystal elbowed Janay off of her.

"New York is downstairs. Come on down," Janay whispered.

"Hell naw. I'm tired, fuck a New York," she answered groggily.

"We got an ounce of that sticky and a bottle of Krüg." Janay snatched a pillow off the bed and hit her with it. "Party pooper. C'mon, Crystal."

"Bitch, get the fuck outta here."

"You in my house." Janay went into her bedroom and threw on some sweats and a T-shirt. When she came back downstairs Skye was still rolling and had popped the bottle.

Janay grabbed a joint and sat down, then quickly bounced up and checked the door. "I thought I locked it," she mumbled as she double-checked it and then went and snuggled up on her love seat.

"You comfortable, homie?" Skye joked.

"Ha, ha, ha, homie. I sure am."

Crystal was now wide awake so she went to the

bathroom. On her way back she heard laughter and paused at the top of the stairs for a few before jumping back in the bed. She lay there on her back wide-eyed, staring up at the ceiling, thinking about how familiar that laugh sounded.

Skye's phone rang. "What up?"

"Everything's cool?" Melky asked.

"Not quite," Skye told him.

"The door is open, right?"

"Not anymore, but I got it. Hit me back a little later, nigga," Skye snapped.

"In fifteen? Let's get this shit over with. I hope you ain't in there tryna get no pussy!"

"Nigga, go 'head," Skye said.

"Aiight. I'm just checkin'. Hit you back in fifteen."

"Yeah, that'll work." Skye hung up.

"You gotta run?" Janay was checking him out.

"In a few, yeah."

Crystal crept down the steps and peeked over the banister. "Unh-uh," she gasped. She stole another glance at Skye and tiptoed back up the stairs. *What the fuck is he doing here?* She closed the bedroom door, opened it and then closed it back, unsure of what to do next. She finally sat down on the bed. "He is up to something." She was now whispering. "Exactly what it is, I'ma find out."

She picked up the phone and dialed Big Choppa.

"Why haven't you touched your drink?" Janay asked him.

"Because."

"Because what?" She took another gulp, looking over the top of her glass at Skye.

"Business. I'm here on business." He picked up the bag off the floor and sat it on the couch. "I gotta eat, Ma." He pulled out rope and duct tape.

When the meaning of a nigga having rope and duct tape registered with her she jumped up and screamed, "What the fuck—"

He shut her up with a punch in the mouth that knocked her backward, sending her flopping over the couch.

"You bitch-ass—"

He cut her off when he jumped on top of her, pinning her down to the floor with his knees. He pulled her head back and slapped some duct tape over her mouth, damn near snapping her neck in the process. She groaned as she unsuccessfully tried to wiggle free.

"Chill out, girl, I'm not here to hurt you. I just need you to come with me." He put her arms behind her back. "We just want a little ransom money." He duct-taped her wrists together and then tied the rope around them. "What you got here in the house?" As if on cue his cell rang. "Hold that thought," he said to Janay and answered the phone. "Yo...she locked the door. I'm on her now. Give me about five minutes." He hung up and made sure her wrists and mouth were secure.

"How much will Big Daddy Choppa give for his heiress?" He led her to the couch. "You ain't got no shoes down here?" She didn't make a sound or a move. "Oh, you calm as hell. I like that in you; you used to this shit, huh?" He went into his bag and pulled out some gloves. "Later for the shoes. Let's take this ride while my boys go through the crib real quick." He grabbed her by her hair and snatched her up.

"Muthafucka get your hands off my sister." Crystal startled him.

"What?" *Shit*, Skye thought to himself.

The red dot was on his hand and as soon as he turned Janay loose, it was on his chest. "Pull that tape off of her mouth." He hesitated and she fired a shot, hitting him in the chest. "See, nigga, you took too long."

"Fuckin' bitch!" Skye fell backward across the coffee table, causing it to crash onto the floor. His upper body was on the floor while his legs rested on top of the table base. Blood was beginning to seep out onto his shirt.

Crystal went over to Janay and pulled the tape off of her mouth.

"Oh my God. Oh my God," Janay panted. "This nigga was getting ready to kidnap me. Fuckin' animal!" she spat. "He has to be fuckin' crazy. He just saw me body a nigga earlier. Untie me so I can shoot this muthafucka myself."

"This is Skye, Janay," Crystal cried out. "This nigga was a fuckin' snake from the get-go. He told me his name was Skye and told you it was New York," she rattled off as she struggled with one hand to untie Janay and had the gun in the other. "All the while his bitch ass was plottin'."

"We gotta call Daddy. He is going to flip," Janay told her sister.

"I did before I came downstairs, but he's not answering. Shit, I can't get this fuckin' rope untied," she snapped. "I'ma need a knife." When she turned for the kitchen, Skye grabbed on to her leg, she screamed and the gun went off by mistake. She then aimed it at him, shooting him in the stomach and another one in the chest. The sisters stood frozen in place staring at him. When they heard a knock at the door they both jumped.

"Shit!" spat Janay. "That's probably his partner." Janay was trying to think fast when his cell phone rang.

"Open the door and we'll shoot him too; we can't leave no fucking witnesses."

"Crystal, we already got a body on the floor."

"He ain't no witness. The muthafucka is dead. Open the door," Crystal pressed. "Fuck it, I'll open it."

"Wait, bitch, untie me first." Crystal ran into the kitchen and grabbed a knife, came back and cut the rope and duct tape down the middle.

They heard knocking again.

"Give me the gun, Crystal. You snatch the door open and jump back."

They marched to the front door. Crystal put her hand on the knob while Janay took a stance with the gun aimed.

"On three. One...two...three..."

Crystal snatched the door open and Janay yelled, "Don't fuckin' move!" They both were holding their breath, but exhaled once they realized no one was there. "Shit!" Janay hissed, then whispered, "Whoever it was is gone."

"Mommy," Marquis called out as he came down the steps rubbing his eyes. "Is my daddy here?"

Crystal slammed the door shut and locked it. Janay dropped the gun and ran toward Marquis.

"No, sweetie. Daddy isn't here. You need to be in the bed, it is way past your bedtime." Her trembling hands swooped him up.

"I want something to drink. Can I have some juice? What's all that noise, Mommy?"

"Auntie Crystal had the TV up too loud. She will bring you some juice upstairs." She hugged him tight as she took him back to his bedroom, praying that he was buying her story.

After they got him back to sleep it was almost two o'clock in the morning.

"Where the fuck is Daddy?" Janay cried. "He missin' in action when we need him the most. Crazy shit is happening."

"He's nowhere to be found. We just got robbed, Janay, call the police." Crystal wanted to get the entire fiasco over with...in a hurry.

"Bitch, this is the second time in months that a bullet-filled nigga lay in my living room. Fuck the police! I need my daddy. But first, we gotta get rid of this body."

They had covered up Skye's body with a sheet and blood had seeped through it. "Won't he start stinking soon?" Crystal asked. "Plus I shot him, not you. Call the damn police."

Janay ignored her. "Bitch, it's almost two o'clock, we gotta move this body and dial Daddy again."

Crystal sighed but did as she was told. "Hello," an unfamiliar voice answered so she hung up.

Crystal had a puzzled look on her face. When she dialed it again that same voice answered. "Who is this?" Crystal snapped.

Janay snatched the phone from Crystal and spat, "Daddy got some hoochie over. Hello, put my father on the phone!"

"Daddy's not available," the male voice replied before hanging up.

Janay's mind went to churning. She ran over to the window and peeked out. Sure enough, law enforcement was getting in position. There were DEA, FBI, ATF and the local police.

"Muthafuckas!" Janay screamed. "Of all the fuckin' days!"

Crystal ran to the window and peeked out. "Shit!" She took off running with intentions of getting rid of the gun.

"Crys, we ain't got nowhere to run. The bastards got the house surrounded. You might as well assume the position."

Janay ran upstairs to put on some shoes, put some money in her pocket and call Miss Ida to come get Marquis.

"Crystal, get some clothes on. We are going to jail."

CHAPTER TWENTY-ONE

Forever Thompson, report to Mr. Moseby's office. Forever Thompson, report to Mr. Moseby's office." Mr. Moseby's voice boomed through the compound speakers.

Forever looked at his watch. "A quarter to eight? What the fuck he want with me?" Forever shrugged it off. "C'mon, niggas, let's finish this hand." He and his partner Rob were trying to dig themselves out of a fifty-point hole in their third game of spades. They were playing against J.T. and Flip, two well-known cheaters.

"Moseby is a lazy-ass unit manager. He only put in work if it's absolutely necessary. So it must be important," Hamilton, the nosy but respected old-timer, slipped in as he walked by the rowdy card game and kept it moving.

After finishing the card game Forever reluctantly got up and headed to his unit manager's office. He was convinced that it was nothing but some bullshit. When he arrived at Mr. Moseby's office he tapped on the door.

"C'mon in," Mr. Moseby yelled out. He was a deacon

of a church and always had gospel music or a sermon playing lightly in the background. "Have a seat, Mr. Thompson, and tell me your inmate number; better yet let me see your ID as well. You haven't been here long, have you?"

"No, sir. I just got here." Forever rattled off his inmate number as if he had an attitude and showed him his prison ID card.

"Okay, then, I'll be releasing the correct Forever Thompson."

"Yeah, eventually," Forever joked, not really catching on to what Moseby was implying. "What can I do for you, Mr. Moseby?"

"Good news and always remember that God is great. Now tell me, does a Lieutenant Billups ring a bell?" Moseby grinned as if he were holding the winning lottery ticket.

"Of course, I saved his ass from gettin' shanked to death and I got myself sliced in the process." Forever lifted his shirt to show the scar.

"Well, does getting out of this institution tomorrow make that little ole scar a small price to pay?"

Forever's heart dove to the bottom of his stomach. He moved to the edge of his seat. "What are you saying?"

"Your early release that you filed over two years ago finally came through. You're outta here first thing in the morning. You saved an officer's life. The Bureau of Prisons takes that kind of thing seriously. They may have screwed up and sent your paperwork to the wrong place"—he let out a hearty chuckle—"but they take saving one of their own very serious."

"Man, do not play with me like this," Forever gritted.

"I'm a man of God. I would not do that to you, young man." He opened a folder. "Here is a copy of the order granting your immediate release. It is official. We got a lot of paperwork that needs to be signed, so let's get started."

Moseby slid the immediate release document over to Forever, who kept reading it over and over. The next two hours and the rest of the evening were all a surreal string of events to Forever.

Tonight was a big night at Briggen's club. Some new hustler who went by the name of Cisco was celebrating his birthday. He had paid for Rich Boy and his crew to perform.

The club was definitely the place to be. Cisco must have really been makin' noise in the streets. There were several BMF cats posted up, so money, drinks and weed were raining all night.

Briggen knew that he couldn't have chosen a better night to go out with a big bang…literally. Everything was going as planned. Woo and damn near everybody else were toasted as he and Briggen watched the partygoers pour out of the club.

"Maine, let's kill the last of this fifth," Woo slurred as he held up a damn near empty bottle of Henny X.O to Briggen.

"Hell naw, I'm high enough and so are you. Yo' ass look like you about to pass out, nigga. I'm probably gonna end up carrying yo' ass up outta here."

"I can walk. But shit, I gots to go to the bathroom."

"Don't piss on my floors, nigga!" Briggen teased. "As a matter of fact, I'ma go with yo' drunk ass."

Briggen stood up and Woo was still sitting. "Nigga, get up. What you gonna do, piss in the chair? Get yo' drunk ass up!" Woo stood on wobbly legs and Briggen couldn't help but laugh.

"Maine, I...am...fucked...up!" Woo slurred as he had to laugh at himself. "You would have thought it was my birthday." Woo was cracking up at his own joke as he followed behind Briggen.

"Woo, did you see that fine honey Rat had on his arm?" Briggen held the men's room door open for Woo as he thought of gettin' with the chick. "I wonder if she got good credit *and* good pussy."

"Yeah, you want me to h-hook you up?"

Briggen smirked. "Since when did I need your help to pull a bitch?"

"Awww, man," Woo hiccuped. "That's low. But she from New York. She fly. You prolly gonna need my help with dat." He stumbled over to one of the urinals while Briggen went to the one next to him.

They both began pissing but Briggen turned toward Woo and began pissing all over his shoes and pants.

"Yo, Brig!" Woo yelled. "What the fuck, man!" Briggen put his dick in his pants while Woo was still taking a leak. "Brig! What the—" His eyes got big as saucers as Briggen pulled out an eight-inch Bowie special hunting knife and rammed it into his stomach.

"Ooooohh," Woo screamed.

Briggen pulled it out and rammed him again. Woo appeared to be in shock. His mouth was wide open and his face was turning purple. Briggen yanked the knife out and stepped back. He watched as Woo grabbed his stomach with both hands as if he was trying to catch all of the blood that was seeping out. He went down on both knees while looking up at Briggen.

"W-why, dawg?" his voice croaked as Briggen plunged him again, twisted it, pulled it out and rammed it into him once more.

"Why? You know why, nigga. Because of your treachery." Briggen pulled the knife out of his stomach and began stabbing his hands while slicing off several of his fingers. While laughing he said, "That was for your greed."

Tears were streaming rapidly from Woo's eyes. Blood was everywhere. He looked as if he was going to pass out.

Briggen, seeing that, said, "Unh-uh, nigga. I'm not finished with you yet." He grabbed Woo's jaw and held his tongue out. He then took the knife and cut out his tongue. "And that, my friend, is because you talk too much."

Woo made some gurgling noises before falling flat on his face.

There was a knock on the bathroom door.

"Yo, Brig." It was Silk.

He hawked and spat on Woo's body before backing toward the door. "C'mon in, man. You right on time," he said to Silk with disappointment evident in his voice. Woo had been his running partner for almost ten years. He wouldn't have even dreamt of having to take him out.

Silk walked in and looked dead at the piece of Woo's tongue laying on the floor. "Damn, Cuz, you butchered that nigga."

"He got his just due. I want him to bleed and burn like the pig that he is. Make sure they torch this muthafucka down to the ground. I want this muthafucka to fry. Start right here with this nigga in this bathroom."

"I need to get you out of here first. Let's roll out." He held the door open for Briggen and they glanced once more at Woo and were gone.

Forever still could not believe the turn of events. Here he was a free man, due to him being at the right place at the right time damn near two years ago. Fo'real, he had given up on getting the time off for that deed.

However, he wasn't actually in rejoice mode. It was more like revenge mode. This was supposed to be a happy day. His loving wife and daughter were supposed to be picking him up and crying tears of thanks and joy. Instead, his homie Ronnie was having his family members meet him at the front gate. Ronnie knew both

Briggen and Forever and wanted to know why Briggen wasn't picking him up. He simply told him, "I want to surprise that nigga."

Forever's gaze fell on the white-on-white Ferrari Spider gliding up the road. Forever let out a long whistle as it cruised to a stop right in front of him. "Gotdamn!" He had to give the whip its props.

The window rolled down and a man's voice said, "Forever, right?" even though a brown-skinned honey dip was looking in his face.

"Yeah, I'm Forever."

The beauty in the front stepped out and two more honey dips stepped out the back, giggling. Forever felt as if he had died and gone to heaven.

"I'm Ronnie's cousin Mason. This here is Ciarra." He pointed at the tall chocolate sister with the short, fly haircut and perky breasts. She waved at him.

"That's Neecy." He pointed to the light brown honey with the cute round face. There wasn't any doubt that she was mixed with something, plus she had ass for days. She waved as well. "And this one right here is Karmel." He nodded to the sister with the sexy smile who was sitting in the front and obviously thought that she owned the world. "You can either ride in the front with me or in the back with the two of them."

"Let me get in the back." Forever wanted to cheese real big but managed to play it cool.

As soon as everyone got settled, the Spider whizzed to life. Forever kept saying to himself that he owed Ronnie big-time. He had no clue as to how much money these Detroit niggas were gettin', and now they were showing him mad love. He could see why Brig had to camp out and set up shop down here.

Six hours later, Forever had a driver's license, some fly gear and a heater, and had enjoyed a couple of blow jobs. He couldn't have been happier. Now they were parked in front of Markeeta's, waiting for her to come home. They were working on their second blunt and third bottle of Moët when she finally pulled up. When Mason saw who she was he said, "Man, that's your people?"

"Yeah, that's my little cousin."

"She fine, man, I saw her before. But listen, you got my digits. If you need anything, *anything* at all, holla. I know you said you going back to Memphis tonight but if you decide to change your mind, get at me. We can continue this. I was just gettin' started." Ronnie had this huge grin on his face.

"I got the number and, yo, you gotta hook a nigga up with a rain check. If I don't get back at you tonight, it will be soon. Believe that. Be sure to tell Ronnie I said good lookin'. He blessed a nigga real nice." He gave Mason a pound, then whispered something in Neecy's ear and headed for the house.

"Bye, Forever," the other two girls sang. He winked at them and they both burst into giggles.

Forever rushed up the stairs, rang his cousin's doorbell and started banging on the door as if he were the po-po. He smiled when he heard her fussing in the background.

"I *said* who the fuck is ringing my bell and banging on my door like they crazy!" She peeked through the peephole. "Who is that?"

"You know who I am. Girl, open the damn door!"

"Oh my God! My big cousin! Oh...mygod!" she squealed. "Tell me I'm not dreamin'." She unlocked the door. "Forever! Boy, when did you get out?" She jumped into his arms, gave him a hug and rained kisses on his forehead and cheeks.

"Girl, what you been eatin'?" he teased her. "You need to get yo' heavy ass down and cover that ass up."

"Boy, I am grown and I ain't covering up shit!" She pushed him back. "Let me look at you. What's in the bags? When did you get out? How you get new clothes so fast?" she rattled off the questions back to back.

"I got out today. My peoples hooked me up. Cat named Ronnie and his cousin Mason. Mason said he be seeing you around."

"Ronnie? Mason? I don't know who you talking about." She grabbed his arm. "Come on in. I just saw your brother yesterday. Why you ain't tell nobody you were coming home, Cuz? We would have done it real big for you, Detroit-style. You know how we do it."

"I wanted to surprise everybody. And I'm asking you to promise me you won't say a word about me being out. Don't tell nobody. I'ma sneak up on everybody. You got that?"

"I got you." She could barely contain her excitement.

"You better have me. Y'all can throw me a party in a

couple of days. This freedom snuck up on me unexpect-edly." She was following him as he walked around the house checking things out. "How long this house been in the family?"

"You older than me, you should know. Shit, I wasn't even born when Mommy and Daddy bought this."

"That's a long time." Forever took a moment to reminisce.

"Are you hungry? You wanna use the phone? Nigga, say something, you actin' all strange and shit."

"I just got outta prison. I'm shell-shocked. How the fuck you expect me to act? Plus, I am a little tipsy."

"I see that. Ain't even been out twenty-four hours and you already trying to get a dirty urine."

Forever sank into the nearest chair. "So who is the broad my brother done got ahold of?"

Markeeta flopped down next to Forever. "Her name is Shan. He brung her from Memphis and he want both of us to run the beauty salon. He put her up in a boss crib, the whole nine. You know I got my cosmo license, right?"

"Of course. You only wrote and told me about ten times," he teased.

She slapped his arm. "You stretchin' the truth, nigga. Maybe nine but definitely not ten times."

"Well, I got my license too. Let me hold one of your whips."

"Not a problem."

"And call my brother to see if he's home. If he ain't find out when he'll be there."

Forever already knew that Briggen had gone back to Memphis the night before. He even had the directions to the house. His only concern was whether or not Shan knew he had gotten out. As Markeeta made the call he was going through his stuff, making sure he had everything.

Markeeta ended her call and said, "Okay, your brother went back to Memphis last night. But Shan ain't sure when he'll be back. I told her to call me when he does. Let me give you the keys to my hooptie."

"Hooptie?"

"Yeah, nigga, you think I'ma give you my Lexus? I love you but not that damn much." She handed him some Volvo keys.

He inspected them and said, "You play too much. I was gettin' ready to say, how you gonna have a boss ridin' a hooptie?"

"Whatever, boy, you can come back and spend the night. And here's a cell phone."

"I got one already."

"Well...excuse me." She twisted her neck around.

"You excused. But let me put your number in this phone and I'ma be out."

"Already? You ain't hungry?"

"Naw, I told you I'm in shock."

"All right then." She gave him the number and he headed out the door.

It took him over an hour to find Briggen's house. "Damn," he said as he slowed down in front of it and parked. He was glad that it was dark. He grabbed the camouflage-patterned bag off the floor and got out. He jogged up the front steps and rang the bell.

The sound of the bell startled Shan. She peeked out the window and saw Markeeta's car. She groaned because she was tired and not feeling like entertaining company.

"Just a minute," she yelled as she turned on the light in the family room.

"What are you up to, Markeeta?" She snatched the front door open to be standing face-to-face with Forever.

"Daddy's home," he said as he stepped inside, shutting and locking the door behind him.

"Oh my God," she mumbled as her heart rate sped up.

"Get that look off your face. And no, I didn't escape."

"Your brother isn't here. So you need to leave." She stood there in an attempt to stand her ground but was scared shitless.

"What makes you think I came here to see my brother? I came here to see you."

"Me? Shouldn't you be trying to see your wife and child?"

"Baby girl, don't flatter yourself. However, I will be paying them a visit. But not until I'm finished with you."

With Woo's body burned to a crisp and Tami's remains put somewhere never to be found, Briggen was pleased to see his plan falling quickly into place. He wanted Sharia to suffer, so he hadn't decided what he was going to do with her. The club that she loved, and had really built up with her sweat, labor and connections, was burned to the ground. Maybe that was enough.

He was now kicking back at Mia's and he had just fucked her into a comatose slumber. Satisfied with his performance, Briggen sat on the edge of the bed pulling on a blunt, trying to get his thoughts together. Once he was totally relaxed he decided to check his voice mail.

"Briggen, this is your favorite cousin. You know, the one who you're buying a beauty salon for?" She giggled. "Well anyways, I got a big secret. My second-favorite cousin told me not to tell anybody but I can't help it. We gotta give him a surprise party. Your baby brother, Forever, he got out this morning. He came by with new gear on, money in his pocket and lookin' good rockin' that jailhouse shine. I told him he could spend the night and gave him my car. Call me back as soon as you get this. Love you." She made a loud kissing noise into the phone before hanging up.

Briggen got out of his voice mail and looked at the phone in disbelief. He then replayed the message.

"Fuck!" He immediately called Markeeta back but it jumped to her voice mail. He then dialed Nyla's.

"Hello."

"Nyla, it's me."

"Hey, Brig, what's up?"

"You got something to tell me?" he snapped.

"Am I supposed to?" she snapped right back.

"What's up with my brother? When did he get out?"

"What! He's out? Briggen, if this is your idea of a joke, it's cruel. I know you are mad at me and I fucked up—"

"Nyla. Forever got out today. He was by Markeeta's earlier."

"Why didn't he call me? Markeeta's? Why is he all the way in Detroit? He just *had* to go see that bitch, didn't he?" Her voice was trembling. "That bitch got transferred out there and so did he." She had no idea that Shan was shacked up with Briggen.

"Shit!" It dawned on him that Forever could be trying to get to Shan. "I gotta run."

"Wait. Are you going to find him?"

"Yeah, Nyla. I gotta run."

"Let me go. Please. Come by and pick me up. Please, Briggen. Do me this one favor. I gotta see my husband and apologize. Please, Briggen, let me go with you."

"I'll call you back."

"Briggen, please, let me ride. I've never asked you for anything."

"Okay, Nyla, damn." He hung up.

She dialed her sister Lisha's. "Lisha?"

"Girl, why is your drama-queen ass crying now?" she answered.

"I fucked up, Lisha. I really, really fucked up. Do you think there's a chance that I could get him back? I gotta get him back." She was crying like a two-year-old baby.

"Nyla, what the hell are you talking about?"

"If only I could have hung in there a little while longer. My man. My husband, he would have been here with

283

me, with us. Now he's home and he hates me. I turned him against me!"

"Forever's home? Nyla! Forever's home?" Lisha squealed into the phone.

"He...he got out today. Oh God, I messed up," she sobbed.

"Oh, shit! Where the fuck is he?"

"I need you to come and get Tameerah. I'm riding with Briggen. He's in Detroit."

"Forever, why are you here?" Shan was trying her best to act as if she were cool, especially when he pulled out a gun and stuffed it under the sofa cushion. He then made himself comfortable on the sofa and pulled out a pouch. She watched as he dumped some coke onto her table and did a couple of lines as if she weren't there in the room.

"You want some?"

"Forever, I think you should be leaving now." She got up and went toward the door.

"Get over here, Shan," he yelled at her. When she started to protest, he pulled out his brand-new burner and pointed it at her. "Bitch, sit the fuck down." He was giving her a look that told her, *If you don't I'ma blow your fuckin' head off.* As she slowly took a seat across from him, his eyes roamed all over her body. "Stand up and turn around slowly. Let me look at you. Take off that robe." He tucked the gun back under the sofa cushion.

Shit, Shan said to herself. Now she was getting scared

beyond shitless. *I know this nigga ain't gettin' ready to rape me.* Trying to think of something, she asked, "Since when did you start getting high?"

"Bitch, you don't know me like that. But since you want to go there, since when did you start fuckin' my brother?" He set the burner on the coffee table. The powder he had just tooted, along with her round luscious ass, was beginning to make his dick hard. He stared at her and licked his lips. "Pull one of them straps down over your nipple."

"Why, Forever? Why are you doing this?" She slowly and methodically did as she was told.

Why am I doing this? he asked his own damn self. *I'm fuckin' mad, that's why. Here I am home and my wife done moved on with the next nigga. Me and my brother ain't even speaking. Me and my cousin Zeke fell out and got into a fight. And this bitch here is carrying my seed but is with my brother. What part of the game is this? How did my shit come tumbling down so fuckin' quick?*

"Can I sit down now?" Shan asked, breaking him out of his self-pity party. The phone rang and Shan ran for it, tripping over the ottoman. She crawled quickly on her knees and picked up the receiver. "Come help me somebody!" she screamed. "Please help me."

"Kill the theatrics and hang up that mutherfuckin' phone! Now, Shan!" he barked.

Peanut turned down his radio. "What the fuck is that nigga doin' to my sister? Shan!" He heard yelling and then he got a dial tone. He called Briggen.

"What?" Briggen snatched up the phone. He was on the highway, pissed that Forever was out and possibly on his way to his crib. He had called Shan as well but hadn't gotten an answer. To make matters worse, Markeeta wasn't answering either.

"This is Peanut and I'm obviously feelin' how you're feelin'. Put my sister on the phone, maine."

"I'm in my car on my way to see her now."

"The fuck you is, nigga! I just got off the phone with her and she was crying. I heard you in the background. If she got one scratch on her...nigga, I put that on my momma, I'ma kill yo' ass."

Briggen beeped his horn. "You hear that. I'm in my fuckin' car. You just said you spoke to her at the house. That's my—"

"You had to have just left. I heard your mouth. I'm on my way to see my sister, and like I said, I better not see one scratch on her," Peanut threatened. He hung up the phone, eager to put his foot in Briggen's ass. Now he had a legitimate excuse. He almost smiled as he dialed Karin.

She must have been looking at the caller ID. "Peanut, to what do I owe this rare phone call?" she asked seductively. She was hoping that it was a booty call.

"Listen. I just called my sister and I think her and Briggen was fighting. I just spoke to him and he was in his car. I'm on my way down there but I need you to go over there and check up on her. Can you do that for me?"

"You ain't said nothing but a word. I'll head over there right now and with my pistol," she teased.

"Tell my sister I'm on my way. Only use the pistol if necessary. 'Preciate it. I owe you one."

"I got you. Let me get out of here." She hung up, threw on some clothes and was out the door within minutes.

Forever had Shan standing in front of him butterball naked. Tears were threatening to fall but she was fighting back hard, refusing to give him the satisfaction.

"How many months are we?" He leaned forward and kissed her stomach lightly. She wouldn't answer so he slapped her ass... hard.

"I'm not sure, Forever."

He slapped her ass once again. "Stop lying. You know how far along you are."

"Forever, this is not right. Just leave and I'll act like this never happened. Go home to your wife and daughter."

He slapped her thigh this time. "Don't insult me like that. You already know she left me to be with your punk-ass brother. So you know one of these bullets got his name on it, right?"

"Why, Forever? He didn't do shit to you. Your wife made her own decision to fuck with him. Just like she made the decision to try and set me up."

He grinned. "This ain't about that. My boy Skye is dead and I know he did it." He looked up at her and saw the surprised look on her face. "You didn't know that, did you? Plus, he took my package that you gave him; your brother owes me money. He knew that was my shit. And he's fuckin' my wife, in my muthafuckin' house! That nigga's in total violation."

She watched as he did two more lines. Then he pushed the table over and pulled her close to him as he slid up to the edge of the sofa.

Oh God, please, she silently prayed. He began caressing her ass. "Why you do me like that, Shan?" He slid a finger up inside her dry pussy.

"Forever, don't," she pleaded while trying to figure out a way to get the gun he had tucked under the sofa cushion.

"Why, Shan?" He was workin' her pussy and it was getting wet.

"Why do you care, Forever? All you did was use me, play with my mind and my feelings." He found her clit and gave it lazy strokes with his finger. "N-no, Forever." She tried to move his hand but all he did was pummel inside her coochie with two fingers, exploring and teasing. She then felt his mouth on her nipples sucking and teasing wickedly, going faster and harder in her pussy. "Oh God, no." She was trying her best to fight the feeling that was threatening to overwhelm her. She exhaled when his fingers came to an abrupt stop and his mouth left her aching nipples alone. But then he spread her legs and her pussy and began eating her out. She clenched her teeth, but that didn't stop the tears from streaming down her cheeks. Her stomach did a wild somersault, her knees buckled and she began cumming all over his face and mouth.

Forever had a devilish smirk on his face that she wanted to smack off. "I knew you missed Daddy." He unzipped his jeans and out sprang a dick so hard that she began shaking her head no.

"Briggen don't eat you out that good and make you cum like that, do he?" he boasted. "Come here. You know you got that good pussy."

"No, Forever," she pleaded as she began backing up. She snatched up her robe and put it on. He snatched up the burner from under the sofa cushion. "I...said... come here."

"Kill me, nigga. Kill me and your seed. That's the only way I'll let you violate me any further," she spat.

He cocked the gun. She froze into place, held her breath and squeezed her eyes shut. She felt his body heat. He was up on her, the gun kissing her temple and his mouth kissing her neck.

"Oh yeah? Try me. You think I give a fuck about killing you and my baby? I ain't got shit no way."

"You have a wife and a beautiful daughter, Forever," she sobbed, refusing to open her eyes.

"Shut up!" he snapped as he took his dick and began rubbing it up against her pussy. "Tell Daddy you want this," he taunted as he massaged her ass with the gun in his hand. "Go ahead, bitch. Tell Daddy you want this." He put the gun to her temple. "Put it in." He was definitely ready to fuck.

Ding. Dong. Ding.

She gasped.

He froze.

He slipped his dick back in his pants and grabbed Shan by the back of her neck. "Who is that?"

"I d-don't know," she stammered.

He squeezed her neck as he tossed her down onto the couch. "You better not make a fuckin' sound."

Karin kept ringing the doorbell and trying her best not to panic. Realizing that Shan wasn't going to answer she headed to her car to call Peanut.

Peanut was doing a hundred on the highway. He fumbled with the phone and dialed Karin. As she searched her bag for her phone it started ringing. She answered it immediately and began rambling, "Hey, Peanut. I—"

"What the fuck is going on?" Peanut hissed.

"I'm over here now and shit ain't right. The lights are on, her car and Markeeta's is parked. She ain't answering the door. Markeeta is out of town until tomorrow, so shit ain't right. What do you want me to do?"

"Fuck! I'm getting there as fast as I can."

CHAPTER TWENTY-TWO

The notorious Jack Brunswick, attorney to drug king-pins, sat patiently waiting for the U.S. Marshals to bring his two clients from the bullpen.

Mr. Brunswick had been Big Choppa's lawyer for almost twelve years. It was because of him that Big Choppa had remained indictment-free all this time. Over the years they had become good friends. Jack kept Big Choppa two steps ahead of the game. He watched as Big Choppa groomed Janay to fill his shoes. He had seen it all in his twenty-one years as a criminal defense attorney, but grooming your daughter to become a kingpin? He was unable to come to grips with that. And now he was facing one of the toughest challenges in all of his career: Janay's indictment on kingpin and murder charges. Even though he had seen it coming, this would be difficult for him because Janay and her sister were like family to him.

Janay entered the room first, dressed in an orange jumpsuit. She wore a grim look on her face that displayed all the stress she was under and the knowledge of how serious this was. Crystal, surprisingly, looked calm. He wasn't sure if she understood the extent of what they were up against. Her orange jumpsuit was two sizes too big.

"So what do they have?" Janay wanted to know as soon as she sat down.

Jack popped open his Valentino briefcase. "The government is coming hard at your family. Since you guys have been untouchable for years, they now feel that they got you by the balls. I'ma be straight up with you, it's not looking good," he said while pulling out a file folder two inches thick. "And you, Janay, won't be going anywhere no time soon. They are trying to put two bodies on you. Crys should be straight. We'll see this coming Wednesday; that's when your bond hearing is scheduled."

"Wednesday?" Crystal shrieked, her calm demeanor flying out the window.

"Hold on, Crys. Let me finish with Janay. For right now, you have a four-count indictment: conspiracy, CCE (continuing criminal enterprise), money laundering, possession with intent to distribute five kilos of cocaine. And...they are most likely going to hand down a superceding indictment to add murder and weapons charges."

"What! Where did they get the five kilos?" Janay needed to know.

"Nay, that's the least of your concerns. I will be getting that dismissed."

"This is bullshit, Jack, and you know it!" Janay spat.

"It sure the fuck is," Crystal agreed.

"Ladies, you know how they play. Believe me, they

are not going to play fair. I've never known them to in all my years as a criminal defense attorney. They are going to come at you with everything they can. You are going to get everything that they couldn't get Big Choppa for. And your father has just up and disappeared."

Crystal popped up out of her seat and began pacing the small space that they called the attorney/client room. "Look at us. We are fucked."

Janay frowned at her spoiled sister. "Crystal, I told you time and time again that no good comes out of the dope game. It's a setup from the start. You either end up where we are now, or dead. But it's a choice that we made."

"I ain't tryna hear that shit, Ms. Gangsta. You got a lot of nerve to be talkin'. I can't even think right now. All I know is that I got a body," Crystal snapped.

"Duh, bitch. I know that. I was there. Right now ain't no time for no dumb shit. We need to put our heads together so that we can figure out the best way to fight this shit," Janay calmly explained.

"Please, girls. Sit down, Crystal. We do have to work together. In order to come out on top, we must work and stick together."

Crystal started to say something but changed her mind, choosing instead to sit back down.

"Okay," Jack continued. "Let's start with your father. Any idea where he could be?"

"You got us fucked up if you think you're going to get away with this!" Shan spat.

He leapt across the room and backhanded her. "Shut the fuck up!" Blood trickled down her chin where her lip was split from the force of the slap.

She watched as he ripped open the camouflage-patterned bag and snatched out a rope and tape. Shan, seeing what it was, went off. She grabbed the nearest lamp and tossed it at him. He moved out of the way and it crashed into the wall. "You think you're going to tie me up? You must be outta your fucking mind!" She ran off into the kitchen with him carrying the rope and dead on her heels. She yanked a kitchen drawer open and hastily grabbed a carving knife. Forever grabbed her by the top of her head and she swung her arm around, slashing him across his rib cage.

"You bitch!" He slammed her head repeatedly against the kitchen counters, drawing blood. He then slammed her into one of the kitchen chairs and proceeded to tie the rope all around her. Then he found a clean dish-towel, wet it and began pressing it against his bleeding wound.

"Forever...untie me...please. I feel sick," Shan gasped as a gash on her forehead leaked blood down the center of her face. Her head was throbbing so bad that she was nauseous.

He kept his back to her as he tried to stop the bleeding. "This was not supposed to go like this, Shan. You know that, right?"

"What the fuck is the matter with you? Untie me, Forever! You haven't been out of prison twenty-four hours and look at you. Why are you trying to go back?"

"Oh, I ain't going back. No sir. Forever will hold court in the streets first. Believe that."

"You're holding me hostage, Forever. I'm fuckin' tied up, if you haven't noticed."

"Chill out. When my brother gets here, we'll take care of everything." He had wet another towel and wiped her face.

"Just leave, Forever," she begged him. "When *my brother* gets here it's going to be ugly. Leave now while you got the chance."

"Not until I do what I came here to do."

"And what's that?" She watched as he nonchalantly walked out of her kitchen. "Forever!" she yelled after him. "Come here, dammit! Forever!"

Forever went to the bathroom and found some gauze, alcohol and Band-Aids to bandage himself up. He then went to the living room, took off the bloody shirt and put on another one. He decided to turn on the CD player and got comfortable enough to snort a few more lines. Shan was screaming his name, so to drown her out he turned the music up louder.

Thinking about the time it takes to drive from Memphis to Detroit, Forever looked at his watch. "Six more hours till showtime." He grabbed the cell phone and called Karmel and found out that they were still all hanging out. Mason jumped on the phone and tried to convince Forever to come out and play, which Forever politely declined to do. After he hung up he took a tour of the house, covering every square inch of it. He couldn't believe that it looked as if Shan had all of her shit there as well as Briggen and they were actually living together as a couple. And to make matters worse they were getting ready to play house...with *his* baby. This shit made absolutely no sense to him.

He flopped down on the king-size bed in the master bedroom and gazed up at the ceiling. Before he knew it he had dozed off.

Forever began to dream...dream about how it was supposed to be. He dreamt that when he was released Nyla was carrying their daughter and was waiting for him at the front gate. His heart and soul filled with joy as he swooped them both up and planted sloppy kisses on both of their faces. Then they got in the car and drove off into the sunset and lived happily ever after. He kept dreaming the same dream over and over, waking up in a hot sweat almost five hours later.

"Shit!" He sat up, startled by his silhouette staring back at him through the dresser mirror. He felt as if his body had been run over by a herd of elephants. But then he froze when he heard a vehicle pull up in the driveway. "Fuck! I don't have my piece!" He flew out of the bedroom and down the stairs. The CD player was still on blast as he turned it off.

"In here! I'm in here! Somebody please help me!" Shan was still screaming, her throat raw and hoarse. He ignored her as he pulled his piece from under the sofa cushion.

It was dark as Briggen entered the house. "Shan!" *Click.* Briggen looked up into the barrel of a piece.

"What's happening, big brother? What? You came to save the day?"

"Briggen, Peanut...please come help me!" Shan cried.

"I'm here, baby, I got you," Briggen yelled.

Forever started laughing. "Nigga, you ain't Superman, how you got her and I'm here holding the gun on you? You done lost your fuckin' mind fo'real."

Shan couldn't hold back anymore as the tears flowed endlessly down her cheeks.

"What the fuck did you do to her, man?" Briggen yanked his piece out a little too slow. Forever fired at his chest, knocking him and his piece backward.

"Chill the fuck out, bruh, we need to talk."

"Briggen! Briggen! Answer me! Oh God, no. Forever...Forever!" Shan screamed.

"Big bruh, what the fuck ever happened to MOB, man? Money over bitches? You let that bitch in there come between us?" Forever heard a car door slam and a pair of feet running. He stepped over Briggen's body, kicked the gun back and went to see who was coming. He opened the door.

"Forever! Forever!" Nyla looked into his face and rushed up to him, hugging him around his neck. He hadn't been expecting to see her. He was definitely stunned and caught off guard. "Baby, I am so sorry. You gotta give me one more chance. We have a family. We have history. Please, Forever, you gotta let me make this right." She hugged him tighter and then he moved her arms. She backed up and looked at him. That's when she noticed the blood on his shirt from the stab wound and the gun in his hand. She put her hands over her mouth and started backing up farther. That's when she saw Briggen's body on the floor. "Oh God, no. Forever, what have you done? Baby, no, please say you didn't kill your only brother. Oh Lord, no!" She fell to her knees, letting out a gut-wrenching scream.

Forever's ears perked up when he heard a car door slam. He watched as Peanut raced up the stairs.

"I should have sent out invitations so that we could have had a fuckin' family reunion." He smirked, ignoring what he felt was Nyla's charade. "So...you must be Peanut. We finally get to meet." Forever stood there pointing the gun at him with a huge grin on his face. "Drop that burner, nigga."

"Fuck!" Peanut gritted as he reluctantly allowed his piece to hit the ground. "Where's my sister? I just came here to get my sister. I don't want shit else."

"Fuck your sister, nigga, you should be coming here to see me. Tell me that you came here to see me."

"See you for what?" *Bock.* A shot rang out, striking Peanut. Nyla yelled out and Shan started screaming once again.

"The next one is going to hit you in the neck. Now tell

me that you're here to see me," Forever ordered, obviously enjoying his reign of power.

"I came to see you...damn."

"That's what I thought. You came to tell me that you owe me for taking my dope and that you got my bread, with interest. You also came to tell me that you merked my boy Skye."

"I didn't touch that nigga. But you can believe that I was on my way to see his punk ass."

"Forever...please. Put the gun down, baby. Your dau—"

"Nyla, shut the fuck up! Nigga, you did Skye. You ain't got to lie about it."

"Maine, believe what you want to believe. He better be glad that somebody got to his punk ass before I did. Because for that stunt that he pulled, I had planned to do him nice and slow."

"Oh, you a cocky muthafucka, huh? Is that why you was able to pull my wife? Nyla, you like to fuck these cocky muthafuckas, don't you? Come over here and stand with your nigga."

"Forever, what the hell are you talking about? I did not fuck him. Tell him, Peanut. Tell him how I told you that I was saving all my love for him. Forever, you're home, baby. Don't fuck up, your daughter needs you, I need you. I didn't fuck him. I swear, baby."

"Maine, I ain't fuck your wife! I don't know where you got that bullshit from."

"Nyla, you forgot you told me you was fuckin' this nigga?"

"No, I didn't," Nyla screamed with conviction. "You *accused* me of fuckin' him."

"Bitch, Skye told me he spent the night in my fuckin' house, Nyla."

"Skye is a gotdamned liar. I would never do that to you, baby. Skye just wanted me for himself. He didn't tell you that, did he? Of course he didn't." She could sense Forever's hesitation and thought that she had him but it didn't last long.

"Y'all muthafuckas think I'm stupid? Get over here by this nigga, Nyla. You want to be with him so bad. Watch what I do to him."

"Forever, stop. I don't want to be with him. I want to be with you and be a family. We have a family. You're home now."

"I don't want your wife, man," Peanut told him.

"Y'all muthafuckas want to play games, huh? *Bock, bock.* "Play with that." He watched as Peanut went down, blood oozing from his mouth, and Nyla screaming her head off. "You like that, didn't you?"

Nyla's face was contorted, her mouth was wide open as she saw Shan looking a horrible mess coming toward them. She was tossing the rope and duct tape aside, as she had finally got loose. She saw Shan bend down next to Briggen and when she came up, she came up firing.

Forever ducked, and when he turned around he slipped and dropped his gun.

"Nigga, make my day and go after that gun!" Shan spat.

Not convinced, he smiled at her. "You ain't gonna kill your baby's daddy." He stood up slowly with his hands raised. "So you might as well give me the gun."

"Nigga, I miscarried your bastard. I'm carrying your brother's baby."

Forever laughed. "All y'all muthafuckas got jokes tonight. Bitch, no the fuck you ain't carrying shit for my brother. You know I planted my seed up in there. That's my seed."

"Shut up, Forever! You wish it was but trust me, it ain't. I was just fucking with your mind, just the way you fucked with mine's. But that ain't important no more. You are a thing of the past. Look at my brother." She moved closer to Forever, pointing the gun at his forehead. "You killed my brother knowing that he's all I had in this world. I'ma make you suffer in hell for that."

Forever grinned. "Get your thong out the crack of yo' ass. That was business mixed with a little personal shit. I had to pay that nigga back." He smirked.

"Nah, nigga, I'ma make you *Payback with Ya Life.*" She fired off, he turned to run and the bullets rained all over his back.

EPILOGUE

Big Choppa and Boomer pulled a straight-up Houdini move. Rumors were floating high and low that they were eating dirt. And guess by whom? Shadee's nephew, Born Mathematics.

However, Dave Carlisimo, the famed gung ho federal prosecutor, refused to believe the rumors. Hell, the bodies had yet to surface so he was on a mission. He even went as far as lying before the grand jury, stating that Big Choppa had recently been seen by a worthy confidential informant.

Janay was sentenced to two hundred and forty months. That is twenty years in federal prison. She would have received a much lesser sentence if she had given up her father, Big Choppa. But that was never an option because she knew without a doubt all she had to do was to sit still. Choppa's reach was very long. So it didn't matter whether he was dead or alive. She knew that she would not be spending the rest of her life behind bars. To date her appeal is still pending.

Crystal was given seven and a half years for conspiracy.

Jack Brunswick was able to beat the murder charge stemming from Skye, being that he was able to prove that killing Skye was self-defense.

Born Mathematics, as he now called himself, was now that nigga. After he gained props for the rumors of bodying Doc, Big Choppa and Boomer, his respect and status grew overnight. He was now running shit with an iron fist, terrorizing anyone that wasn't getting money with him, and was bodying niggas left and right.

Zeke had the FCI on lock. He was the person to see. Be it weed, crack, cocaine, meth or heroin, whichever one you wanted he had it. His cousin and Born kept him well supplied.

Lieutenant Scott was found hanging from a rope in his office. His death has yet to be ruled a suicide. The investigation is still pending. His trusty sidekick, Lieutenant Marion, transferred immediately after the death. No one was gonna cut into Zeke's profits, not family, friend or foe. Not on the streets and definitely not in the joint. Didn't niggas know that?

Shan swatted at the stubborn bumblebee that refused to leave her alone as she was in deep thought about the past.

Forever was paralyzed from the neck down, confined to a wheelchair for the rest of his life while serving a life sentence at the FCI in Milan, Michigan. She was glad that his payback went exactly how she'd wanted it to and she had only one regret. That was that Nyla was sticking by him. Shan wanted him to suffer...alone.

She couldn't help but shed a tear for the loved ones that she missed so much. Some days she felt as if she would cry a river. Other days she would find herself moving forward, being strong and enjoying life like any other successful person. That's how both Peanut and Brianna would want it. She had to thank the Creator for her businesses: a beauty salon, day care center and hotel. She was grateful for all of her financial gains, especially since she didn't have to set foot in another prison again.

However, all of this didn't make her feel complete or as if she had closure on the people she'd lost, and deep down she knew that. Therefore, Forever being paralyzed could not remain on the same earth as her and just like that, the last laugh would be hers. But in every curse, there is a blessing. Forever had almost succeeded at killing her, mentally and physically. In his current state he may as well have been dead, physically and mentally. *Maybe I should let it go.* But she told herself hell no, she swore that he would payback with his life.

She shook her thoughts and broke into a grin as she watched Anthony, aka Lil' Peanut, as he ran around in circles trying to catch a butterfly. She rubbed her big stomach and was praying that this time she would have a girl, so that she could name her Brianna. She loved her son and unborn more than anything. They were all that she had left . . . well, almost.

"Shan, I want you to meet somebody. Come here, baby," her hubby, Briggen, yelled. "This here is Nick."

Reading Group Guide

Reading Group Guide

1. Do you think Shan should have accepted another prison job?

2. Was Shan wrong for getting back with Briggen?

3. Was Peanut's hatred of Brianna and the other women in his life justified?

4. How different do you think Shan's life would have been if she had not lost Forever's baby?

5. Should Janay have accepted Doc's help?

6. What are your thoughts on Woo? Did he appear to be jealous of Briggen?

7. Was the crew wrong for canceling Doc's authority?

8. Was Tami justified in having an affair with Woo?

9. Since Forever and Zeke are blood relatives, should they have overcome their differences?

10. Should Born have pulled the plug on Shadee?

11. Did Skye get his just due?

12. Did Forever submit to the pressure? Or do you think he just wanted to get some payback?

13. In the end Nick shows up. Why do you think he does?

14. Should Big Choppa have disappeared on his daughters?

15. Who do you think received the ultimate payback?

More

Wahida Clark!

A preview of her next novel,

THUG LOVIN'

Available April 2009

old beginnings
The Cali Move

Boom! Boom! Boom! Tasha peeked behind the curtain of her apartment window and saw jackets with huge lettering—FBI, ATF, DEA—and regular squad cars. She placed her hands on her pregnant belly as her knees hit the floor.

"Baby, throw something on." Trae was rushing to put on some boxers and some sweats. "You see they are coming in. C'mon, baby, get up." He hopped over to her, one leg in the sweats, one leg out.

"I love you, Trae." She looked up at him, still in shock.

"I know you do, Ma, but I need you to put something on."

"Then why are you doing this?" she screamed. "Why do you keep leaving me?"

Trae's adrenaline pushed through his veins as the sounds of combat boots rushed up the stairs. "C'mon, baby, you gotta put something on." Concern over Tasha's frame of mind was evident in his voice. Seeing that she wasn't going to move, he snatched up his T-shirt, put it on her then hurried to the dresser and grabbed a pair of panties for her. "C'mon, baby, they're at the door. Get dressed." He managed to get her to stand up. Just as Tasha pulled up her panties the front door flew off its hinges and they were on their way into the bedroom, screaming.

"On the floor! On the floor, now! Let me see your hands! Get down!" Trae could decipher those orders if nothing else.

"She's pregnant, man!" he yelled as they threw a distraught Tasha to the floor and were handcuffing her. "Why the fuck are y'all handcuffing her? Y'all came here for me!"

"That's right," the agent in charge said. "We don't need her. Not yet." He smirked.

"It'll be okay, baby," Trae assured Tasha as they led him away with nothing on but some sweatpants.

"Okay? Trae, you promised me. You promised me you wouldn't leave us, baby." Tasha was trying to run toward Trae but the female DEA agent was holding on to her.

As they began tearing up the apartment the agent in charge yelled, "Oh, he's leaving you all right. He's leaving for a very long, long time. That baby you're carrying will be raising a family of its own!" The entire room burst out laughing.

"Aaagh!" Tasha sat up, gasping for air as her fingers clenched the bedsheets so tight her knuckles were turning white. Her breathing was rapid; her body was pulsing from the thundering of her heart as it tried to beat through her chest. She tried hard to shake her head clear of that horrible nightmare. As she wiped the sweat from her brows, Trae sat up and turned the lamp on.

"What's up?" he wondered as Tasha kept shaking her head no. As he reached over to comfort her he realized how badly her body was shaking and saw the tears rolling down her cheeks. He pulled the sheet off her to make sure she wasn't bleeding or anything. He sighed a sigh of relief as he looked between her legs. "Baby, what's the matter?"

"That dream. It's starting again."

"Its okay, baby. It's over, I ain't going nowhere." He used his thumbs to wipe her tears away. "Are you listening to me?" He grabbed her face.

"It was so real though. Oh God, it was real," she gasped.

"It's not real, Tasha. I'm free. Me, you and the babies are far away from New Jersey. Aren't we?"

She hugged him. "Sorry, baby."

"Don't apologize. It's okay. It was only a dream." He could still feel her shaking. "I need to be the one apologizing. It was my lifestyle that got you so shook. I'ma make it right, baby. I promise."

"Just tell me you'll never leave us." Tasha felt she could never get enough of his reassurances as she held on tighter.

"I'm never leaving my family. I promise." He reached down and rubbed her stomach.

Since the day that Tasha picked up Trae and Kaylin

from the courthouse they had been at the bungalow in Ochos Rios. They had the same bungalow where he had promised her that after he got out of the game they would come back and chill until they got tired of it. Their first couple of nights there, Tasha began having that same nightmare, but after about a week it stopped. Now, exactly three months later, they were starting again.

Trae broke her thought pattern. "Maybe it's time for us to raise up outta here. What you think?" He felt her nodding her head yes as she buried her face against his chest.

Two hectic and exhausting days later Trae hopped out of the limo before it had fully stopped, as it pulled up to the entrance of the Wilshire Grand Hotel, one of the best-kept secrets in LA, sitting on the corner of Wilshire and Figueroa. Being that it was downtown it was rarely crowded with tourists. Trae watched carefully as the bellman got their luggage and the driver helped a sleepy Tasha out of the limo. He decided right then and there that this spot would suit their needs perfectly as relocation central.

They were so exhausted that after they settled in they slept until almost noon the next day. They were chillin' while waiting for Tasha's cousin Stephon to come over. They had about six houses to look at and he was going to be their tour guide. They were sitting on the couch in front of the big screen, which was on mute while watching ESPN2. Trae was on his cell phone talking with a Realtor. Tasha had her legs thrown across his thighs as she watched and listened to him take care of business.

"My wife is pregnant and I need something that we can occupy immediately. We're expecting twins so we need to get settled in as soon as possible." Trae reached over and began doing his favorite, rubbing Tasha's belly. He was silent as he listened to what excuse the Realtor came up with. Tasha placed her hand over his as she guided it to where the movement was.

"What's up, twins?" Tasha whispered.

"Call me within the next hour. If I don't hear from you I'm moving on to the next man." He pushed the end button then leaned over and began kissing Tasha on the lips. "Man, these clowns out here got so much money they act like they don't wanna make no more! I have no understanding of this bullshit."

"Give the poor man a chance, baby." Tasha laughed. "I mean, what you want the man to do? Throw the people out of their houses today?"

"Hell yeah! Daddy needs a house."

"And Ma Ma needs for Daddy to chill out."

"I need to chill?" He tongued Tasha down.

"Mmmmmmmmmm-hmmmmm," she moaned as she came up for air. "Yes you do. That's my job, to clock out on niggas."

"Aiight then. You got that."

"Thank you. Now go answer the door."

"I love you more than anything, you know that, right?"

"Of course I know that. You show me that every day."

"Aiight then. Just don't forget that shit."

"Open the door, nigga!"

Trae winked at her as he walked across the room to open the door. Tasha watched nervously as Stephon came in. She hadn't seen him since they were teenagers. He was the one to bring her the bad news about her brother getting shot to death. He was around when both of her parents got hauled off to prison. He was there when Social Services came and took her sister Trina and brother Kevin into custody. When she saw him it was a mirage of her childhood. She felt that seeing him was like reopening the door to her past, something that she felt she wasn't ready to do. She didn't like that feeling.

He had spoken with Tasha and Trae over the phone on several occasions. Especially when they had confirmed that they were coming to LA, which he called his playground. He promised them that he would do everything to make their transition as smooth as possible.

"What up, man?" Stephon greeted Trae. They gave each other the dap followed by a brotherly embrace.

"Good to finally meet you in person," Trae told him.

"Same here, man. My cousin sounds like you're keeping her very happy."

"Well, actually, we do that for each other," Trae said

with sincerity. Then yelled out, "Yo, Tasha, your family is here!"

"Damn, look at this room. Y'all rollin' like this?" Stephon was admiring the plush suite.

"Illlk!" Tasha teased when she got up on her cousin, immediately forgetting those bad feelings she was having. "You look just like Uncle Bill." She gave him a big hug while Trae stood back and watched his wife.

"And you look just like Aunt Seleta. So I don't know why you turning up your nose. My dad and your moms is sister and brother remember?" He held her back to get a good look at her. "Even though I look better, you do look good. You look very happy. I'm happy for you." He hugged her again.

"I feel good too. But you wrong about looking better than me. You trippin' already! So where you taking us? I'm ready to get out and smell some of this Cali air. That Realtor you referred us to is moving too slow for 'Mr. Make It Happen Right Now' over there," she said, referring to Trae.

"Later for that bum. That's what I wanted to tell Trae. What I got to show y'all you're gonna love. I should be able to get the keys in a few days if you want it and if you got the paper, which I know you do. My man out here got other moves he tryna make and plus he got the connections to make the deal close very fast. Y'all couldn't have come at a better time."

"Now that's the shit I'm talking about. Somebody that's tryna get paid!" Trae exclaimed. "How big is it?"

"Trust me. It's big enough. It has a guesthouse and a pool in the backyard. Master bedroom, about four or five other bedrooms, living room, dining room, family room, den and I don't know how many bathrooms. I'm telling you, y'all won't have to ever move again."

"Sounds too big to me." Tasha was turning up her nose.

"Cousin, you sayin' that now, but wait until you see it. Trust me." Stephon was getting more excited by the minute.

"Aiight then. Can we go check it out?" Trae asked, catching on to Stephon's enthusiasm.

"Let me call my man right now."

"Babeee!" Tasha squealed as she entered the master bathroom for the third time. Her eyes glittered as they roamed the his-and-hers commodes, two-person shower, sunk-in Jacuzzi that looked like it could seat four or five and the his-and-hers marble sinks. "Oh my God!" she gasped as she looked around.

"C'mon, let's see the rest of the house again." Trae grabbed her hand.

"I don't have to see it again. I want this; no, I gotta have this house," she whined.

Stephon was grinning at her excitement. "Damn, girl. What about the man of the house having a say-so in the matter?" Then he turned and whispered to Trae, "Who do she think she is?"

"I heard that, nigga!" Tasha shot at him. Then she said to Trae, "Baby, school this nigga on what time it is."

"If my baby says she gots to have this house, then it's my duty to make it happen for her," he informed Stephon and winked at Tasha.

"Aiight, Cousin." Stephon raised his arms in surrender. "I didn't know it was like that. My bad!"

"Well now you know, playboy," Tasha scolded him.

"Aiight, Tasha. Anyways, where did Tasha come from? You went out and got a name change on me? Roz!"

"No, Cornelius!" she mocked, emphasizing his middle name. "I didn't get a name change. That's my middle name."

"I got your point. But for your info I did change my middle name; it's now Neal."

"Oh my gosh. No you didn't!"

"Yes I did."

"Whatever tickles your fancy. I see that fake-ass LA done got the best of you! I ain't mad. Go ahead and let your man know we want the house. C'mon, baby. I do need to see the pool again." She grabbed Trae's arm and began pulling him down the stairs.

"Yeah, you do that while I make it happen," Stephon agreed as he pulled his cell out of his pocket.

One month later . . .

Trae and Tasha had been trying to get situated in their new home. It was so monstrous to the both of them that the challenge of getting it furnished and decorated were almost overwhelming. However, Tasha was so excited about their new Brentwood estate, and Trae was more worried about Tasha overdoing it with her pregnancy. Nevertheless, Tasha was in heaven. And as far as Trae was concerned if Tasha was in heaven, everything else would fall into place.

"Baby, pick up the phone!" Trae was yelling from the family room. He was posted in front of his big flat-screen TV.

"Hello." Tasha was going to get it anyway because she knew Trae wasn't going to answer it.

"What's up, girl? How you doing?"

"Ho, when are y'all coming over? Can I see my peoples for a change?"

Kyra laughed. "I miss you too, smart-ass! I told you we'll get over there. It's not like I live right around the corner. I'm taking two classes, Marvin has been doing some things and I know you and Trae are trying to get settled in. And I know your busy ass is overdoing it."

"No I'm not. I'm just excited and anxious at the same time. Trae just put up the cribs for the twins, so my main concern is their room and our bedroom. I'm dying for you to see it. It was empty the first time you saw it, but now I got some thangs!"

"Trae told Marvin that you are getting big and fast. How are you feeling?"

"Tired. But like I said I am soooooo excited!"

"Look, Tasha, you don't need to be overdoing it."

"I'm not. When I feel myself getting a strain I chill out."

"Umm-hmm." Kyra doubted her. Plus she knew how

Tasha was. "Ho, I think I need to come visit your ass for real now!"

"Yeah, I miss you. I need to see my people," she whined. "You gotta see the twins' bedroom and I need to see my niece. You know she gonna help me with the twins, right?"

Kyra laughed. "Let her help, 'cause I ain't having none no time soon that she can play house with."

"Yeah right." Just then Tasha's phone beeped. "Hold on, Kyra, let me take this call."

"Girl, just call me back."

"No, Kyra, hold on." Tasha didn't want her to hang up.

Kyra sucked her teeth. "Girl, go 'head."

"Hello. Hey, Nana." It was Trae's mother. "I'm fine, thank you. How's Pop Pop?" Trae magically appeared in the doorway.

"How long you gonna be on the phone?"

"It's your mom," she mouthed.

"Give me the phone."

Tasha rolled her eyes at him. "Nana, here's your rude son. I love you too." Tasha covered the mouthpiece. "I think something's wrong," she whispered before passing Trae the phone.

"Hey, Ma. Everything aiight?" Trae was silent as Tasha watched his facial expressions. When he ran his hand over his head she knew something wasn't right. "Ma, calm down. Put Daddy on the phone."

"What's the matter?" Tasha was now up and standing in front of Trae.

"Dad, what happened?" Tasha watched as the tears rolled slowly down his cheeks.

When he hung up, Tasha asked, "Baby, what's the matter?"

"We gotta go back to New York."

About the Author

WAHIDA CLARK was born and raised in Trenton, New Jersey. This Trenton native owned and operated L.M. Clark Printers & Publishers Inc., a printing and publishing company in Trenton. She decided to write fiction while incarcerated at a women's federal prison camp in Lexington, Kentucky.

She was crowned the "Queen of Thug Love Fiction" by Nikki Turner, a mogul in urban fiction. Her *Essence* bestselling novels include *Thugs and the Women Who Love Them*, *Every Thug Needs a Lady*, *Payback Is a Mutha*, and her latest and highly anticipated *Thug Matrimony*. In June Wahida was released from the federal prison camp in Alderson, West Virginia, and is now back in New Jersey, where she is hard at work on her next book.